A TOAST TO THE ESTABLISHMENT

Eyekon THE UNION

BY

Edward Wilson Jr

Copyright © 2025 Edward Wilson Jr

This is a work of fiction. Names, characters, people, places, incidents, or locales are the product of the author's imagination or used fictitiously; any resemblance to actual persons, living or dead, business establishments, or events is entirely coincidental.

ISBN:
978-1-968973-65-0

Dedication

This Book is dedicated to Viola Wilson.

Thank you for being the blessing you are. I love you.

Acknowledgment

This Book is dedicated to all who dare to believe. No situation is impossible to overcome; no condition is stronger than the human mind.

Also, to the Universe! Thank you for being the blessing you are. I love you.

Additionally, Tacarra A. Brown, Brandon M. Florence, and Kevin J. Allen (my kids, forgive me guys for being absent over all these years); Inez, Cynthia; (I miss you both dearly...RIP); V. Wilson, thanks for the growth. You are simply Beautiful (without your tough love, this accomplishment could not have occurred...I will be loving you for you for a couple of forever). Cassandra White and Larry White, thanks for the inspiration. Oh, C, you inspired the Protagonist Sire. Thanks.

Also, Rodney and Lois Davis (thank you, big brother and sister, for the support over the years {RIP, Lois}; Rodney Jr. Rabbit/Main, love you, nephew...stay focused).

"Special Thanks" to my editor, Joyce White, for her valuable guidance and insight. For which I am forever grateful. Thanks, Joyce, and Thanks to The Authors Central.

And to every individual on lockdown across this great Nation of ours. If you courageously go with confidence inwardly, you'll find those bridges (s) that may permit the crossing of many troubled waters.

About the Author

Edward Wilson Jr. is an entrepreneur, author, and advocate for post-conviction reform whose life story reflects resilience, reinvention, and purpose. After serving more than 34 years in prison, he was released in December 2024 and has since dedicated himself to legal education, public service, and creative empowerment.

He is the founder of E. Lee Wilson & Associates, LLC, a Florida-based consulting firm that assists attorneys and families with post-conviction case reviews. Drawing from more than three decades of hands-on legal research and analysis, Mr. Wilson provides and supports both pro se litigants and legal professionals in their pursuit of justice.

Mr. Wilson is the author of Florida Post-Conviction Relief: A Guide to Rule 3.850 Motions, a widely accessible legal manual designed to simplify complex processes for laypersons and practitioners alike. His forthcoming works include The Super Post-Conviction Self-Help Litigation Manual, a comprehensive guide to both state and federal post-conviction procedures, and his debut novel, A Toast to the Establishment: Eyekon The Union, currently in professional editing. He is also expanding into children's literature with ABC Safari: Learn, Rhyme & Color!, an alphabet-themed coloring book that encourages early literacy and joyful learning.

Through his writing, consulting, and community

engagement, Mr. Wilson seeks not only to advance legal understanding but also to inspire others navigating life after incarceration. His journey from confinement to creativity stands as a testament to perseverance, growth, and the belief that transformation is always possible.

Born in 1963 in Fort Myers, Florida, he continues to build a legacy rooted in service, education, and empowerment.

PREFACE

A king does not begin or end with the description of a male ruler of a country; a king is also a man or thing regarded as supreme.

Ascendancy will never be inherited in a place where the only legacy passed down is penury.

Most men and women alike are capable of being supreme, but only after a burning desire is sparked, fanning the flame of achievement within them.

Oftentimes, that spark will only be noticed and become accessible when a person falls or is knocked to the knees in defeat. However, it can only be realized through the refusal to accept total defeat.

No matter the game you choose or the one you're forced to play in life, somebody must lose, and somebody will win; a real winner can take a loss and still come out being boss.

Such is the epitome of a character required for supremacy.

Your own kingdom will never reach you until you recognize its spark, allowing the flame to burn a pathway to your subjects.

PROLOGUE

The black Mazda going in the opposite direction makes a U-turn in the middle of Michigan Avenue. The male driver's attention focuses on the female driver of the powder blue and white 2010 Chrysler 300 as it enters the highway. She pulls into traffic from the parking lot of Shoemaker's Florist. He begins to follow her. The Chrysler's windows are tinted, but they are rolled down; the lady is avoiding the new-car smell that is found in most new automobiles; it upsets her stomach. She makes a turn on Henderson Street and heads to the cemetery, where she parks and gets out.

The black Mazda follows the same route but does not stop. The driver notices the flowers in her hands and drives to Handy Court Park at the south end of Henderson Street. The Henderson Street Cemetery is accessible through three different entries: two by vehicle and one on foot. The guy enters the park and exits on the backside near the ditch on Ford Street. After turning right, he turns right again and makes his way to Blount Street, where he walks through the worn-down path leading to Indian Street. A few moments later, he comes to a second ditch across from the graveyard. He crosses the small walk bridge and enters the Cemetery.

The lady locates plots 50 and 51 and then begins to clean the windblown debris and wild weeds from the grave sites. After a while, the graves are neat, and she is about to leave when she hears the sound of an old twig snapping. She turns in time to see a wild-eyed man bolting towards her with a large stick in one hand and a gun in the other. The thing is pointed directly at her head. The fear immediately immobilizes her. The man's lips are drawn back into a grimacing countenance, displaying what was left of a few badly damaged teeth.

The look on his deranged face gives her the feeling that she is staring into the eyes of the devil himself. She wants to scream; she needs to scream. However, when her mouth opens to do so, nothing comes out. The fear is total. Then something deep inside her being commands her to run. Now! She turns and attempts to run away from the rapidly approaching madman who is hell-bent on reaching her. However, her instincts kick in a fraction too late; the heaVee truncheon in the maniac's filthy hand comes crashing down hard on the back of her shoulders, knocking her to the ground between the two graves.

The pain is too great; it becomes a struggle for her to remain conscious.

"Bitch!" the madman utters threateningly, "if you try and run from me one mo' damn time, yo' ass will neva see the sun rise again..."

Table of Contents

Introduction

SIRE

...Before his kingdom is granted the chance to materialize, Sire must journey from the pits of the ghetto to the halls of corporate America, an odyssey marked by unrelenting, in-your-face mayhem.

Though no stranger to crime, he is forced to spend over 25 years in the Florida prison system for a crime he did not commit. Yet instead of growing bitter toward a society long riddled with grave injustices, he vows to confront it on a scale never before attempted.

...Little Teddy Hilson, just 8 years old, is thrust into a life on the streets. There, he navigates a dark world filled with pimps, prostitutes, drug users, pushers, wine-heads, robbers, and killers, all of whom expose him to harsh lessons unimaginable to most.

Quickly adapting to and surviving in an environment that has claimed many adults, Little Teddy carves out a name for himself in the very heart of this unforgiving world. But will he escape the inevitable destruction of the ghetto, where law and order are dictated by the meanest and deadliest? Or will he, like so many before him, spend his life in prison or worse, end up dead?

Upon his release from prison, Sire is reminded that society sees him only as a convicted felon, unwelcome and unemployable. With quality job opportunities nearly impossible to find, he returns to what he considers soft crime to raise capital for a business venture of his own.

Things begin to take shape and offer a promising future. That is, until an old enemy picks up his trail, intent on fulfilling a deadly promise: Sire must die.

The enemy is no ordinary hitman. He's a fearsome, lethal killer who has never failed to complete a contract. This time, however, money isn't his motivation. His vendetta with Sire is deeply personal and deadly.

As bodies begin turning up across the city, police intensify their investigation. In the midst of this chaos, Sire and his devoted partner Tish resolve to leave hustling behind and earn their living within the bounds of the law by launching his brainchild, Eyekon, a union for the nearly one hundred million convicted felons across America.

Eyekon holds the potential to make Sire one of the richest and most powerful men in the country. But can he and Tish survive the assassin's ruthless pursuit? Can they live long enough to bring their revolutionary movement to life, The Eyekon Empire?

A gripping tale of raw determination in the face of staggering odds, SIRE is a powerful journey through danger, betrayal, and resilience. Informative, enlightening, and emotionally charged, it's packed with the intensity of a street novel and the depth of a mainstream epic. This unforgettable story is poised to transcend urban fiction entirely, birthing a brand-new genre: Urba-Main, a seamless marriage of urban grit and mainstream power.

Chapter 1

The Debt Paid in Blood

(Circa 2019)

The sky was bleeding color, red and gold smearing across the horizon, the sun sinking low like a boxer staggered in the final round. Rain drummed against the windows of Sire's house, a place he half-jokingly called The Palace. It sat tucked behind a stretch of scrub palms on a half-acre in South Fort Myers. Not quite regal, but spacious, four bedrooms, quiet, and his.

Tonight, it felt less like a retreat and more like a bunker. The storm wasn't asking permission. It just took. Rain fell in thick sheets, tapping the windows in erratic rhythms like someone testing the perimeter. Inside, the shadows settled in the corners, and the walls held the weight of memory. He had built this place to be a sanctuary, but even sanctuaries aren't immune to ghosts. Sire, lounging in a jacuzzi that steamed up the windows, wasn't the kind of man who panicked over the weather. But tonight was different. He had business. Pool Shark Willie. Tee-Tots Pool Hall. High-stakes. Reputation-leveling, wallet-busting business.

The last time they met, Sire walked away twenty-five grand richer. Word spread fast in the underground, pool sharks, corner hustlers, dice slingers, everybody was watching now. And Sire? He didn't flinch under pressure. He flipped the remote, paused the grainy footage of Ali vs. Frazier, Round 4 frozen mid-punch, and switched to the weather channel.

The meteorologist said the rain would clear in an hour. Perfect.

The bell rang again on screen. Round five. The phone rang in real life.

"Yeah," Sire said flatly, barely glancing at the caller ID.

Tish. Loyal. Smart. And fierce with the books. She was dropping off the money collected from Black Pearl and Ice Man, Sire's weed runners. Half his distribution chain was in her hands tonight. He trusted her like a soldier trusts his sidearm.

"I'll be in the jacuzzi," he told her. Click.

Time passed. Keith Sweat crooned through the bathroom speakers, the soulful pain of "In the Rain" drifting with the steam. Sire reclined deeper, eyes closed, mind in ten places at once. He didn't hear her heels click on the tile— just felt the presence, the pause.

Tish stood in the doorway. A silhouette framed in quiet reverence.

"You look so peaceful and desirable lying there," she said, her voice like velvet soaked in devotion. "May I join you?"

Sire didn't open his eyes. Not at first. He let the silence stretch like a sermon.

"Tish…" he finally said, voice low but steady, "if you

climb your fine ass in this jacuzzi, it's going to interfere with the business we have at hand."

She tilted her head, lips curling in a smile, familiar with the rhythm of his wisdom.

"Success comes from learning, understanding, and handling your business," he continued. "Pleasure has a way of dulling the senses. You mix it in at the wrong time, and you miss the details that keep you alive."

Tish nodded, the heat in her eyes replaced by pride.

"There'll be time for pleasure later," he said, softer.

"A girl can't argue with that. Especially when her man's so on point," she answered. "Want me to fix you something before I go?"

"No, Baby. I'm good. Tell Stella I said to keep her head up. Tell her to let us hear from her."

Tish winked, blew a kiss, and disappeared down the hallway. Sire eased back into the warmth. The song changed, "Just One of Those Things", but the peace didn't last.

Because in the silence, Sire's thoughts turned sharp. Gorilla Seville.

That name came with heat. History. A vendetta dressed in bruises and bad blood. And Sire knew—knew without needing to ask—that Seville wasn't done. The beating he gave him last month during The Tribute would not go unanswered.

Sire had embarrassed him. In public. At a gathering where legends were remembered and ghosts toasted. It was a Fort Myers reunion of pimps, players, and polished street generals. Held at the New Phase II Lounge, the Tribute honored the kind of street royalty who once moved entire neighborhoods with a whisper.

Seville had just been released from prison weeks before. That night, he showed up with old scars and fresh rage. And Stella.

Stella had been his for a while, more like owned than loved. He broke her leg once with the very Cadillac she bought, selling herself for him. She stayed because fear shackled her tighter than affection ever could. But after Seville caught a 25-year bid for shooting another pimp in the head, she got out. Clean. Quiet. Gone.

Until the Tribute. Until she walked back into the room like a ghost, nobody was ready for her.

Sire was there for his partner, Pimpwell, a boss hustler with style. Tish was at his side. The lounge pulsed with bass, bodies, and throwback laughter. Then her voice broke through it all.

"That motherfucker is kicking that girl!" someone yelled outside.

Sire moved without thinking. Out the door. Through the crowd. Into the chaos.

There was Stella, blood smeared down her face, her all-white outfit a canvas of horror. Her mink coat was soaked in it. Gorilla Seville stood over her, rage in his fists, madness in his eyes.

"Hey, man! Have you lost your mind? You're gonna kill that woman, and a thousand witnesses will see it!" Sire barked.

Seville turned. Blood lust and ego flaring behind his glare.

"Suckah," he growled, "if you don't mind your own business, it's your ass they'll see me tear up."

What happened next was a pure blur.

A crack. A blur of muscle. Sire's right hand exploded against Seville's nose, blood gushed, and cartilage snapped.

"Augghh! Your sonofabitch!"

Sire didn't hesitate. He stepped in, turned his hip, and unleashed a brutal uppercut to the chin. Seville's teeth cracked before his head did. He was unconscious before he hit the pavement.

The girl with braids helped lift Stella. Tish met them at the door. They slipped inside. Cleaned Stella up. Someone whispered, "Seville's gone. But he's coming back with a gun."

Sire's eyes were steel.

"Tish. Grab your things. We're leaving. All three of us."

He turned to the new girl, who had helped Stella. "You rolling too? Let's go."

Back at the apartment, the night stretched long. Tish had taken Stella to the bus station. Sire was soaked in the tub, but the water no longer relaxed him. Too much had shifted.

He stood, dried off, dressed, and stepped to the middle of the bedroom. He peeled back the thick polar bear rug, revealing a hidden safe. The click of the lock echoed in the stillness.

He took out fifty thousand of the ninety he had stashed since prison. He counted it carefully.

The streets weren't going to stay quiet after tonight.

And neither was Gorilla Seville.

The streets glistened beneath the dim orange of the city lights, slick with the remnants of the earlier downpour. Sire's Escalade cruised through the Fort Myers night, navigating traffic like a shark cutting through still water. He turned onto Edison Avenue, then veered left onto Cranford. Just ahead, like a beacon in the shadows, the back end of Tee-Tot's Pool Hall emerged from the gloom.

The lot was packed, a sea of polished chrome and attitude. Cars lined up like a dealership from another planet—candy-painted CheVees on sky-high rims, beats thumping from within, windows tinted black as secrets. Some of the vehicles were jacked up so high they needed ladders just to climb inside.

"Too much for me," Sire muttered under his breath, shaking his head.

The only available spot sat beside a cluster of trees, too shadowed for comfort. He stepped out, clicked the lock, and activated the alarm with a soft chirp. As he walked toward the back entrance, his instincts kicked in—those trees could easily conceal a threat. He noted it and moved on every step, alert.

Inside, the atmosphere hit like a wall. Sweat, cigar smoke, cologne, liquor, and anticipation. Sire's first move wasn't toward the bar or the game—it was toward awareness. He scanned the layout. Front door? Decorative only. Real players used the back.

Pool Shark Willie arrived shortly after, wearing a face carved from stone. Around the pool table, the city's underground elite mingled and flexed: East Coast, Train, Tampa Red, Silky Dee, Ho Bender. All suited in exotic threads—ostrich-skin shoes, crocodile belts, Tom Ford jackets. The sparkle of diamonds rivaled the shine of ambition in their eyes.

Tee-Tot, the aged owner with a finger still on the pulse of the streets, raised his hand. Game time.

The ladies working the room weren't exactly dressed to serve food. Two Black women, a Latina, and a white girl— all gorgeous, nearly nude, carrying trays of drinks and snacks. They moved through the crowd like walking temptation.

Sire handed over the ten-thousand-dollar stake. Willie matched it. Then a familiar presence drew his attention—Pimpwell, slick as ever.

"What's happening, my Brotha?" Sire greeted, offering a dap.

"What a surprise, Playa," Pimpwell grinned. "Heard you left for Chi-Town. That Pimp of the Year ball ain't kicking off tonight?"

"Midnight tomorrow. I flew back in just to watch my partner take this chump's money—again."

"That you can count on, Pimpin'," Sire said, confidence low and lethal.

The room hushed. Eleven o'clock sharp. Tee-Tot signaled the start.

"Crack!"

Willie broke hard. Three balls down instantly. Then six more. Perfect game. Not a single shot for Sire. Murmurs rippled across the room. Willie was focused, locked in. And for Sire, a creeping irritation itched beneath his calm exterior.

"Double it. Five more grand if you do it again," Sire offered.

"Make it ten," Willie barked, chest swelling.

"You got it."

Another break. Balls flew. Four sunk. And once again,

Sire didn't get to touch the stick. Spectators grew bolder in their betting. Setback hollered, "I still like Sire for ten grands in the long run!"

"Shit," Ho' Bender replied, "Pool Shark Willie finna get that ass tonight."

But for Willie, this was more than ego or money. His son—his only son—needed a kidney. The transplant cost fifty grand. Insurance wouldn't touch them because of Willie's record. This hustle? This tournament? It was a father's last hope.

"Crack!"

Willie's third game began. Nothing dropped. The table stayed quiet.

Finally, Sire's turn. He made six straight before missing a tricky bank shot. Willie grinned, thinking victory was in hand. But then came the angle. The cue ball lay in the dead zone—between the corners, against the cushion.

He lined it up. Hoped. Shot.

The ball sank.

"I'll be damned," Sire muttered, jaw tight. "The bastard made the fucking shot."

The room erupted. Cheers for Willie. More money was thrown. Ho' Bender howled in joy.

Fourth game. Same result.

Four to zero. One more game and it was over.

Willie looked like a man on the verge of salvation.

Then Sire spoke.

"How much are you holding? Outside of the ten?" he asked, voice cool as ice.

"Thirty-one thousand. Counting what I took already."

"I'll put up thirty more grand to your twenty," Sire said. "Winner takes all."

Willie hesitated, eyes wide. Then nodded. "You got a bet."

The room went silent. Not quite—silent. You could hear breathing. Heart hearts.

The side door creaked.

Tish entered, calm and confident. Sire met her eyes. No words. Just recognition.

He chalked his stick.

And then, like a machine, Sire did not miss.

Four games straight. Clean. Deadly. Not a sound beyond the crack of the cue and fall of balls. Willie began to sweat. First on his brow. Then he soaked his collar. Sire closed in. Three balls. Then two. Then just one.

He paused. Chalked the stick again. Took a breath.

Then—

BOOM!

The side door exploded inward and blasted off the hinges. Screams. Chaos.

Four men stormed in, black clothes, black boots, and black masks.

One raised an AK-47 and fired into the ceiling.

"Get your fucking hands in the air! This is a got-damn stick-up! Anybody who moves dies. No mo' warnings!"

Panic swallowed the room.

Sire's eyes snapped to the pool table. $50,000. Then to Pimpwell's chain. $30,000 is easy. Then, to the terrified faces in the crowd, eyes darting to their rings, watches, and necklaces.

A scream tore through the air.

"No! You ain't taking Ho' Bender's Rolex! I sold pussy for a whole month for that watch—"

CRACK!

The goon pistol-whipped her mid-sentence. She hit the ground hard. Blood soaked her temple.

In the chaos, Willie saw a moment. He grabbed the pile of money and ran.

"RAT-TAT-TAT-TAT!"

The Uzi tore through him like wet paper. Bullets raked his back. He stumbled, twisted, and fell face-first, dead before he hit the ground.

His final thought was for his boy.

Tish crouched near the counter with the waitresses and flashed Sire a look. She pointed subtly to her thigh—her Beretta. She was ready.

Sire shook his head.

No.

Not now. Not here.

But something clawed at his thoughts. A thread he couldn't grab.

The leader. His voice. His posture.

I know this fool from somewhere…

Before Sire could place him, another voice called from outside.

"Yo! Five-O on the way!"

Sirens in the distance.

The robbers vanished like smoke, out the side door. The crowd scattered, not one person wanting to explain a dead body or a room full of stolen goods to the police.

Pimpwell touched the space where his chain used to be.

"That chain can be replaced. I'm good, partner. But you? You need to be gone. Cops won't come asking questions. They'll come looking for answers. And I know you got heat on you."

Sire nodded once. Cool. Calm.

"Yeah, Playa. You're on point."

He glanced at Willie's still body. So much hustle. So much loss.

"Hit me later," Sire said, already moving toward the back. "We'll be at the place if you need me."

He paused.

"Oh… and enjoy the ball, Pimpin' 76."

Chapter 2

Ghost in the Alley

(Circa 1970)

No one pays much attention to the child as he moves in and out of the throngs of people, most of whom begin and end each day of their lives with something to do with street life. Maybe the lack of acknowledgment is because the kid's mannerisms so closely mimic their own, quick, alert, and soaked in survival instinct. Then again, it could simply be the ways of the jungle out here, that if you are in these streets, then you are entitled to no sympathy, child or not.

The boy, no older than ten or eleven, carries himself like someone who's seen more than he ever should have. He doesn't play. Doesn't smile. Don't speak unless necessary. His eyes flick from person to person like searchlights in the dark, scanning for weakness and opportunity.

He walks with a purpose, pretending to stoop and grab beer cans here and there, like so many black kids do in this neighborhood. Hustling recyclables for a few coins ain't just a hustle, it's survival. But tonight, that's just a front. He ain't out here for cans.

He's hunting.

The city hums around him. It's Friday night. All the jukebox joints and neon-lit bars are alive, pulsing, breathing, and filled with the scent of sweat, cheap perfume, cigarettes, and spilled gin. Men laugh too loud. Women sway to Marvin

Gaye or Al Green. On these corners, everyone wants to forget something.

Inside Tamp's Bar and Grill, the air is thick with soul music and chatter. A man, red-faced and slurring, rises from a cluttered table where the ashtray overflows and liquor dances in half-empty glasses. He stumbles toward the single bathroom in the back, bouncing off chairs.

"Damn, somebody in there," he mutters, tugging at the locked doorknob.

Frustrated, he pivots and hurries toward the back exit, hands pressed tight against his crotch like a dam about to burst. He bursts through the rear door into the dark, muggy night, unaware he's about to become part of a different story.

Out here, the streetlights don't reach far. Only the club's glow spills a few feet past the doorway. He turns left, heading toward the shadows near the dumpster, where the stench of piss is thick and hot, curling up his nostrils like ammonia gas.

As the man unzips and leans into the wall, groaning with relief, the child emerges, silent as fog, sudden as a whisper. It is as if the night itself peeled open and let him slip out.

He's fast. Calm. Focused.

In one hand, a sharp single-edged razor. With the other, steady fingers reach toward the back pocket of the man's slacks, right where the outline of a wallet presses.

With a swift, practiced swipe, he slices the pocket clean

open. The fabric parts with a whisper. The wallet falls effortlessly into his small palm.

The man flinches, twisting his head. "Hey, what the?"

But it's too late.

The kid is already gone, darting down the alley with the agility of a shadow. His feet pound the pavement like he's done this a hundred times before. And maybe he has. Maybe this is who he is now. Not a boy. Not a thief.

A ghost in the alley.

Just another night in a world that teaches boys to be wolves before they ever get to be kids.

Chapter 3

Lessons from the Avenue

(1970)

Teddy Hilson sits at his desk, barely able to keep still. His knee bounces under the table. His eyes flick constantly to the clock above the chalkboard, willing the minute hand to move faster. The last bell can't come soon enough.

There was a time when he hated this moment—the end of the school day used to mean a return to a tense home, chores, or silence. But that was before the move to Anderson Avenue. Before the streets started calling his name louder than any school bell ever could.

Now, his heart races for what waits outside.

Twelve years old. Sharp as a tack. Good-looking, with a pair of curious brown eyes that seem to scan the world with more hunger than most grown men. And that hunger isn't for food or toys. It's for knowledge—the kind you don't get from books or classrooms. The kind you earn from the hustle, from watching, from surviving.

His world is small but complicated. His mother, Inez, is the sun it orbits. She's loving in her way, a fighter when sober, and a wanderer when drunk. The bottle has her heart in a chokehold, but she still tries. She still shows up the best she can. Teddy knows that. Their bond is more partnership than parenthood. It's built on necessity, on unspoken understanding.

"Ma always says, 'We got each other, baby. That's more than some folks ever had," he once told his older sister Cynthia as they counted dollar bills on the kitchen table.

Teddy often takes on more than a boy should. Making sure rent gets paid. Saving for school clothes. He moves through life with the silent pressure of being both a child and a caretaker.

The year is 1978. America isn't at war, and jobs are plenty. But for kids like Teddy, Fort Myers is still a battlefield. Anderson Avenue is his university, and the tuition is paid in bruises, lies, and quick lessons.

Their house sits between Shorty's Bar and B.C.'s Jukebox Joint. The front porch is screened in, and from it, Teddy watches the parade of street life unfold every day. He studies the men with gold chains and heaVee cologne. The woman with wide hips and sharper eyes. But it's winter when he gets most excited, when long sleek Cadillacs glide to the curb like sharks, and outstep the pimps, dressed like technicolor dreams. Big hats. Fur coats. All flash, all power.

After three years on Anderson Avenue, Teddy has stopped dreaming of fire engines or football fields. No more fantasies of law degrees or jerseys. Those have all been replaced with something real, something right in front of him. The streets have shown him a new kind of ambition.

By the time he finishes sixth grade, something unexpected happens. The school administration sees something in him, a brain too sharp to be held back. They skip him straight to eighth grade. It's a surprise to some, but

Teddy knows he's always been ahead. Just not always in the way teachers can measure.

That promotion lands him in a new program called "Work Studies." It's perfect. School from eight to noon, and then he's free to roam. Free to work. Free to learn in the only classroom that ever really challenged him in the street.

The truancy officers don't bother him now. He's got permission. But even before this, Teddy was already making his rounds. He'd been hanging around pool halls since age eleven, nursing sodas, watching, learning.

It's in his mid-teens that the regulars start taking notice. The old heads at Club 21, Jack's Pool Hall, and Club 82 start talking.

"That boy got hands like silk," one man murmurs, watching Teddy line up a corner shot.

"Smooth like butter and eyes like a hawk," another replies.

Word spreads fast. Teddy's name begins to carry weight. He's not just a kid with a stick. He's a hustler with instinct.

But being fourteen comes with limitations. Bars and clubs don't care how straight you shoot if you're too young to drink.

On Wednesday night, Teddy shows up at Club 82. The last time he was there, Dave, the club owner, ran him off, muttering about rules and age. But tonight, Dave has just returned from a trip. He steps inside and stops in his tracks. The crowd is massive, all eyes locked on the single pool table in the center.

"What the hell?" he mutters under his breath.

He pushes through the wall of bodies, past the smoke and murmurs, only to see Teddy, his once unwelcome guest, running the table with calm confidence. Cash is flying. Bets are high. And everyone is watching the kid.

Dave squints, scratching his chin. The businessman in him speaks louder than his pride.

He nods to the bartender and mutters, "Let the boy play."

From that night forward, Teddy is never turned away again.

School fades into the background. Not that it ever really had his full attention. Now, the streets are his school, his temple, his battleground. He wakes and sleeps to its rhythm.

But this education has no grades, no report cards. The stakes are higher. A missed lesson doesn't mean summer school.

Out here, failing a test can cost you your life.

Chapter 4

Blood, Brotherhood, and Blanks

"You know," Rodney's voice crackled through the phone line, low and heaVee, "that could've easily been you instead of Willie. These new thugs out here? Cold-blooded. Not like when we were coming up. It's a damn miracle everybody in that pool hall didn't end up in a body bag. You got any idea who did it?"

Sire leaned back against his kitchen counter, his hand absently stroking his jaw. The memories of the previous night still flickered behind his eyes like a dim film reel.

"No. Not yet," he said flatly. "But I will. Believe that. When more than one person is involved in a murder, keeping it quiet becomes damn near impossible. There were five of them. That many mouths? Somebody's bound to slip."

Rodney sighed, the kind of exhale that carried both worry and weariness. "But why just Willie? Why was he the only one killed?"

Sire rubbed his temples, letting the truth sting him again. "Because Willie didn't listen. Ignored the guns. Ignored the shouting. He went for the stack of cash on the pool table like it was his birthright. I guess he thought he could make it. He couldn't."

Rodney's tone shifted from inquisitive to admonishing.

"Sire, listen to me. You're too old for this shit. You've got too much potential to still be swimming with sharks. Remember what you told me when you got outta lockup? Said you'd get a job, save up, and open your own business. Said something about starting a union for ex-cons. Man, what happened to all that?"

Sire chuckled humorlessly. "Rodney, slow the hell down. You firing off questions like a damn news anchor. Let me speak."

He took a breath, the air heaVee with bitterness and truth. "That job dream? I tried, man. You know I did. Got my GED in there. Took college courses. Became a damn bookworm. I knocked on over thirty employers' doors. Thirty. They liked me until they heard I was a convict. Then it was always, 'We'll call you back.' But the phone never rang."

Rodney's voice sharpened. "But not every business turned you down."

"They might as well have," Sire shot back. "You think I was gunning for a broom and mop job? With my credentials? I was overqualified and still under-considered."

On the other end, Rodney's laugh came through, warm but tinged with sadness. "Same old Sire."

"Look, man, I gotta go. Got a call to stop by and see Bandy Welks at the precinct. Might be a break in the pool hall case."

"Alright, Sire. Watch your back. These streets don't

24

play fair."

Click.

As he slid the phone into his pocket, Sire heard Shauka's deep growl erupt outside. He stepped out onto the porch. The pit bull, now a broad-shouldered beast of reddish brown muscle, was going wild, barking furiously at a leashed dog walking by with its owner.

"Chill out, Shauka," Sire muttered, pulling him back. "That dog ain't looking for trouble…"

That's when it hit him.

The walk. The toes.

The image came flooding back, the slight, almost dancer-like gait of one of the masked robbers. A tip-toe stroll, like someone strutting to a beat only he could hear. Only one person walked like that.

Rock Blanks.

It all rushed in now. Last summer. The dog fight. Shauka versus Sho' Death, Rock's prize fighter. It had been hell in a backyard.

Sho' Death had ripped Shauka's ear clean off. Blood soaked the dirt, turning Shauka's coat crimson. Everyone thought it was over. Then, in a miracle twist that even seasoned dogmen couldn't believe, Shauka planted all four paws and launched upward, flipping Sho' Death into the air like a WWE suplex.

The stunned silence had turned into a roar as Shauka, dripping blood, went savage. Bite after bite, tear after tear, he dismantled Sho' Death like a wolf with vengeance in its eyes.

"GET 'EM, BOY. AARRGGH. TEAR HIS ASS UP, SHAUKA." Sire had screamed, voice cracking from the rush.

Rock panicked. "I'll give you five thousand. Just call him off!"

Sire had smiled then, a cold smile. "Down, Shauka."

The dog obeyed.

That memory, now vivid, gave way to a darker realization.

The pool hall. The robbery. Willie dead.

It wasn't just Rock. No. If Rock was involved, the rest of the Blanks crew probably was too. Sammy Blanks, the oldest, is a killer for hire. Billy Blanks, short-tempered, was always the muscle and the others.

This wasn't just a robbery anymore. This was a war brewing, and Sire wanted no part of it.

That evening, Sire drove to a storage unit tucked behind Bay Shore Road in North Fort Myers. The place smelled of metal and secrecy. Inside was ten pounds of weed, bagged, sealed, and ready for the streets. Also stashed were a Tec 9 and two Glock .40s. Street insurance.

Tish had secured the shed using the name of a former lover, an attorney she'd played like a fiddle. Tish Henry didn't do half measures.

Smart. Dependable. Fine. At 39, she wore strength-like armor and had the intense gaze of a woman who'd lived through a fire. Like Pam Grier in a Blaxploitation flick, beautiful, bold, and deadly.

Sire met her eighteen months ago at his old lawyer's office. She'd challenged him and said she'd leave everything behind if he made her his. He warned her, his world came with shadows, bullets, and blood.

She didn't blink, now she was in it. His phone buzzed. Skinner. Asking about the "meal."

"On the way now," Sire said, grabbing the bags. He usually avoided mixing hardware and products, but today was different. He needed to move fast.

In Dunbar, he parked near Skinner's place. Five pounds of weed per bag, topped with Lays chips. The drop went off without a hitch.

Driving through town, he passed Guava Street, where Mama Blanks lived. No interest in her. Rock was on South Street. Sire parked by the old STARS Complex and hoofed it through the projects.

He found an abandoned house with a view of Rock's

place. The grass held a shiny motorcycle, Billy's Ninja. A Ford F-150 and a van sat nearby.

He watched for nearly an hour. One figure came out, gold teeth gleaming, and mounted the bike. Billy. Sire considered tailing him but decided against it. No need to tip his hand just yet.

As he turned to leave, a creak echoed from the attic above. Sire froze. In one swift motion, he had the Beretta out, safety off, eyes scanning.

Silence.

Could be a raccoon, it could be worse.

In the attic, Bo Bo clutched his crack pipe. Paranoia swallowed him whole. His sweaty body trembled as he saw a man in black staring out the window.

That's Rock's house, he thought. Who the hell is crazy enough to mess with Rock Blanks?

Then, the man turned and looked up at him. Bo Bo stopped breathing. Then, the man disappeared.

The next day, Sire, Tish, and Vee visited Graddic's farm for target practice.

"One more time, Tish. Vee, you watching?" Sire barked.

Tish tore her shirt, splashing red nail polish over her chest and face. She staggered forward, moaning like she was dying, eyes wide with mock desperation.

"Help me… please…" she whispered.

Most men would drop their guard. Women, Sire said, could either raise a man to glory or lure him to his grave.

Vee nodded. "It's reciprocity. My psych class at FAMU broke it down. Give something, even a flower, and people feel obligated. That's how Tupperware and Krishna hustled folks. Human nature, especially men, can't ignore a wounded woman. Especially when sex is a distraction."

Sire smirked. "Damn, college girl. That's deep."

He pulled her close, brushing her lips with his. Tish joined, wrapping her arms around both of them. They stood still, three hearts beating as one, for just a moment.

Driving down Anderson Avenue, still, Anderson to him, not MLK Jr. Blvd, Sire saw Trick Baby, bent at the waist, slobbering and swaying on heroin legs.

Inside Golmer's Grocery, he bought orange juice, soda, and peach. Tish and Vee laughed like sisters. No jealousy. No power struggles. They lived to protect him. That was rare.

Outside, chaos.

A man curled on the ground, beaten. Above him stood Billy Blanks, rage exploding.

"You wanna die, motherfucker? This your last warning!"

Sire's blood ran cold.

That voice, that limp.

It wasn't Rock who pulled the trigger that night, it was Billy. They both walked on their toes, but only Billy had that limp. Sire backed away. Got in the car. Drove off with his women.

"Damn," he muttered to himself.

He hadn't wanted this war, but the war had come anyway.

You play the hand you're dealt or fold.

And Sire? Sire didn't fold.

Not then, not ever.

Chapter 5

Cool Blood, Cold Streets

The 1970s: a decade steeped in soul, swagger, and a sense of self-definition. Everywhere you looked, from neon-lit corners to back-alley dice games, from juke joints to barbershops, there was a collective performance of cool. People didn't just walk, they glided. They didn't just speak, they preached. And for Black America, "cool" wasn't just style, it was survival. It was armor. A performance. A rebellion.

The country was shifting fast. Television had begun its reign, slicing into the film industry's box office profits. Studios were desperate, scrambling for a new formula to bring people back to the theaters. In their panic, they turned to the very audience they had long ignored: Black America. The result was the rise of a controversial, electric new genre called Blaxploitation. Films, like Cotton Comes to Harlem, Shaft, Coffy, Foxy Brown, and Superfly, flooded the screens with fast-talking, sharply-dressed antiheroes who didn't play by the rules, they rewrote them. Some cheered these films as revolutionary. Others saw exploitation wrapped in rhythm and velvet. But no matter the take, one truth stood out: a generation was watching. Imitating. Dreaming, and in Fort Myers, Florida, one of those dreamers was Little Teddy.

Tonight. Saturday night. The air is sticky with summer heat and the promise of trouble. Teddy steps into the night dressed in a uniform of young Black cool. Rust-colored corduroy jeans stiff as cardboard, a brown silk V-neck tee hugging his slim frame, brown Stacy Adams shoes that shine like polished copper, and the pièce de résistance: a tilted brown derby hat. The angle is deliberate. It's not just style, it's a signal. He's a boy playing a man's game.

He should be up on The Avenue, where the grown folks prowl, where the real stakes lie. But tonight is for the teen dance, the training ground. Inside the dim, sweaty rec center, the bass thumps like a second heartbeat. Bodies grind. Eyes watch. Status is earned in sweat, in rhythm, and in who gets chosen when the slow jam plays.

Lynn Murray is stealing the show, her limbs moving in robotic precision to the Commodores' Brick House. The crowd roars. Teddy watches, half-impressed, half-bored, until he spots it. A wad of cash, thick and heaVee, jutting from the pocket of Lynn's dance partner. It's not just money, it's an opportunity. And Teddy, even at fifteen, already understands the power of taking something that wasn't given.

He doesn't hesitate. He moves like a whisper and brushes past the man once, then again, this time with purpose. A practiced bump. A subtle tug. The money vanishes into Teddy's own pocket, and just like that, he's gone. Out into the night. Onto The Avenue.

The Avenue is alive with lights and lies. A melting pot of hustlers, hookers, dreamers, and dealers. The air smells of hair grease, cheap liquor, fried food, and danger. Teddy stops by the Tasty Freeze, Fort Myers' ghetto answer to Dairy Queen.

"Gimme a gizzard cone with heaVee hot sauce," he tells Mrs. Seawood.

"Young man," she says warmly, "how you doin' tonight?"

"I'm alright," Teddy replies, even though the street hums beneath his feet, tempting him with more.

Gizzard cone in hand, he heads toward Jack's Pool Room, passing a dark alley next to Galmer's Grocery. That's when the voice slithers out.

"Hey. Hey. Jitter-bug, come here."

Teddy freezes. "Fuck you. What the hell do I look like comin' in dat dark ass alley?"

The voice comes again, harder now.

"If I have to call your lil' ass again, umma bust a cap in it."

A figure steps forward, emerging from the shadow like something out of a nightmare. A man with a pistol so large it gleams like chrome lightning in the dim streetlight. But Teddy doesn't flinch. Not much, anyway.

"You might as well get to bustin'," he snaps back, "cause I sho ain't comin' to you now."

The man laughs. Hard. So hard that he almost buckles. But his grip on the gun never wavers. He's amused.

Intrigued.

"I need you to do me a small favor," the man says, his voice calm now.

"I'll give you fifty bucks."

Teddy listens.

All he has to do is deliver a brown paper bag to two dope boys in front of Sam Bo Bo's Greasy Spoon and tell them one name: Joe Kearse.

Teddy agrees. Why not? Fifty bucks for a simple errand? That's grown-man money.

He approaches the dealers with the same cocky confidence he wore in the rec center.

"See that man over there by the alley?" he says, nodding toward Joe. "He told me to give y'all this bag and tell y'all that Joe Kearse said un-ass the money and dope."

The name hits them like a thunderclap.

The tall one deflates. The other one goes pale. Whatever bravado they had evaporated. They hand over fat rolls of cash and two zip bags full of dope, grumbling under their breath but obeying. Teddy watches them, awestruck. Joe Kearse didn't lift a finger. That was power.

Teddy brings the bag back across Anderson Avenue.

"Man," he says, eyes wide with newfound awe, "you are

a badass dude for real. Those dope boys almost pissed in their pants when they saw you. Who the fuck is you?"

"Joe Kearse, young blood."

Teddy swallows his pride. This is it. His moment.

"I don't want those fifty dollars you promised me," he says. "Instead, I want you to teach me how to be like you."

For a long second, Joe doesn't speak. His cold eyes scanned the boy, searching. There's something in them. Pride, pain, a warning. A glimmer of his own ghost.

Finally, Joe speaks.

"Son, listen. This is no way to live a life. When people fear you, it's more dangerous to you than to them."

He speaks of courage and wisdom. Of the delicate line between bravery and stupidity. Of survival.

"Always remember, the dope game is one of the richest and slimiest games out here. The hate dope boys have for jack boys like me is equal to what they feel for cops. So whatever you choose in this cold-ass world, make damn sure your mind's made up. Everything else will be at your command."

Then, without a word more, Joe reaches into the bag, hands Teddy a fat wad of cash, and disappears back into the darkness, leaving only the echo of his truth and the gleam of that big-ass pistol behind.

Chapter 6

The Palace and the Pact

A week had passed since the gun range session with Tish and Vee. The morning sun now streamed through the sheer curtains of the living room, casting a warm, golden hue across the tile floors and worn leather sofa.

Sire sat still, absorbing the silence. The same house, his Palace, that had once felt like a fortress in a storm now exhaled peace. Nestled on a half-acre in South Fort Myers, the four-bedroom home was more than brick and drywall. It was still a sanctuary, but one that changed with him, restless in the rain, reflective in the sun. A mirror of the man inside it.

The recently remodeled home had everything he could want: a split floor plan, a cozy fireplace, a luxurious master suite with a private den, and a sparkling pool complete with a built-in bar. It was a far cry from the concrete coldness of prison cells and sleepless nights behind bars. For the first time in years, he could stretch out on his own couch, walk barefoot in his own yard, and breathe without tension.

He had moved into The Palace over six months ago. Back then, the walls were bare, and the rooms echoed with emptiness. But then came Tish. She didn't just move in, she breathed life into the place. Her presence filled the spaces with warmth, laughter, with purpose. After all those years alone, waking up next to her made each morning feel like a blessing he never knew to ask for.

He'd once asked her why she gave it all up, her business, her comfort, her world, just to be by his side. She didn't even hesitate.

"You enable my spirit to soar," she told him, her eyes calm and unwavering. "You give me a kind of freedom I never knew existed."

She had a poet's way with words, weaving philosophy into everyday conversation. Tish believed that growth came from discomfort and that the soul stretched its wings when challenged. Her words stuck with him: "There are no accidents in life… I'm just seizing my moment."

Sire often thought to himself how lucky he was. Tish wasn't just sexy, though she absolutely was, she was also wise, strategic, and fiercely loyal. And then there was Vee, the other woman in his life. Together, the three of them had formed something rare, something balanced. Still, with both women out of town for the past few days, the house had grown far too quiet.

"I'll be glad when they get back," Sire muttered, wiping his hands after feeding Shauka, the protective beast of a dog that guarded The Palace like a sentinel.

Just as he rose from the patio, the growl of the Escalade's engine pulled into the driveway. Shauka barked his greeting, tail wagging as Tish and Vee stepped out, radiant under the Florida sun.

"Hey, you two," Sire called out, cracking a wide grin.

"Hey, to you, back. Did you miss us?" Tish purred, her

voice like silk sliding across bare skin.

"More than you know, sweetness. More than either of you can imagine. I've been out here living like a caveman, cooking my own meals. It's tragic," he said, feigning a pout.

Tish raised an eyebrow. "Daddy, don't start. We tried to take you with us, remember? You said you'd be just fine. What, now you trying to guilt us?"

He smirked. "Maybe I am. But I might be willing to forgive… for a tiny little touch."

The two women exchanged mischievous glances before rushing toward him in a playful frenzy. Tish, in her satin mini skirt that shimmered under the sunlight, pressed herself close. Vee, in tight pink biker shorts, moved with deliberate sensuality. Their laughter filled the air, and Sire's hands, eager, grateful, found familiar places on their bodies.

They were teasing, arousing, and connecting in that wordless language built on trust, history, and raw desire. But Sire, always the tactician, pulled back before things escalated.

"Go on," he said, his tone shifting slightly, "unpack, get refreshed. We need to talk."

He waited until they disappeared into the house, then walked over to the stereo and slid in a Maze CD. The smooth rhythm of "We Are One" pulsed through the room, a soulful prelude to a conversation he'd been rehearsing in his head for days.

Moments later, Tish returned.

"Daddy," she said, "we stopped by the weed connection. I told him you wanted five hundred pounds like before. He only had two hundred. Said he'll need a few days for the rest."

"What'd you tell him?"

"That we'd take the two hundred for now. He offered it fronted, but I told him I'd call him before midnight. Didn't want to drive around with product in the Escalade."

"Good call," Sire nodded. "Bring me a glass of melon juice to the den. I need your thoughts on a few things."

"I'll get it!" Vee volunteered, dashing off with a smile.

Tish followed Sire to the den, her heels clicking softly on the polished floor.

"What's eating at you, my king?" she asked.

"Let's wait for Vee. But I'll say this much. I know who robbed the Pool Hall."

Tish's eyes sharpened. "Oh yeah?"

"Blank's brothers."

She inhaled sharply. "Damn. If their rep is even half true, we'll need both hands for that heat. And believe me, both will be full."

Just then, Vee returned, handing him the glass of melon juice. He nodded his thanks and motioned for them both to sit.

"Here's the deal," he said, voice steady. "I walked into Tee Tots' with fifty grand. Left with twenty, and only because the old man held it as table stakes. Now, normally, I'd be riled up. But here's what's keeping me calm…"

He laid it all out, pound-for-pound profit margins, worker pay, and the bottom line. They were about to clear ninety thousand dollars. He could eat the thirty grand loss.

"I can live with it," he said finally. "But I want your take."

Tish leaned in, voice warm. "Sire, I gave up my world for yours. Whatever you decide, I'm with you."

Vee, always the firebrand, had more to say. "I agree, Daddy. But what about the violence? The brother who got killed? Pimpwell's chain? It's too much. We blame the system, but look at us. We're doing this to ourselves."

Tish gave a nod of approval. "Well said."

"I hear you," Sire said, "but nothing was taken directly from me. They went after the pimps, the hustlers. Still, we're not waiting for trouble. We're ready for it."

He turned to Vee. "By the way, you impressed me. The way you handled that Glock…"

Vee smiled, her cheeks glowing. "Thanks. But don't let the curls fool you. I grew up with four older brothers who all taught me how to survive. I'll never betray either of you. And if it ever came down to it, I'd risk my life to protect you."

Sire looked at her, then at Tish. "That's deep. But I need you to understand something. What you're offering is commitment, not love. Love is rooted in emotion. But commitment? Commitment is a pledge. It's a duty. It's everything."

Vee grinned. "I can dig it. And I don't even need a shovel."

Their laughter broke the tension, just as the phone rang. Tish picked up.

"It's the connection," she said. "The rest of the order's ready."

Sire gave quick instructions. Meet at the Brown Derby, use the payphone at Publix, and grab a paper while you're at it.

As Tish headed out, Vee stayed behind.

"Let me ask you something," Sire said, shifting his tone. "Where'd you really learn to shoot like that? And no more 'my brothers taught me' lines."

Vee hesitated, then took a breath. "Alright. Real story? I was with a man named Carlton. We met at FAMU. He left college to lead a chapter of the New Black Panther Party. He was passionate, fearless, and driven. He taught me everything, especially how to defend myself."

Sire listened closely. "Where's Carlton now?"

"Dead. Shot by police three months ago in Fort Lauderdale. He knew it might happen and told me to stay away."

Sire's brow furrowed. "So why leave after?"

"I destroyed files. Closed out accounts. Gave Ishmael, his second in command, half the cash in the safe. I had no ties left there. I'm from Atlanta."

Sire was quiet for a long moment.

"You've lived a whole other life before we met."

"I have. But I'm here now. With you. You're my man."

Sire looked at her with a new layer of respect.

"You're full of surprises, Vee."

She smiled gently, her eyes shimmering with truth.

"And I've still got more to show you."

Chapter 7

Blood on the Jukebox

The tall, caramel-colored woman stood by the jukebox, her arms wrapped tightly across her chest like a barrier against the world. Barbara's eyes scanned the flashing buttons of the dusty old machine, but she wasn't interested in Marvin Gaye or Aretha tonight. The jukebox was simply a place to escape the noise, the judgment, the looks, especially the looks.

She shifted her weight to one leg, the toe of her pump tapping against the stained linoleum floor as cigarette smoke hung in the air like gauze. Club 21 reeked of cheap beer and crushed dreams. The laughter from the next table felt jagged like glass scraping against a chalkboard. She winced and looked down, the corners of her lips tightened in silent suffering.

Barbara wasn't here for the music. She was here because she had nowhere else to go.

They had been evicted that morning.

Red Man, her man for eight years, sat hunched at the corner table, nursing a watered-down drink and the weight of two months' unpaid rent. He watched her carefully, a mix of guilt and helplessness carved into the lines of his face.

They had tried to go straight. That had to count for something, didn't it?

Red Man had hustled his whole life, but the streets never forgave you, not fully. Barbara had held a job at the packinghouse, steady work, decent hours. Then came the layoff, the silence, and the pink slip that folded her future into quarters and threw it away.

Now they were drifting again.

Barbara sighed, her finger hovering near the button for "What's Going On," when a screech ripped through the thick air.

"I know damn well you ain't selecting none of my songs. That's my damn money in the machine!"

Barbara blinked. A short, stout woman stormed from the bathroom, her wig tilting slightly to one side as she stomped toward the jukebox like a madwoman on a mission.

The bar fell into an eerie hush. Conversations died mid-sentence. Heads turned.

"Excuse me?" Barbara asked, her voice flat but polite.

"You heard what the hell I said," the woman growled. "You better not have used my selections."

Barbara didn't flinch. She didn't want trouble. She wanted peace. Help, maybe. Kindness, if it still existed in this city.

"I didn't use or select any of your songs, and I'm sorry if I did anything to upset you." Her tone was calm and controlled. She had learned long ago that in places like this, it was better to yield than to fight.

She turned to walk away. Red Man was already half-rising from his seat, lips parted in a warning.

"Barbara, watch out!"

Too late.

The woman rushed up behind her and shoved her hard. Barbara's feet lost traction, and she hit the floor with a thud, sliding across the grimy surface. A burst of pain shot up her hip, but her pride ached more. The room blurred with rage.

The woman charged again, fists raised. But Barbara wasn't broken. She was bruised, yes, but she still had her spine. Gritting her teeth, she sprang to her feet and rammed into the oncoming woman like a linebacker, sending both into a tangle of limbs and curses. Chairs toppled. Drinks spilled.

"Get off me!" the woman shrieked, but Barbara was done playing nice.

From the edge of the room, Red Man's hand moved fast, too fast to be noticed. His fingers dipped into his left pocket and pulled something out, something small and glinting.

As the brawl spiraled into chaos, another man stepped in, grabbing Barbara by the shoulder.

"Let go of me!" she shouted, twisting in his grasp. But

the stranger wasn't just holding. He was holding her firmly, giving the other woman the advantage.

Red Man's eyes narrowed. His face darkened with fury.

In one smooth motion, he slashed the stranger's forearm with a flick and a drag of his blade. Two fast swipes.

The man howled. "Arrgghh. Shit."

The skin of his forearm peeled back grotesquely, tendons glistening beneath the bar lights. Blood sprayed onto Barbara's blouse as the man staggered backward, reaching under his shirt with his good hand and pulling out a gun.

"He's got a gun!" someone screamed.

Chairs clattered. Glass shattered. Club 21 erupted in chaos. Patrons ducked behind booths and bolted for the exit. But the man's eyes widened as he looked at the dangling flesh from his own arm. He dropped the gun and slumped to the floor, his lady friend screaming as she tried to wrap a dirty towel around his wound.

Teddy, who had just stepped inside, stood frozen halfway across the room. He had seen the whole thing unfold like a slow-motion movie. The fall. The brawl. The knife. The gun. He spotted the revolver skittering across the floor, landing in the shadows between the jukebox and the wall.

Calmly, he walked over, scooped it up, and disappeared out the front door with the fleeing crowd.

Chapter 8

The Price of Truth

The tall, sinister-looking man with an old, ugly wound along one side of his face put forth his hand and touched the other man, indicating that's enough. The battered person strapped to the old wooden chair was unconscious again from the severe beating Jabbo gave him.

"He's telling the truth. If he knew more, he'd spill it," Sammy explained.

"Get his ass out of here and clean up your mess. Put some crack in his pocket. Also, give him the fifty dollars he asked for in the beginning."

Both of Bo Bo's eyes were swollen shut. His jaw was broken, and his discolored front teeth were covered with blood. The left side of his bloated lip was deeply gashed, the result of being repeatedly struck there by Jabbo's fist. The K-9 tooth had penetrated the lip.

Bo Bo had approached Sammy Blanks, offering information about something he saw a few nights ago. He told Sammy what he saw. A guy dressed in black was spying on Rock's house.

Sammy was the oldest of the Blanks brothers. There were five of them in total: Rock, Billy, Byron, and Jabbo. Sammy was aware that the cops had Byron under watch. Byron was a major drug dealer and had been in the game for a long time. All the brothers favored a specific craft out in the streets, but each could perform the mission of the other. They shared a strong bond and sense of comradeship.

Sammy was also aware that Bo Bo had been observed on more than one occasion getting out of the unmarked police vehicle of Detective Bandy Welks. This fact was the primary reason for the beating. The brothers thought that Bo Bo was trying to play both ends against the middle in an effort to support his crack cocaine habit by being the eyes for the police and then turning right back around and claiming to be the eyes for the crook.

But after sticking to his story in the face of the severe beating, Sammy now believed him. He was seriously concerned over who the spying individual could be, and what the hell they were looking for. It simply didn't make sense. If it were someone planning a robbery, there simply wasn't a need to spend that much time keeping Rock's crib under surveillance. No, Sammy thought, it wasn't someone casing the joint. It was much, much bigger. If it was a hit, the next question was, why would a contract be out on his younger brother? When Rock got back in town, Sammy would have to find out exactly what he had been into lately.

Chapter 9

Sugar Bear Rises

"Love and happiness... something that'll make you do wrong... something that'll make you do right, yeah..."

Al Green's voice oozed from the dusty old RCA 45, filling the small living room like a slow-moving fog. It was three in the morning, and Inez was dancing. Not with anyone, just with herself. She swayed with an original two-step, eyes closed, holding a glass of Canadian Mist in one hand and the half-empty bottle in the other.

The carpet beneath her feet was worn. The lamp on the side table flickered. Outside, the city was sleeping, but Inez was in her world.

Teddy heard her from his room and knew immediately what it meant. Usually, when she was up this late, singing and drinking, it meant she had company. And the company meant cash.

He padded softly through the hallway and peeked into her bedroom. Just as expected, two bodies sprawled across the bed. His mother was half-covered with a floral sheet, and the man beside her snored deeply, the bottle still gripped between his thighs.

Teddy moved silently. Like a shadow, he crept into the room and rifled through the man's pants on the floor. A wallet. Folded bills. Jackpot.

By the time the pair stirred, Teddy was gone, already heading toward The Avenue. The wide street, slick from last night's rain, glistened under the early sun. The Avenue was his teacher, his playground, his proving ground.

It was around ten in the morning when Teddy cut through the back lot of Buck's Place, a spot known for good food, bad pool games, and parking lot drama. Under a giant oak tree, he saw a commotion unfolding.

A group of wine-heads were drinking and laughing, but their joy was shattered when three young thugs jumped them. One of the goons yanked the wine bottle from an old man's hand. The man tried to retrieve it, only to be sucker-punched and dropped to the ground. Another goon drew back, ready to kick the fallen man square in the face.

But the old man wasn't done.

In a sudden burst of agility, the wine head shifted onto his right elbow and swept his left leg low and hard. The kicker never saw it coming. His feet flew out from under him, and he landed flat on his backside.

Stunned, the old man jumped to his feet. His movements were clean and practiced. Another thug stepped forward, cocky and smiling, assuming a boxer's stance.

"Come on, old man. Let's dance," he sneered.

The puncher launched a wild right hook, but the wine head dipped just in time. The thug stumbled forward, off balance. The old man stepped aside and countered with a precise left hook to the temple. The young man collapsed, knocked out cold.

The last goon tried to intervene. He ran behind a crate and picked up a large brick, holding it high to strike.

Teddy had seen enough. He pulled the pistol he had found behind the jukebox a week ago and pointed it at the thug.

"If you don't put that damn rock down, umma bust a cap in yo fool ass," he shouted, trying to channel Joe Kearse's voice.

The thug froze. So did the wine-head.

The brick hit the ground with a dull thud. The three assailants ran, disappearing down the alley like rats from a flood.

The old man exhaled and looked at Teddy. His jaw was bruised, his lip bleeding, but his eyes gleamed.

"If the man rolls down on you, young blood, with that heat, you're going downtown. That's only if a cop decides to ask questions first instead of shootin' first and askin' questions last," he said.

"What man? Who are you talking about?"

"The police."

"Oh. Why didn't you just say police? And it ain't like I walk around showin' everybody that I got a gun."

"Take it easy, young man."

"If that joker hadn't picked up that brick to hit you with, I never would've pulled it out."

"Don't misread me, young blood. I'm glad as hell you were here. Otherwise, I might not be rappin' with you right now."

Teddy looked at him sideways. He wasn't sure whether to believe this drunk or not.

"I'm only speakin' matter-of-factly. Most cops are itching for a chance to smoke one of our black asses. Havin' a gun is like giving them a license to kill you."

"Not if I kill his ass first," Teddy snapped.

"No. No. No. Son, that's the wrong attitude. Never declare war on the law. That's suicide. Even if you escape death, you'll be dead inside. Behind that badge is the force of the whole government. And the government of the United States is one bad mother. You kill a cop, especially a white one, and the law comes down on you so hard the ground you stand on will vanish."

"Well," Teddy said slowly, "That doesn't sound right to me. If the police are supposed to protect people, how does that badge give 'em the right to kill us?"

"That's not exactly what I mean, son. And what's your name anyway?"

"Teddy."

"I'm Frank. Dig this, young blood. What I meant was that carryin' a gun gives the cops a reason to kill you. So don't get it twisted. Even the law must obey the law. No one is above it, not even the President. But carryin' a gun out here raises the stakes. Just be careful. You hear me? Be careful, even if you can't be good."

Frank turned toward Roger's Package Store.

Teddy hesitated, then called out.

"Hey, Frank. Will you teach me how to fight?"

Frank paused and smiled faintly.

"We'll see, kid. We'll see."

A week later, Teddy returned, hoping to see Frank again. But Frank was nowhere to be found.

On The Avenue, the sun was cruel. People packed themselves beneath shade trees, trying to escape the heat, but business kept moving. Boosters hawked clothes and meat. Dice games clattered in the shadows. Dope fiends buzzed like flies. Prostitutes flaunted more skin in the heat.

As Teddy waited to cross the street, a woman's voice called out.

"Hey lil' daddy, what's hap'nin'?"

He turned. A prostitute leaned casually against a tree, smiling like she'd known him forever.

"You talkin' to me?"

"I'm sure not talkin' to Casper the friendly ghost," she purred.

Teddy smirked. "How you know Casper ain't my name?"

She laughed. "Not bad. Especially for someone so young."

"If you worried about my age, why'd you speak to me?"

Her smile faded just a bit.

"Hold up, lil' playa. I said something because I like your style. And to answer your first question, I don't know if your name is Casper. I just said that to make you smile. I'm not worried about your age if you can handle what I might give you. You got potential."

"What's that supposed to mean?"

"Your persona. That special something others see in you. Not everyone will recognize it. But those of us who do, we need you."

"I don't know what you talkin' about."

"You may be young, but sugar, you're definitely ready."

"You don't even know me," Teddy interrupted. "Why do you need me?"

Before she could answer, a pearl-gray Lincoln pulled up. She waved and headed to it. Just before opening the door, she looked back.

"My name's Betty, but everybody calls me Doll Baby. And if your name ain't Casper, may I know what it is?"

"Teddy."

"I like it. But if you don't mind, I like Sugar Bear better. You'll be sweet to women but strong like a man. I'll explain more later. We'll meet again…"

The car rolled away, and Teddy stared after it.

Later, Teddy hit Jack's Pool Den on Cuba Street. He baited an older player into a few games. A dollar a match. They traded wins and losses. After an hour, Teddy was up seven bucks. Jimmy called it quits, and Teddy left.

Outside Club 21, he noticed an older man selling marijuana joints and stacking cash. Teddy considered robbing him, but the man spoke first.

"What's goin' on, jitterbug? Still got that gun you picked up last week from behind the jukebox?"

"I don't know what you talkin' about," Teddy lied, arm brushing the weapon at his waist.

"No beef, son. I'm just lookin' to buy if you wanna sell. I came back to town, and this joint business is hot. Someone's bound to rob me. I need protection."

"I dig, man," Teddy said. "But I ain't sellin' nothin'. How 'bout I got your back when I'm on the stroll?"

"Cool. I'm Hubert. What's your name?"

"They call me Sugar Bear."

Hubert smiled. Once he sold out, he handed Teddy twenty bucks and ten joints.

What Teddy didn't know was that Hubert had hustled for decades. He saw the greed in the boy's eyes. And just in case, Hubert had a loaded .357 derringer strapped to his wrist.

For the next few months, Teddy trained with Frank and soaked up every lesson. When he finished, he'd clean up and meet Doll Baby on The Avenue. She always had a bankroll for him. But today, she was different.

"What's wrong with you, Betty?" he asked.

"Nothing, Sugar Bear. Just a situation needing attention."

"What do you mean?"

"We need to talk. I believe you're ready."

"Ready for what?"

"First, let me ask you something. Here's five hundred and fifty-three dollars. That's everything I made since I last saw you. I've been giving you money for over three months. What have you done with it?"

"I've been lettin' it build up. With this, I got close to fifteen hundred. Still got every penny."

"I figured you'd say that."

"So why'd you ask?

"Sugar Bear, don't take me for a fool. I'm from the old

school. Out here, if a woman chooses a man, she gives him everything."

"Chooses what?"

"Her man. Her protector. Her daddy. If a smooth-talking player's game is tight, it's his job to make her surrender to him."

"Quit lookin' at me like that, Betty. You makin' my dick hard."

"Listen, Sugar Bear. I got a room at the Sheridan downtown. Would you mind spendin' some time with me?"

"No, Doll Baby," he said softly. "I don't mind. How we gettin' there?"

"A cab," she answered.

And just like that, Sugar Bear's journey into manhood took another step.

Chapter 10

Shadows Beneath the Cypress

"Doggonit! I wish they'd have this thief of a machine repaired or replaced. I lose at least eight bucks a month in it," Detective Bandy Welks grumbled, slapping the side of the ancient vending machine with the same frustration he'd shown it for three years running. The stale bag of corn chips clung halfway inside the coil, taunting him.

"Did it get you again?" Sonny Ferrells laughed from across the break room, cradling a steaming cup of black coffee like a sacred relic.

Bandy shot him a sidelong glare.

"Yeah, Sonny. The thief has struck again. The chief needs to retire this antique. Or at least give it a proper burial."

The two detectives made an odd but effective pair. Bandy, a wiry, sharp-featured Black man with eyes like lit coals. Sonny is a massive white man with a booming voice and shoulders like stacked bricks. Around the department, they were jokingly dubbed "Super Foot and the One-Man Gang."

Sonny took a slow sip. "Oh, before I forget, Lewis from Homicide was lookin' for you. You run into him yet?"

"Nope. Not lately." Bandy's brow furrowed. "Funny, he hasn't had much to say to me since he got passed over for

Detective. I figured he might be nursing the wound."

"Word is," Sonny said, lowering his voice, "one of Lewis's informants spotted Bo Bo. Said the poor bastard's beat to hell. Any guesses who'd do that?"

Bandy leaned back, jaw tightening. "Hard to say without talking to him directly. Could be anything. Bo Bo's an addict. Crack, mostly. And that world…" He shook his head slowly. "That world doesn't care if you had a family or graduated from high school. Crack's not just a drug, it's a plague."

He stepped away from the vending machine and began pacing slightly, the weight of memory settling on his shoulders.

"In the early eighties," Bandy continued, "when crack hit Fort Myers, it hit the Black community like a wrecking ball. We'd barely pulled ourselves out from the heroin mess, and then crack came in with promises of escape, of fast highs. That first hit? It's like heaven. And after that, you spend your whole damn life chasing it, paying for it. It turned people into shadows of themselves. Took away refrigerators full of food and replaced them with emptiness. Little kids openin' the fridge to find nothin'. That drug ain't just poison. It's a damn curse."

Sonny let the silence settle before nodding.

"You gonna talk to Lewis?"

"I'll track him down later," Bandy said, grabbing his coat. "But first, I'm gonna need a real snack. One that doesn't come from a machine with a grudge."

*   *   *

"Damn man!" Jabbo cursed, slamming the passenger door of the low-slung Monte Carlo. "Ya'll be gone three damn days longer than we agreed."

Byron tossed his duffel into the trunk and shrugged. "Jab, you know the deal. Rock saw a piece of ass he couldn't pass up."

Rock lit a cigarette and blew smoke out the side of his mouth. "Business was handled, alright? Byron was back at the motel, and I took care of my own. Don't forget, you told us to delay returning. What's three days if the job got done?"

Jabbo ran a palm over his shaved head, frustration slowly cooling. "It's not a problem. But listen, Sammy's inside. Wants a word. Says somebody was spotted sniffin' around your place."

Rock's eyes narrowed. "So that's the real reason you told us to lay low."

Inside, Sammy sat in a recliner, eyes fixed, sharp as ever.

"Rock," he said as the younger man walked in, "someone's been casing your place. Not random. Purposeful. You have been into anything lately I need to know about?"

Rock hesitated, then nodded. "Maybe."

"Don't give me that maybe shit," Sammy snapped. "This one moves like a hitter. Could be a cleanup crew, could be a vendetta. But this is serious, blood."

"Alright," Rock relented, dropping into a chair. "A few weeks ago, Billy, Zack, his little brother, and his partner knocked off that pool hall across from Styleland's."

Sammy's eyes darkened. "The one where that dude got shot?"

"Yeah."

"So that means you stirred up the nest. And some of them cats you crossed might know someone who kills for money. You think they forgot?"

"I don't give a damn who they are."

"You should. You're not invincible, Rock."

Sammy's voice dropped an octave.

"Tell me everything."

Rock outlined the robbery. Ray-Ray outside, the rest busting in, roughing up the place. Then a guy grabbed a stack of cash and tried to run.

"Billy shot him," Rock said. "Dropped him cold."

Sammy cursed under his breath. "That man had a name. A life. And now you've got a bounty on your back. Byron, make sure Rock and Billy got enough cash to disappear for a while."

"What about the guy sniffin' around?" Rock asked.

"I'll find him. And if I do, I'll bury him."

*   *   *

"Sire," Tish called out from the kitchen, holding a newspaper. Mount Herman Church of Christ is doing a car wash on Saturday. Trying to raise money for a young boy, Willie Palmer Jr., who needs a kidney transplant. It says his father was killed in a robbery at a pool hall."

Sire stepped out of the bathroom, shirtless, towel slung over one shoulder. He took the paper from her hands.

"Pool Shark Willie…" he murmured. "Yeah, that was him."

Tish watched his expression darken with a mix of anger and compassion. Her man was fierce and full of contradictions. That's what pulled her in. That, and the way he loved.

"Before I forget," she added, "the connection says he's ready to deliver the other three hundred pounds."

Vee strolled in with a towel draped over her shoulder. Tish took it gently and began drying her hair, an intimate sisterhood between them.

Sire rolled a few joints and passed one to Vee, who coughed like a busted radiator. Tish rubbed her back, chuckling.

"Easy, girl. That's the real stuff."

Sire stood and zipped up a windbreaker. "You two handle the pickup. I'm going into town. Need to ask around and see if anyone's been offloading stolen jewelry. Wanna find Pimpwell's necklace. And we still need to visit my mom and sister. I'll meet you at the cemetery around four."

"Don't be late," Tish said, smiling. "We're stopping at the Dr. Ella Piper Center first. Bringing some joy to the old folks."

"Y'all stay focused," he said.

They blew kisses as he headed out to the backyard.

Sire crouched beside the dog. "Shauka, what's up, ole boy?"

The dog wagged its tail madly, whining.

"Calm down. It ain't been that long."

He fed the dog, cleaned up, and was about to leave when the phone rang.

"Hello?"

It was Pimpwell, calling from Chicago. Bragging about his second straight win at the Playa Ball Contest.

They laughed, chopped it up for a few minutes, and then Sire hung up and made his way across town.

The pool hall felt like a ghost house. Sire hadn't been back since Willie's death.

"Hey, young'un," said Tee Tot, the old man behind the

counter. "How's it going?"

"Just tryin' to stay above water, Dad."

The word "Dad" always lit a spark in Tee Tot's eyes. He had no kids of his own, but Sire was the closest thing.

"Business?"

"Slow now. But hell, one man dyin' ain't gonna stop the grind. Streets move too fast."

Sire nodded. "Ain't that the truth?"

Tee Tot leaned in, his tone turning serious. "Couple days ago, this dude came around saying he was lookin' to gamble. But the questions he asked? They were all about the robbery. Who was here? What went down, Names?"

"Cop?"

"If he was a cop," Tee Tot said, "he was the devil's own cousin. Coldest black eyes I ever saw. Nah, Sire. He ain't the law. He's huntin'. And he's close."

Sire nodded slowly. "Thanks, Dad. I'll see you again soon."

*   *   *

The black Mazda going in the opposite direction made a sudden U-turn in the middle of Michigan Avenue. The male driver's focus locked onto the female driver of the powder blue and white 2010 Chrysler 300 as it merged into traffic from the parking lot of Shoemaker's Florist. He began to follow.

Inside the Chrysler, the windows were tinted but rolled down. The woman, Vee, was trying to escape the factory smell of the new car, which upset her stomach. She took a turn onto Henderson Street, heading for the cemetery, where she parked and stepped out.

The black Mazda continued but did not stop. The driver noticed the fresh flowers in her hands before turning onto the south end of Henderson Street and heading for Handy Court Park. The cemetery could be accessed through three entries: two by vehicle and one on foot. The man followed the same route but veered off at the park. He exited the back of the park near the ditch on Ford Street, turned right, then right again, making his way toward Blount Street. From there, he walked down a worn path toward Indian Street. After a moment, he reached a second ditch near the graveyard. Crossing the small walk bridge, he entered the cemetery.

Vee had spent nearly thirty minutes clearing debris and wild weeds from the gravesites marked 50 and 51. The work had given her a moment of peace, but as she straightened up to leave, a twig snapped behind her.

She froze.

A man came charging toward her, his eyes wide with madness. One hand clutched a large stick, the other gripped a gun, pointed directly at her head. The shock paralyzed her, and a wave of terror flooded her chest.

His lips peeled back into a grotesque grimace, revealing a few broken, rotting teeth. The look in his eyes was one of pure insanity, like she was staring into the very depths of hell.

Vee's mouth opened to scream, but no sound came. Fear had her throat in a vice grip. Yet, something deep inside her, the last shred of survival instinct, urged her to run. Now.

She turned, but the madman was too close. His stick slammed into the back of her shoulders, driving her to the ground between the two graves.

Pain exploded in her back, and the world tilted. She struggled to stay conscious, her vision swimming.

"Bitch!" the man hissed, his voice a low snarl. "If you try to run from me one mo' damn time, yo' ass won't see another damn sunrise..."

Chapter 11

Lessons in Power

The night air hung thick with tension and temptation. The motel room, dimly lit by the soft, flickering orange glow of a single bedside lamp, was a paradox of intimacy and instruction. The sheets on the bed were tangled, still holding the scent of the sea breeze slipping in through a cracked window. Betty, nude and unashamed, moved across the room like a queen pacing her throne chamber, confident, commanding, deliberate. Her every step was a performance.

Teddy watched her, his eyes trailing the sway of her hips, the curve of her breasts, the coarse triangle of dark hair that she made no effort to conceal. His erection strained visibly beneath his boxer briefs.

"Are you gonna keep walking around this room flashing your hairy coochie and pretty titties," he said, his voice low and gruff, more of a declaration than a question, "or are you gonna gimme some? I know you see how you got me all hard and shit."

Betty stopped. She turned to face him, her hands on her hips, her lips curled in a smirk that didn't quite reach her eyes. She glanced down, and then slowly back up, letting her gaze rake over his body like a velvet blade.

"Lil' Daddy," she began, her tone thick with amusement, "if I didn't really dig you, there'd be nothin' I'd like more than to get it on with you. Especially with all that you're toting." Her eyes lingered on his arousal, then flicked back up with a knowing gleam. "But that's not why I'm walking around here necked."

She walked to the edge of the bed and perched herself on it like a teacher settling in for a lesson. Her body remained bare, but her words were clothed in purpose.

"The truth of the matter is, I'm giving you your first major lesson in dealing with a woman. Especially a whore. See, there's this old saying: Money is the root of all evil. But I'm here to set the record straight. Pussy," she said, her voice thickening into gravity, "pussy is a lot more powerful."

Teddy blinked, confused but clearly listening.

"Think for a moment," she said. "Right now, I'm supposed to be teaching you about getting Ho' money, pimping, in other words. But look at you. You ain't thinking about no money right now. You don't give a damn about the almighty dollar. You just wanna bury that tool in this hairy pussy." She spread her thighs slightly for emphasis, her voice low and hypnotic. "That's power, sugar. Power made flesh. You're experiencing it right now."

She stood again, slowly walking toward him, each word a silk lash across his conscience.

"You're sleeping on your strength, Teddy. You've got that rare kind of magic. A gift. When I met you weeks ago, I knew right away you weren't average. I told you then, my instincts, my womanly senses, they recognized you."

Teddy swallowed hard, nodding, his throat tight.

"God blessed you, baby. But you gotta learn it. Learn yourself. Understand that a woman... constantly needs to feel loved, desired, deeply, genuinely. Yeah, she might get pleased for a night with good sex. But when she feels loved by the one pleasing her? That's what makes her soul catch fire."

She stopped in front of him, placing a hand gently on his chest. "Even if she's with another woman, even if she's hard as nails out here in these streets... she still wants to feel cherished."

"When I first saw you," Betty said, her eyes softer now, "I wanted to love you with everything inside me. That's the power you have, Teddy. And that power? It will make women flock to you. The real ones. The ones who can feel that special need that most men can't even touch. You've got it."

She paused, gauging the weight of her words.

"Some of this might go over your head now, but I have to say it. My spirit demands it. So listen. Don't be a sucker for anything or nobody. Especially not for me. Not for this or any other pussy. You hear me?"

Teddy shifted, a blush creeping into his cheeks.

"Yeah, Betty. I ain't no dummy. But what do you mean by money being some kinda evil root? Are you talking voodoo or some shit?"

Betty chuckled softly. "No, baby. My precious Little Daddy"

"Stop calling me Little Daddy," he said sharply, the adolescent edge in his voice belying the man he was trying to become.

She took a long, searching look into his eyes. "Okay, Daddy," she said, at last, the new title tasting different on her tongue. "Let me break it down for you. In this world, two forces are always at war, good and evil. When I said 'root,' I meant the source, the beginning. And actually, I misspoke. The saying goes, The love of money is the root of all evil."

"Anyway," she continued, sitting beside him now, "money is important. With it comes power, and with power comes control, dominance, ascendancy."

Teddy squinted. "What does that mean?"

"What does what mean?"

"That word you said. Assendy or whatever."

Betty smiled without mockery. "Ascendancy," she repeated. "It means having the upper hand. Being on top."

She leaned forward, her breasts brushing lightly against his arm. "Now. You said you still have every dime I've given you. What are you gonna do with it?"

"I'm saving it."

Betty raised an eyebrow. "And how do you plan to live if you're just saving it all? Look, saving's smart if you're working nine to five. But if you're hustling out here, baby, that money's gotta move. You gotta make it work. Plant it in the right soil and it'll grow."

Teddy rubbed his chin, thinking. "I don't know, Betty. Never really thought 'bout it."

"I respect that honesty," she said, reaching out to stroke his cheek. "But if I care enough to give you my money, you'd better make it grow. Learn the game before you play. Out here, only the masters win. And when you lose? The streets make you pay in full."

She stood, her eyes gleaming now with ambition. "You've got a power, Daddy, a way with women that'll make the game work for you. But if you want to win, you gotta be sharp, focused. We'll need a place. A car. A future."

"You already said I was young but ready. What, you forgot?"

Betty laughed freely this time, the sound like rain on a tin roof, sudden and beautiful. She pulled him close and kissed him deeply. Then, with deliberate care, she took him in her mouth and worshipped him until he climaxed, swallowing every drop like a promise.

When it was done, she stood again, stretching like a cat. "Enough lessons for now, if I may call it that," she said, her voice light again, playful. "Come on. Let's go for a walk along the sandy shore and watch the stars."

Her hand slipped into his.

"I think I'm falling in love," she whispered, sounding suddenly like a girl again. A girl with dreams, in the arms of a boy learning to become a man.

And just like that, the night folded its wings around them.

Chapter 12

Sire's Purpose

Sire's feeling pretty good about the way things are shaping up. The additional money raised from the 300 pounds will finally give him enough funds to finance a legitimate business.

Going back to prison is not an option.

However, as long as he continues to play with the dirt throwers, it's only a matter of when, not if, some dirt gets on him, too. Sire learned long ago that out on the streets, Murphy's law is always in effect: what can go wrong, will go wrong.

There are a number of businesses he can choose to open: auto detailing, car washes, strip clubs, lawn services, or game rooms. But these lines of business fail to satisfy his thirst to do something bigger. In fact, they only limit his uncovered sense of purpose. He'd like to try and make a real difference in the lives of the downtrodden. Having himself come from that segment of society, Sire understands the struggle.

It took going to prison for him to get a real idea of why underprivileged individuals are those who make up the vast majority of those incarcerated. Most people who grow up mentally and emotionally malnourished are also those individuals who, when they grow up, have no true sense of what value really means. It's no wonder that crime seems appealing. Money is the only thing those impoverished souls are sure to learn the value of. Their life becomes so much better when they have money.

During his incarceration, Sire had taken several courses in psychology, and in those courses, one study in particular brought to light an interesting fact.

In counseling with neurotic patients, emotional problems usually originate in one of two places, if not both: the unloving or non-nourishing relationship with parents, or the inability to gain acceptance and respect from peers. In other words, most emotional disorders (except organic illness) can be traced to destructive relationships with people during the first twenty years of life.

It didn't stop there.

Members of society who are fortunate, privileged, and accepted by their peers often view those on the lower rungs of life as misfits. Ironically, such a viewpoint creates a hidden undercurrent that fuels a systematic tool of division.

In other words, an epidemic of inferiority is raging throughout our society. From the moment our children enter the world, they are subjected to an unjust value system that reserves respect and esteem for only a select few. Those who fail to measure up to society's systematically structured standards, primarily in areas of beauty (which is not limited to a physical perception), and intelligence (normally not found in the uneducated), must cope with feelings of inadequacy and inferiority. Those who lead and guide children must understand the impact of this inferiority if they are to respond effectively to their needs and longings.

Yes, Sire reflects to himself, I have to do more to make a difference.

Eyekon just may be the key, Sire thought. Start the union.

It's 4:30 as Sire turns into the cemetery. He's 30 minutes late. There is no sign of his woman, and the Chrysler 300 isn't in the parking lot. Maybe they'd come and gone. His cell phone begins to vibrate, indicating an incoming call. It's Tish.

"Hey, lady, what's good?"

"I'm not sure, Sire. Vee was supposed to pick me up over an hour ago. I'm unable to reach her on her phone. It goes straight to her voicemail box."

"Well, since I'm here, I'll go on and put these flowers on my mother's and sister's graves. I'll come and get you. Where are you?"

"I'm still at Dr. Ella Piper's old folks' home."

"OK."

"She wanted to surprise you," Tish begins. "We—"

"Tell me about it when I pick you up. I'll see you in half an hour."

Approaching his sister's grave, Sire notices the freshly cut flowers scattered in the immediate area. A familiar sound comes to his ears from the place between the two graves in front of him. It's Kesha Cole's "Remember." Vee uses the song as her ringtone. He clearly hears the ringtone, but Vee is nowhere to be found. Intrigued, Sire moves closer to the sound. Now, he sees the bright pink phone lying partially obscured under the edge of his sister's grave. He picks up the phone, which is still ringing, and answers it.

"Hello." It's Tish. She lets out a sigh of relief when she hears Sire's voice, thinking Vee has been located and is safe.

"Not so fast," he says into the phone.

"I found her phone between two graves. But not Vee. Something is definitely wrong. Listen, get your things together, I'll be right over to get you."

* * * *

Detective Bandy Welks was on his way to clock out for the day when he ran into Larry Lewis, second in command at the department and commander of the homicide division. He's been with the Fort Myers Police Department for 28 years. It's everyone's guess that Lewis will be the next Chief at the station, as he's worked in every division. Over the years, he has put together a decent line of snitches.

"Lewis," Detective Welks calls out as the two men enter the elevator. "Sonny told me that you received word that Bo Bo Scurry has been banged up pretty bad?"

"How's it going, BW? Yes, you heard correctly. I was informed by one of my best rats. Whoever did it to him worked him over severely. No other information was given concerning Bo Bo. However, we did receive a juicy tip on the homicide at the pool hall last month. Two streets over from Tee Tot's, I was told, a van was sitting at the corner for maybe 20 minutes when four people in dark clothing hurriedly entered an orange van and quickly left the area. There aren't that many orange vans in the Dunbar area. So hopefully, it'll lead to an arrest for the death of Willie Palmer." Lewis finishes as he steps out of the elevator to leave the building, then turns and says, "Bo Bo's at Lee Memorial; his jaw is broken in three places."

"Thanks."

Detective Bandy Welks continues to the clock-out room, calling it a day.

Chapter 13

Sweet Touch, Cold Game

"What's up, Sweet Touch? Is that thing really as good as you say it is?"

"I'm not sure if I can answer that question, sugar pie, because I can't get it. All I can do is give it if the price is right," she says to the dark man sitting behind the wheel of the Ford F-150.

"How much time will a C-note get me, sweet thing?"

"If you make it good to me, I may try and squeeze you in for a whole hour," she responds as she opens the passenger's door and climbs in.

"Do you have someplace to go?" the man asks.

"Yes, I've got a room at the Tide Motel."

In the room, the man says, "Listen, baby, all I want you to do is get naked and walk around the room for me and just talk with me."

Ignoring him, Sweet Touch gets completely naked. She lies on the bed, spreads her legs wide open, and says:

"You sure you don't want to see for yourself just how good this juicy pussy is?"

"I'm sure. Tell me, how did you get that ugly gash over your left temple? Did it happen at the pool hall?" The man already knows the answer to the question.

"Yep. The bastard wanted my man's Rolex, and I tried to stop him, and that's when he hit me with a gun."

"Was he alone?"

"Hell naw. There were three or four of them muthafuckers."

"How many people were in there besides the robbers?"

"15, 20, maybe 25."

"Did you know any of the people?"

"Most of the people there were pimps, hustlers, whores, and only a few squares. My man, Ho' Bender, Train, East Coast, Fat Back, Rabbit Taylor, and his hustling ass brother, Sole Daddy. Plus, a couple of slick cats from out of Miami."

"Who was shooting pool with the guy who was shot and killed?"

"That was Sire. I heard he recently got out of prison.

"Okay. Is that it? Was anybody else there?"

"As a matter of fact, yes. That pimpin' ass Pimpwell was there too. They took his shit too."

While Sweet Touch was talking, she had been walking around in the room, twisting and swishing her bouncing ass, as if strutting across a runway, which is starting to affect Sammy. He now has an erection. But he wasn't about to stick his Johnson in this whore. Sammy squeezes her soft ass and tells Sweet Touch to lay down again and bust it open for him. he only wants to see her cute pussy one more time before he leaves.

Chapter 14

The Unseen Threads

"Tish, let's go back to the cemetery and have a good look around," Sire said, his voice low, serious, thick with a tension that hadn't left since Vee's disappearance. "Whatever happened to Vee started there. We can safely assume one of two things is going on here. She's new around Fort Myers, so unless something from her past has caught up with her, a debt unsettled maybe, I'm betting this is about us."

Tish glanced at him, brow furrowed with concern, her fingers tightening on the seatbelt strap. "What makes you think it's an abduction, honey?" she asked quietly. "I mean, I get that we've got her phone, but maybe it was just an attempted kidnapping. When you think about it, her car isn't even in the parking lot."

Sire's gaze didn't shift from the road, but his grip on the steering wheel tightened, knuckles whitening. "Didn't you tell me she was long overdue for picking you up? Surely if she were able to contact us, we'd have heard from her by now, Tish. Don't you think?"

Tish didn't respond. The silence settled between them like a thick fog as the Escalade rumbled down the street toward Henderson Street Cemetery. The further they drove, the heavier the atmosphere grew, as if the air itself knew something had gone terribly wrong.

When they arrived, Sire didn't move right away. He stared out across the burial grounds, his eyes scanning the familiar rows of weathered headstones and wilting flowers. Shadows stretched long beneath the trees. There were only two cars in the lot, neither of which had been there earlier. Visitors, no doubt, are mourning quietly.

Sire finally exhaled and stepped out. Tish followed close behind. He approached a group of cemetery workers, all dressed in green uniforms dusted with earth and sweat. The closest was a broad-shouldered man whose nametag read "Tom."

"Excuse me, sir," Sire said, voice respectful but urgent. "Did any of you see a young lady near plots fifty and fifty-one, maybe an hour or so ago?"

Tom glanced up, squinting at him beneath the brim of a sweat-darkened cap. "No, I didn't," he said after a moment, then turned to shout the question to his coworkers.

The other two shook their heads.

"Zilch," Tom said, shrugging. "Sorry, man."

Sire nodded, pulling a business card from his wallet. "If you hear anything, anything at all, give me a call."

Back at the plot where they'd found Vee's phone, the ground offered no new answers. The grass still looked flattened where someone may have stood or fallen, but no signs of struggle. No clue. No Vee.

On the drive to the Palace, Tish finally broke the silence.

"To have Vee disappear is one thing," she murmured, "but for the car to vanish too? That's not as easy. Should we involve the law?"

Sire shook his head slowly. "That's a good point, Tish. But not just yet. With Vee's past affiliation with Carlton and the New Black Panther movement, the cops might paint her into a corner she doesn't deserve to be in. Hiding a person is one thing, but hiding a Chrysler? That takes muscle. For now, we do what we can. Just us."

The Palace greeted them like a silent sentry. Inside, they stripped away the grime of stress under a shared shower, letting the steam wash over their tangled thoughts. Later, with music pulsing low and smoke curling lazily from a joint, Sire leaned back and exhaled.

"Baby girl," he said, "I have a feeling the shit's about to hit the fan."

Tish arched a brow. "Yeah?"

"I stopped by old man Tee Tot's. He told me someone came by, asking questions, wanting to know who was around the night Willie died. The description matched Sammy Blanks."

Her eyes widened. "Sammy?"

Sire nodded grimly. "While I may not be sure about the other two robbers, I am dead sure about Rock and Billy. Sammy? I don't think he was in on the robbery. But he's dangerous. Known hitman back in the day. My guess? He's trying to clean up his brothers' mess. Tie up any loose ends."

Before Tish could respond, the sharp bark of Shauka cut through the music.

Sire stood and walked to the door. As he opened it, the familiar sight of his longtime friend and partner, Pimpwell, met him like a long-forgotten rhythm.

"I wonder," Pimpwell grinned, "has Shauka forgotten his first master? Or is he warning me that if he weren't tied up, I'd be lunch?"

Sire chuckled and stepped aside. "I thought you were still in Chi-town, basking in the glory of victory."

"I've been back a few days. Missed Ma Dear's cooking too much," Pimpwell said, opening the rear of his Rolls and pulling out two heavily foiled plates. The scent of seasoned meat, slow-cooked greens, and cornbread danced in the air.

"Say, partner," Sire said, "you haven't met Vee yet. She was out of town last time."

"Vee? Who's that?"

"I won't call her an accident, because that would imply regret. She's nothing of the sort. I met her the night of the New Phase II tribute."

"And where's she now?"

"That's the thing. We don't know." His voice tightened. "She wanted to surprise me, clean my mother's and sister's graves. When I got there, she was gone. Just her cell phone was left behind."

"You report it to the police?"

"No."

"Any enemies?"

"She's new here. Except maybe Gorilla Seville."

"How'd she get there?" Pimpwell asked, his tone sharpening.

"In our powder blue Chrysler 300," Tish answered firmly, stepping into the conversation like a co-captain.

"This is the ghetto," Pimpwell said flatly. "Nothing happens without someone seeing something."

"Exactly," Sire nodded. "And it gets deeper. Tee Tot says someone matching Sammy's build and face was sniffing around."

"You mean the Sammy Blanks, Mr. Mercenary himself?"

"One and the same."

Sire leaned in, voice low. "Rock and Billy, his brothers, were in on the robbery. Billy shot Willie. I tailed Rock and scoped out his place."

"Could they have seen you?"

"Doubt it. I was disguised. Looked like an old darky."

"You want me to reach out to one of my people? Sammy's the real deal. You don't want him on your tail."

Sire glanced at Tish. She moved to his side and laced her fingers with his.

"Appreciate it, Pimp, but no. This is mine to handle. Vee became part of us, Tish and I. And she swore, without hesitation, that she'd give her life for us. I won't give her any less."

Pimpwell saw the fire in their eyes. "Alright, Sire. You need me, just say the word."

"Count on it, partner."

Pimpwell turned to go. "Tell Ma Dear, I said thanks."

"Oh, and remember Sexanna? Her mom lives on Indian Street. I'll check with her and see if she saw anything."

"Appreciate that, Pimpin'."

* * * *

In a pale, sterile hospital room, the acrid scent of antiseptic filled the air like an invisible fog. The blinds were half-drawn, letting only a dull gray light fall on the man in the bed.

Detective Bandy Welks stood in the doorway, eyes narrowed as he took in the sight.

Bo Bo lay beneath a hospital-issue blanket, his body still, broken. His jaw wired shut, face swollen and bruised, he looked more like a victim of a train wreck than a man who once moved through backstreets with swagger.

Welks stepped inside, the click of his boots soft against the linoleum. "Word is you ran into a Mack truck," he said, trying to inject some levity. "Hell, that's an understatement. You look like you collided with a whole damn locomotive."

Bo Bo's bloodied eyes opened, slowly locking with the detectives. Pain and something deeper burned behind them.

"I'm gonna ask you a few questions," Welks said, pulling a chair beside the bed. "Just nod. Yes or no."

Bo Bo blinked once.

"Did you get caught with your hand in someone's cookie jar?" Bo Bo shook his head. No.

"Do you know who did this to you?" A pause. Then, a slow, grim nod.

Welks leaned forward. "If you know who did this, and you didn't bring it on yourself, why would someone do this much damage to you?"

Bo Bo didn't speak, couldn't speak, but his eyes never left Welks's. And then, quietly, he tilted the crown of his head toward the detective. Welks's stomach dropped. "Are you saying this happened because of our arrangement?"

Bo Bo broke eye contact, staring instead at his feet beneath the blanket.

That answer was enough.

Chapter 15

Rules of the Game

"Sugar Bear," Betty said while adjusting her earrings in the mirror, "I'll be gone for a few days with this date. He's paying me fifteen hundred to go on a business trip."

She moved about the room with efficient grace, grabbing her overnight bag and checking her look once more.

"The landlady will be by tomorrow for the rent money," she continued, slipping on her heels. "I told her you'd be here. I had to handle some business out of town. This is our third month living here, and you're the man of the house now, so it's only right that Mrs. Brown finally meets you. And tell her I said thanks for that pound cake she brought us."

"Okay, Doll Baby," Teddy said with a nod, watching her.

She came over and kissed his cheek gently. "And watch your back out there with those joints you're selling. You need to be careful, both from the cops and the robbers. Don't take any chances."

Outside, the town car honked twice. Her date was waiting.

Teddy watched her walk out, her hips swaying in confident rhythm. The car pulled away, and with it went the momentary peace.

Later that evening, he took a long shower, steam clouding the bathroom mirror as he collected his thoughts. After dressing in one of the crisp outfits Betty had laid out for him, he headed out with a fresh batch of a thousand joints tucked away. The car, Betty's newly acquired 1978 Oldsmobile Deuce and a Quarter, was clean, bold, and turned heads wherever it rolled. Before she let him drive it, she'd made sure he got his license.

Feeling sharp, he decided to make a stop behind Buck's Place. It had been too long since he last saw Frank. Underneath the familiar old oak tree, Frank sat on an overturned crate, looking parched and half-lost in thought.

"C'mon, dude, go three rounds and win yourself a fifth of wine," Teddy teased, jumping out from behind the tree with a playful boxing stance.

Frank's eyes lit up. "What it is, Young Blood," he said, standing slowly with a grin. "I thought you'd moved on. Word is, you a pimp daddy now. Got a nice whip too. Damn! Ain't life good when everything's sweet?"

Frank leaned against the tree, his face serious now.

"But listen, my advice? Always remember this: for everything sweet, there's something sour waiting on the flip side. Up is down. Day has night. Good times have their bad shadows."

He paused, rubbing the back of his neck.

"Son, if you remember that principle, it gives you power. See, choices got you where you are now. Make the same kind of choices, and you keep that sweet life. But slip up, make just one wrong move, and that sour life will catch you."

He sat back down, voice thickening with memory.

"Take me, for example. High school grad. Solid athlete. Had a real shot at going pro as a prizefighter. Then one night, I went to a party. That's the night I took my first sip of wine. Tasted so damn good, I couldn't stop. It became an everyday thing, even during training. By the time anyone noticed, I was deep in. An alcoholic. That was thirty years ago."

"I can dig it, Frank," Teddy said softly.

"In other words," Frank went on, "I broke the rules that made champions. Eat right. Rest. No drugs. No booze. That's the formula. I knew the rules, and I still chose wrong. And that's why I'm sittin' here now."

Teddy nodded thoughtfully. "I think I understand. But let me ask you something. If a fighter only needs to follow the three golden rules to win, why would he ever need to make adjustments?"

Frank's eyes lingered on him. There was something in Teddy's voice, curiosity, sure, but also intelligence. Something rare in a street kid barely seventeen.

"That's a good damn question, son. See, when something has a million ways it can go, you can't master all of 'em. Sometimes, you've gotta adjust your game."

He leaned in, voice shifting into teacher mode.

"Let me break it down with some boxing knowledge. Most fighters are right-handed. Left foot out front. Left arm bent, hand up by the eye. Right fist guarding the chin. Now, if you're up against another righty, it's all familiar. But what if your opponent's a southpaw? Do you keep your stance the same, or do you adjust your game with different offensive and defensive moves?"

Teddy tilted his head. "I don't know, Frank. But I guess it makes sense to learn how to deal with any kind of fighter."

"Exactly. That's the point. Life's like that, too. Even if you know the basics, there's always room to improve. But timing is everything. If you've truly learned the fundamentals, your instincts will tell you when it's time to shift gears."

Frank tapped his chest. "It becomes like a sixth sense, screaming at your soul when it's time to pivot."

Teddy nodded. "Frank, I got it. I hear you loud and clear. Let me ask you something else, though. Why can't you make that adjustment and get your life back on track? You're way too smart to be out here living like a bum."

Frank raised an eyebrow and gave a lopsided smirk. "Careful, Young Blood, with that 'bum' talk. I just might take you up on them three rounds you mentioned earlier."

But he didn't answer the question. He couldn't. It was

the same one that haunted him every morning.

Before leaving, Teddy dropped a twenty in Frank's hand, and Frank gave him a nod of respect.

Teddy decided to visit his mom and sister. It had been months. Thanksgiving was just around the corner, and he knew how happy it would make Inez to see him.

The year was 1989. Headlines were still buzzing about the Exxon Valdez oil spill. Oliver North's conviction in the Iran-Contra scandal had been all over the news. Hurricane Hugo had torn through the Carolinas. And all eyes—Black and white, were watching L. Douglas Wilder's historic campaign for governor.

Inez lived on the corner of Lime and Evans Street in the Dunbar section of Fort Myers, affectionately known as "The Bottom." Their house sat across from Prather's Laundry, and the yard was so small that parking required creativity.

As Teddy pulled up, he hadn't even cut the engine when Inez came bursting out of the house with a wide smile. "There's my Baby!" she cried.

He stepped from the car, arms open. She wrapped him up in a mother's embrace, the kind of hug that lingered deep in your bones.

"Hey, Baby Cakes," Teddy said, kissing her forehead. "Where's Mr. Harold? I want to thank him for keeping you happy and sober."

"He's out back cleaning the fish we caught yesterday.

You staying to eat?"

"Yes, ma'am. I've missed your cooking. And I know you're gonna throw down for Thanksgiving."

"If God's willing, honey, I sure am."

"You must really like Mr. Harold. Is he why you're staying clean?"

She looked away. "He drinks too. We just… don't drink every day now."

Just then, a voice called from the back. "Hello there, young man."

Mr. Harold appeared, drying his hands on an old dish towel.

"What's up, Pops? Momma said y'all caught a nice mess of fish. Mind if I help knock some of them off?"

"Teddy, are you kidding? You're always welcome home. Your momma talks about you all the time."

They told him his sister had gone to Tampa to visit her father.

After two heaping plates of fried fish and grits, Teddy felt full and grateful. He slid fifty dollars under his plate before saying his goodbyes.

Back on the Avenue, the sidewalks were thick with people. The crowd was lively. Business would be good tonight.

At Club 21, the jukebox sat silent. Teddy dropped in a quarter and selected two songs before heading to the bar for a glass of coconut milk. He took a table in the corner.

Word spread fast. People came in a steady stream, buying joints two or four at a time. Business was booming. The ready-to-smoke joints were in high demand.

Within three hours, he'd re-upped several times at three hundred per trip. Only thirty or forty joints remained.

Teddy decided to walk down to Dave's Club 82. He'd sell the rest there. But he never made it that far. He was passing Coach Graddic's and Him-John's Wigg Wamm Restaurant when gunfire erupted. Screams followed. People scattered, diving for cover.

Teddy ran past a row of parked cars before realizing he needed to get down too. He ducked and peeked in the direction of the shots.

His heart froze.

Joe Kearse was fleeing. Blood streaked down the left side of his body. He turned every few steps, returning fire, desperate and wild.

Teddy sprinted back to the Deuce. His gun was in the glove box. Within minutes, he was back in the car, barreling through the parking lot. Ahead, Joe stumbled across Anderson Avenue, trying to reach the alley behind Galmer's Grocery.

Teddy cut into traffic, pushing the car hard. He saw Joe

fall. One of the shooters was gaining. Teddy hit the horn and leaned out the window, gun aimed. He fired.

The shooter collapsed.

Teddy stopped the car, jumped out, and spotted the second gunman. Another shot. The figure turned and vanished behind a building. He ran to Joe's side. Joe was on the ground, pistol still in hand, grinning through the pain, blood everywhere. And his eyes locked on Teddy's with fierce recognition.

Chapter 16

No Mercy in the Shadows

She cannot remain in this position much longer, the woman thought, her body slumped in the hard, splintering wooden chair, wrists bound tight behind her back with a fraying cord that bit into her skin. The air was damp and smelled of mildew, urine, and something metallic—blood, maybe. A single cracked window let in slivers of dusty sunlight that barely reached the corners of the room.

It had been a full week now. Seven long, nightmarish days since Vee had been snatched from the street and locked in this forgotten hellhole, raped, beaten, and starved like some disposable rag doll. Her captor, that bastard Gorilla Seville, had slapped her so hard on the first day that the ringing in her ears hadn't left since. His breath reeked of rot and drugs when he leaned in close, demanding things no man had a right to ask.

And when she resisted, refused to put her lips anywhere near his filthy body, he had punished her the only way a monster could, violating her with no mercy. The pain of that first brutal assault haunted her still. Her lower back throbbed, and her dignity felt crushed beyond repair.

The room she was trapped in looked like the afterthought of an abandoned crack house, with dingy linoleum floors streaked with grime, and bare walls stained with the residue of time and smoke. Besides the creaky chair she was tied to, there was an old, dented dresser leaning against a wall, its legs uneven, propped on a chipped brick. A wooden lamp with a long, slender neck lay discarded in the center of the room, like a forgotten relic. Could that work as a weapon? she thought grimly. She hadn't eaten much. Just a few stale, dry bites of chicken shoved into her mouth by Seville. Her stomach felt hollow, her limbs leaden. If no one came soon, she knew she wouldn't last much longer. The thought of dying here, nameless and degraded, ignited something in her.

Her chance might be coming. Occasionally, Seville would leave the door cracked when he went into the other room. Through that narrow slit, Vee had seen him many times, nodding off from the drugs he injected, leaning forward, mumbling, drooling like some grotesque marionette with snipped strings. She studied him again now. Slouched, half-asleep, the needle still fresh in his arm. This could be it.

"Hey! You out there?" she called out, voice rough but edged with baited seduction. "If you really want some of this smoking head I got, why don't you share some of that good dope you're on?"

Gorilla Seville stirred. His bloodshot eyes rose slowly from the slump of his chest.

"Don't just sit there looking dumb," she said louder. "Didn't you hear me, man? I'm saying if you give me some of that good shit, I'll do anything you want."

The change was instant. His slack face curled into a disgusting, anticipatory grin as he stumbled to his feet, trying to appear suave but looking like a walking hangover.

"What'd you say, baby?" he slurred.

"I said I'm tired of being tied up like a damn dog," she pouted. "I'm ready to be with you if you make me feel good first."

He swayed against the doorframe, using it like a crutch, the drug having claimed almost full dominion over his body. His knees buckled slightly, like a drunk balancing on a shifting boat.

"Wake your ass up and untie me," Vee purred, "so I can give you that nasty head you've been dreaming about."

That was enough. Seville shuffled over, mumbling something unintelligible, and started loosening the cord around her wrists.

* * * *

"Answer that call, Tish," Sire said, gripping the wheel as he made a tight turn onto Edison Avenue. His jaw was set, brows knit in a storm of worry. The Avenue was alive as ever—kids on bikes, folks sipping from brown paper bags, deals going down in alley shadows, but none of that mattered to him right now.

Tish answered her phone, listening briefly. "It's Pimpwell, honey. He says he might know where Vee is. He's at the Wagon Wheel across from Club 21."

"Tell him we'll be there in ten," Sire replied, already changing lanes.

Minutes later, he parked the car outside the bustling soul food joint. The thick, rich smell of frying chicken, smothered beef, onions, and potatoes rolled through the air like a warm blanket from someone's grandma's kitchen. It tugged at his stomach, but not enough to distract him.

"Now that's the smell of soul food," Sire said. "Let's eat first, talk while we chew."

Inside, the restaurant was buzzing, with laughter, dishes clinking, and impatient murmurs of waiting patrons.

They spotted Pimpwell in the far corner, seated near a window like always, able to see both doorways, inside and out. That was how he liked it. Sire led Tish over and greeted his man with a dap.

"What it do, Pimpin'?" Pimpwell said through a mouthful of cornbread and gravy.

"I'm straight, but not right, not until we find Vee."

Ms. Williams came over, radiant as always, pad in hand. "We'll have what he's having," Sire said. "And whatever he's drinking, too."

Ms. Williams smiled warmly, gave Tish a knowing wink, and disappeared toward the kitchen.

Pimpwell leaned forward. "Sexanna got the word. Seville was seen nearby when your girl disappeared. He got out of a dark whip and went through Handy Court Park, headed toward the cemetery. You embarrassed that clown in front of the hood, Sire. That ain't the kind of wound a fragile ego like his can take."

Sire's eyes darkened. "So you're saying this is payback?"

"It ain't a guess. It's logic. And if we find Seville..." Pimpwell scooped the last bite of his collards. "...you'll find her."

"Old Man Pops owns the rooms on Borden Street," he added. "Eight units. Seville's likely posted up there."

"I know where they are," Sire said, voice clipped.

Ms. Williams returned with plates heavy with steaming food. For ten minutes, their mouths were too full for anything but grunts of appreciation. But Sire, despite the flavor, couldn't taste a damn thing anymore. His mind was with Vee.

Finally, he pushed his plate aside. "Let's ride," he said to Tish. "If we don't get to her soon..."

Pimpwell stood and gave him a solid handshake.

"Make him pay, partner."

"Oh, he'll pay."

* * * *

Once her hands were free, Vee gasped at the sensation of blood rushing back into her fingers. The pain was sharp and hot, but it meant she was still alive. She rubbed her wrists furiously, breath quickening. In that moment, she made a quiet, sacred promise: he would never tie her again.

100

And if she had her way, he wouldn't walk out of this room alive.

"Bitch," Gorilla Seville grunted. "Don't just stand there like a fuckin' statue. Get over here and work that mouth."

"Oh, sugar," Vee cooed. "You promised me a little taste of that high first. You want the best, don't you? Let Mama feel good, and I'll have you begging me not to stop."

His pupils dilated. She could see the lust and the heroin duking it out in his brain. He turned, motioning for her to follow him into the kitchen. His legs moved slowly, heavily.

"The dope's in here," he muttered. "Try some stupid shit and I'll stomp your guts out."

"Baby," she said sweetly, "the only thing I plan on trying Vee is this wet ass on your lap."

The kitchen was a mess, with peeling linoleum floors, a table that wobbled with the weight of cigarette burns and dried food spills. An aluminum salt-and-pepper set sat next to a dirty plate full of syringes. One was already filled, half-used, cloudy, with a smear of blood at its tip. A spoon with a blackened underside sat nearby.

Seville picked up a matchbox and opened it with one hand, revealing a ziplock of off-white powder.

"This here is China White. Pure as angels," he chuckled. "So good it'll make you wanna suck your own—"

She cut him off with a fake giggle. Soon, motherfucker. Keep laughing.

"Hey," she said, "I need to freshen up a bit. You want a clean kitty, don't you?"

He gestured lazily at a door missing its knob. The bathroom was filthy. The floor had shoe prints and soap scum, but it was what sat on top of the toilet tank that caught her eye.

A bottle of bleach. Her pulse quickened. Her fingers twitched. Just a few drops in his dope… That's all it'll take.

* * * *

"Tish, turn on Borden and drive all the way to Edison," Sire said, his voice calm but coiled like a whip. "I need to see what's around those units. Look for dogs, obstacles… anything."

They rolled past the duplexes. Tish tapped the window.

"There's our ride," she pointed. "Next to the last room, under that crooked tarp."

Sire's eyes narrowed. Rage and resolve burned behind them.

"We got thirty minutes before dark," he said. "When you hit Highland, drop me behind the Flat Top Club. There's a cut through there—leads to Holland Lakes. Borden's is just one street over."

He reached for his Beretta, checked the clip, then slid another into his jacket pocket.

"If you don't hear from me in twenty, circle back. But

stay low. And stay sharp."

She nodded, clutching the wheel.

The hunt had begun. And this time, there would be no mercy.

Chapter 17

A Dangerous Game

Vee stepped out of the bathroom, the faint scent of bleach still clinging to her skin. She felt a little cleaner, physically, at least. Her hands trembled slightly as she wrung out the last of the bloodstains from her panties, the water running red and tinged with memories she'd rather forget. The bleach stung her nostrils, mingling with the sharp, sterile smell of the room, and she shuddered, wishing she could wash away the fear in her veins as easily as the blood from her clothes.

Her reflection in the cracked mirror seemed foreign, her eyes darkened by sleepless nights, her skin pale and taut from stress, but her gaze was sharp and determined. She couldn't let this man break her. Not now.

Taking a steadying breath, she made her way back to the dimly lit room, her mind racing. She needed answers, no matter how much the truth might wound her.

"Seville, sugar," Vee began, trying to keep her voice smooth, yet the edge of frustration bled through. "Now that I'm willing to do whatever you want of me, will you tell me why you kidnapped me? I need to know if I ever did something to you."

Gorilla Seville, sitting in a worn-out chair, shot her a glare. His eyes were cold and calculating, and the smug grin on his face deepened with his words. "Come on, lady, don't try and pretend you don't know who the fuck I am."

Vee raised her chin, steadying herself. "I've never said I didn't know who you are. You used to be Stella's pimp. She told us all about you. I just want to know why you're fucking with me... sweetie?" Her words dripped with a calm venom, but she could feel her anger bubbling underneath, clawing at the surface, desperate to get free.

"Oh, that mothafucka's kicking that girl," Seville mocked, leaning forward, a nasty grin twisting his face. "Out of all the men and women on the scene that night, you were the only bitch who opened her mouth to get in my business. And when I showed up back at the club? I learned you and your little walking dead man kidnapped my woman."

Vee shook her head, the bile rising in her throat. "That's not true. We didn't kidnap Stella. Any decent person would have helped that woman. You beat her, Seville. You beat her like she was a damn man."

Seville's laugh was dark, low, a sound that crawled under her skin. "What I do to my woman is my damn business. What part of that ain't you understanding, Ms. Bitch?"

Her breath caught in her throat. She couldn't hold back anymore. "Stella described a different picture. You use violence and fear to keep her. She said she didn't leave you before you went to prison because she wasn't ready to leave

Fort Myers, her hometown."

Seville slammed his fist on the armrest of the chair, his voice rising with fury. "Hold it! Hold it right there with that shit."

He stood up, towering over her, his bulk filling the room. "My game is tight when it comes to keeping my Ho' in check. It's pure strategy. When she's out there on my mission, my Ho' is supposed to keep her mind focused on my mission. Which is to get my money. The only man she is to look at or talk to are Johns and Squares who will pay for pussy. If she strays from my priorities, she gets straightened out when I see her. It's as simple as that. Those are my rules."

Vee couldn't suppress the disgust that twisted her stomach. The air in the room felt thick, suffocating. How could anyone think like this? The man in front of her was demented, a monster disguised in a facade of control and power. She knew, with cold certainty, that the only way out was to outsmart him. Find a way to slip something into his syringe, poison him with his own arrogance.

Her left arm hung useless by her side, pain gnawing at the muscles that wouldn't obey her. She needed to move, to think, but her body felt betrayed.

Suddenly, a sharp knock-knock-knock echoed through the silent room.

Seville's eyes narrowed. He reached beneath the cushion of his chair and pulled out a sleek 9mm handgun, the cold steel catching the faint light. He stood, his movements slow and deliberate, as he made his way to the kitchen window. His gaze swept the outside, ever-watchful, ever-paranoid. "Get yo' ass back in the room and close the door," he ordered, his voice hard, final.

"Make one sound," he added with a malicious grin, "and I won't hesitate to use this."

Vee hesitated for only a moment, a fire kindling in her chest. She wasn't afraid of this man. Not anymore.

"You still didn't answer my question," she pressed, her voice sharp. "Why did you kidnap me?"

Seville glanced back over his shoulder, the gun still clenched tightly in his hand. "It'll come to you before this night is over. Now, be a good little girl and get the fuck in that room."

Another knock-knock-knock rattled the door, the sound ominous in the silence that followed.

Vee's heart pounded. She had to act before it was too late.

The game was far from over.

Chapter 18
The Price of Survival

"Look, man, I remember everything you've been telling me for the past week. I ain't no dummy," Teddy said, his voice steady, though his heart was hammering in his chest. He had come a long way since first meeting Joe Kearse, but tonight, everything felt different. More real. Dangerous.

Joe Kearse, cool as ever, gave him a side-eye, sizing him up before speaking. "Is that right? Okay. So, if you come to a place which has three or four different directions to approach it and you have just as many people there whom you'd like to get the ups on, how would you go about accomplishing your goal?"

Teddy thought for a moment. His eyes flickered with the sharp calculation of a seasoned player. "I should approach them from the angle that will give me the best escape route."

"Okay. Why is this?"

"Because dangerous situations are easy to get into but hard to get out of, and I must assume that all situations are dangerous when I'm about to take somebody's shit."

Joe let out a low whistle, impressed. "Good. Good. What do you do then?"

Teddy nodded, more focused now. "Then, I'll locate the biggest threat and throw down on them first. If I control the strongest link in the chain, I control the whole chain."

"Very good," Joe Kearse complimented. "Tell me this, Sugar Bear, what if the threat is a situation and not a person? How do you deal with that?"

Teddy's face tightened as he processed the question. "First, I would observe the circumstances to choose the best course of action, including calling the job off if the conditions don't look good."

Joe smiled a rare smile. "Good job, S.B. Now, you may be ready."

As the fading light of dusk settled over the park, the two men moved quietly, slipping through an opening in the fence and weaving between the wooden shacks that were supposed to be homes. The smell of dust and old wood hung heavy in the air, mixing with the scent of diesel from a nearby truck. Their footsteps were muted, as if the earth itself was holding its breath.

Upon reaching the last house behind the store, a man suddenly burst from the front door, clutching the side of his head where blood streamed down in thick, dark rivulets, where his ear once was. He ran past Joe and Sugar Bear, shouting frantically for help, his voice raw with panic.

Hot on his heels, a wild-eyed woman—Henrietta Baptist- emerged from the shadows. She was the Haitian bootlegger, infamous for her volatile temper. "Mutha pucka," she shouted in broken English, "I'll 'tut cho' damn head off. Don't chu' neba brang cho ass 'round henh!"

Joe nodded to Sugar Bear, a silent command to follow him into the cover of the trees at the back of the Wagon Wheel I.

As they moved stealthily through the dark, Teddy's mind was elsewhere. He thought of Pretty Tony, the lieutenant who was always in the thick of the drug game. Tonight, Tony was returning from his re-up house on Douglas Street, carrying a grocery bag heavy with 100 packs of rock cocaine. He was the muscle behind Chuck Williams, the man pulling all the strings in Fort Myers, and his job was to keep the dealers stocked, ensuring the money never stopped flowing.

The night had turned into a game of shadows, and Pretty Tony was the piece in the middle.

"Yes!" Pretty Tony muttered to himself, his voice sharp with excitement. "Get money, you pretty ass mothafucker." He leaned back on the hood of his car, basking in his success, oblivious to the plans that were unfolding around him.

Joe's voice broke through the stillness, calm and calculated. "Sugar Bear, listen. I'm going over the ditch across Ford Street and through Mr. Green's gas station. Then I'll cross the Avenue and go behind the American Legion. From there, I'll come out on the side of Club 21, close to where Tony is sitting. When I get in place, I'll flick my cigarette lighter twice; that will be your signal to move in and throw down on Tony from the front. I've got the back."

Joe turned his head, his eyes locking with Teddy's. "This could easily turn into a kill or be killed situation. Is your mind made up to win?"

Teddy didn't answer immediately. Instead, he watched Joe make two long strides, bolting across the debris-filled ditch. His heart raced, not out of fear, but with the cold thrill of what was to come.

As Joe crossed Anderson Avenue, Teddy followed, nerves stirring in his gut. He was about to step into the big league, where every decision could be a matter of life and death. He thought of Betty and her warning about getting involved in dangerous work. But Betty had always known that Teddy was a survivor. He wouldn't be held back, not now.

Teddy observed Joe's lighter flickering twice from across the street, a silent signal that the plan was set in motion.

Just then, a small brown car pulled up and parked beside Tony's car, its engine rumbling low. A tall, slender man in all black exited, his movements sharp and purposeful. He walked straight to Pretty Tony, and Teddy knew this wasn't a cop. Joe had made it clear: no police interference, and this guy didn't look like an officer.

Teddy closed the distance, moving quietly, every step bringing him closer to the target. His fingers tightened around the grip of his .357, the weight reassuring in his hand. He'd been trained for moments like this, where timing was everything.

Just as Teddy was about to make his move, the man in black reached for the small of his back, pulling out a gun with fluid precision. At the same time, he grabbed Pretty Tony from the hood of the car and fired a shot toward where Joe had been. The situation was already slipping into chaos.

But Teddy's instincts kicked in. The man in black didn't see him coming. He pulled his gun, aiming at the back of the man in black, ready to make him drop the weapon.

Suddenly, a car horn blared behind him. He spun around, narrowly avoiding the vehicle speeding towards him. Without thinking, Teddy fired three quick shots into the windshield, the sound deafening in the quiet night.

In a blur, he turned and ran down Cuba Street, the echoes of gunfire and chaos trailing behind him. But as he looked back over his shoulder, he froze.

The man in black was still standing, his gun now pointed directly at Teddy. The cold black eyes staring back at him were filled with malice, like the depths of a bottomless pit. Teddy's heart skipped a beat, a chill crawling up his spine.

The man fired, but nothing happened. The gun was empty.

Teddy didn't hesitate. He fired his own weapon until the chamber clicked empty. The man staggered back, clutching the side of his face as he fell to the ground. The car that had tried to run Teddy down crashed into a parked 1972 Fleetwood Broham.

Teddy knew this wasn't over. He could disappear behind Rogers Package Store and slip away unnoticed, but he couldn't leave Joe in danger. He had to go back.

As he rounded the corner of Club 21, gunfire erupted, the sounds of battle filling the air. Teddy's heart pounded as the gunshots gradually stopped. The quiet that followed felt heavier than the chaos.

Then, a figure limped into view. It was Joe Kearse, his arm dangling lifelessly by his side, the blood staining his clothes.

"Joe! Joe!" Teddy called out, his voice cracking with urgency. "This is Sugar Bear, man. Come on. Let me help you. We've got to get the fuck away from here."

Joe was not a coward, and he hesitated at the idea of running. Joe had also recognized Sammy Blanks. He was also aware that Pretty Tony had put a contract out on his life. What Joe really wanted to do was demonstrate that he was the baddest jack-boy around. But Joe was not stupid.

Joe's voice was barely a whisper, the pain evident in every word. "Another day," he said, his voice strained. "Live to see another day.

Teddy moved to help him, draping Joe's arm around his shoulder for support. The two men began the slow trek toward the rendezvous, but they didn't get far.

A ghetto army, twelve men deep, surrounded them. Weapons drawn, they looked ready to take everything.

"Lose them damn guns or get ch'all's ass smoked," one of them said, his voice sharp. The gun he held was unfamiliar, sleek, and futuristic, unlike anything Teddy had seen before.

Betty Wright's soulful voice floated on the wind from a nearby car, her song "After the Pain" filling the silence. Teddy felt the barrel of a gun pressed to his temple, and his own weapon was ripped from his hand.

Joe's gun was taken, too.

A heavy-set man in green suede loafers approached, eyeing Joe with a mixture of respect and disdain. "Joe, baby, you've got to leave my money alone. I won't accept it any longer. Let me put it this way: I'm willing to create a position for you as my chief of security. You'll be paid $25,000 a month to keep my operation safe from Jackboys."

Joe's face was unreadable as he listened, but Teddy could see the weariness in his eyes. Joe had been a notorious jack-boy, but now, he was being offered a seat at the table, a chance to live.

The man turned and left without another word, his gang following him without hesitation.

Pretty Tony, lingering in the background, had heard the offer. His jaw tightened, and it was clear he had no intention of letting Joe Kearse become a protector. Not while he still breathed.

Teddy didn't miss the way Sammy, standing in the corner, watched him. There was no love lost between them, and Sammy had his own reasons for wanting to see Teddy dead.

As the tension thickened, the young punk felt the weight of the moment. He'd survived another night, but in this world, survival always came at a price.

Chapter 19

Echoes of Death

"Seville," a voice called out, the tone thick with impatience. Gorilla Seville squinted through the grime-coated kitchen window, trying to make out the figures standing at the door. The night outside was dark, lit only by the flickering streetlights and the soft hum of distant traffic. A cold breeze cut through the cracks in the walls, but Seville barely noticed. He had lived in this shoddy, cluttered house long enough to grow numb to its uncomfortable stillness.

"We need to rap, man," the voice continued, cutting through the stillness. "I've got a message for you from a mutual associate. The sooner you open this door and hear it, the sooner you can go back to your nods." The voice finished with a low chuckle, one that Seville recognized all too well.

He didn't have to look hard to know who was on the other side. Rock and Billy Blanks. They were here for one reason, and one reason only. Either they wanted trouble, or they were here to collect the five thousand dollars Seville owed to Theo from Bassie Court. It had been four weeks since Theo fronted him that ounce of heroin, and Seville had yet to come up with the cash.

Seville gritted his teeth, his fingers brushing the cold handle of the door. He thought about backing out, maybe pulling some bullshit story to buy more time, but the truth was, he didn't have the money. He didn't even have a fraction of it. He could only hope they took what he had—

116

he could give them that. They could take a piece of his pride or his stash, but not both.

He opened the door slowly, squinting into the low light that spilled from the porch. "Listen," Seville started, trying to keep his voice steady, "I don't have—"

"No, you listen," Billy interrupted, stepping forward with a sneer. Rock followed, his heavy footsteps punctuating his arrival. The two men entered without invitation, filling the cramped, cluttered room with their presence. "Theo gave you plenty of time to get the money together. So, what you need to do is unass it without all that extra lip, and we'll leave you in one piece."

Seville straightened, his hands clenching into fists. "I owe Theo," he spat, "but I don't owe you a goddamn thing. Furthermore, you motherfuckers need to get the hell—"

Before Seville could finish, Rock's punch came out of nowhere. It landed with a sickening thud against Seville's temple, sending him reeling to the side. As he stumbled, his hand shot out toward the armrest of his chair, gripping it for balance. His fingers brushed the cold metal of the gun strapped to his side, but before he could reach it, Billy's sharp eyes caught the movement.

Billy's gun was already drawn, aimed directly at Seville's head. The barrel was cold and shiny in the dim light, a perfect extension of the death it could deliver. For a moment, time seemed to freeze between them. Seville, dazed and gasping, met Billy's cold, unflinching stare. The world outside seemed distant—everything outside of that gun, that moment, seemed to fade away.

Then, Billy's hand jerked, and the heavy gun bucked in his grip. The shot rang out like thunder, shattering the stillness of the room. The bullet entered just below Seville's left eye, instantly cutting his life short. The force of the impact sent Seville's body to the ground with a sickening thud, his blood pooling on the worn, stained carpet.

Elsewhere, the night crept on, thick and full of tension. Sire moved with practiced stealth through the backyard of several houses, his figure swallowed by the darkness. The faint rustling of leaves and the occasional creak of a fence were the only sounds that accompanied him. He rounded the corner of a set of duplexes, careful not to alert anyone nearby. The muffled sounds of a young couple making out drifted from behind one of the houses, but neither lover noticed Sire's presence.

The sweet, familiar scent of the night filled his nostrils, earthy, damp, and alive with the hum of insects and the distant rumble of thunder. The storm had yet to break, but the air was heavy with the promise of rain. Sire stood motionless for a moment, his eyes scanning the area, waiting. His target, Vee's car, was only a few yards away, but something felt off as if the night itself was holding its breath.

He moved toward the house, his body a shadow against the wall. As he approached a side window, he noticed the faintest sliver of light seeping through a crack in the door, casting a narrow beam onto the dusty floor. His senses heightened, and he reached for the .380 tucked into his waistband, the cold metal reassuring in his grip.

He noticed the door was slightly ajar, a bad sign. His instincts screamed for caution, but he couldn't turn back now. He knocked gently on the door, the sound barely a whisper in the thick air. When the door creaked open wider, he stepped inside.

The house was dark, save for the faint light coming from a room at the end of the hall. The bathroom, probably, though it didn't matter. The stillness of the room was unnerving, as if it had been abandoned.

And then he saw it.

A body, Seville's, lying sprawled on the floor, an awkward twist in his limbs as if death had come too quickly for him to brace. There was no sign of Vee. Maybe she had escaped, armed herself, and done what she had to do to get away. The thought was fleeting, disappearing as fast as it came. There was something more pressing now, a deeper concern gnawing at the back of his mind.

Sire stepped further into the room, his eyes scanning the cluttered space. Papers and empty bottles lay scattered on the floor, evidence of the chaos Seville had left behind. On a nearby table, a damp pair of panties caught his attention, next to a set of keys. Vee's keys.

His hand hovered over the keys for a moment before he turned away, unwilling to linger any longer in the house that now felt like a tomb. His mind was racing, but he knew one thing for certain: he needed to find her.

Sire moved quickly, his footsteps silent as he made his way out of the house. He uncovered Vee's car and slid into the driver's seat, his fingers gripping the wheel tightly. The engine roared to life, breaking the silence of the night. He pulled out of the yard, the headlights cutting through the darkness, and vanished into the night, leaving behind the house of death that had once been home to Gorilla Seville.

The hunt was far from over.

Chapter 20

The Price of Protection

"Sylvester the cat only had nine lives. I know damn well I've gone through a full nine count of 'should-have-been dead,' and I'm at least halfway finished with a second nine count. Let me share a little secret with you, it's not because I was lucky."

Joe's voice was steady but solemn, like someone giving a eulogy that no one wanted to hear.

"Over the past 20 years that I've been takin' people's shit, I've been protected by a force much stronger than man. Or a weapon. Every day before I leave the house, I read from the Bible: Psalms 74, 83, and 125."

He reached into his coat pocket and pulled out a small red flannel bag.

"See this right here?" he said to Teddy. "Inside is the entirety of Psalm 125, written on parchment, anointed with protection oil. I carry it with me when I'm on the streets. Also inside, Mandrake root. It's said to protect a person from harm. That little bag has walked me out of hell."

Joe paused and looked Teddy in the eye, something behind the stare pressing against the weight of the moment.

"Now that we've been offered a job, I won't be needing my root bag anymore."

"If you come to work with me, Sugar Bear," he

continued, "I'll pay you eight grand a month."

"Joe!" Cassandra's voice rang out from the kitchen. "You and Sugar Bear come on in here and eat before this food gets cold!"

Joe smiled and motioned toward the kitchen.

"Come on, son, let's eat. Cassandra can burn too. Who is yo' people anyway?"

"They call my momma Ally Queen, and my daddy is known as Brain," Teddy answered.

"Brain?" Joe sat up straighter. "Boy, I knew your daddy! Didn't he get killed by the police in a shootout up around Gainesville?"

"Yep," Teddy said. "That's exactly what Murray and Curt told me.

"No wonder you're as ready as you are," Joe said. "Yo' daddy was a gangsta all the way."

Over the next week, Joe's healing went better than expected. The bullet wound closed up cleaner than the doctor predicted. He still walked with a little hitch, but he carried himself like a man reborn.

The next Friday was the 13th, and the air carried a charge of finality with it.

Joe and Teddy, and Sugar Bear were to start working security for Mr. Williams' drug distribution ring. It was official.

Teddy had moved in with Joe and Cassandra.

Returning to his mother's house wasn't an option, not after what happened with Betty. When he went back to the apartment, it was empty. Betty had left a note inside a heart: "Going up north to be with family. Stay focused. You're special." That was it.

So he moved his things and settled into Joe's home, a place that, despite the shadows around it, felt safer than he'd known in a while.

*　　*　　*

"I don't give a fuck what the boss told that bastard, I want you to finish the job, man," a gravel-voiced Tony said into a burner phone.

"I'll give you Otis's pay along with your $25,000. I'll be damned if I let Joe Kearse protect me."

"Bizness will be handled," the hitman replied coldly. "Go on and give me my pay now. I intend to disappear right after it's done."

Chapter 21

The Day Everything Changed

That morning, Sugar Bear awoke to the smell of bacon frying in the kitchen. Cassandra was at the stove. The scent took him back to when his mother was still whole, still loving, before the bottle robbed her of everything.

He decided: he would go see her and his sister today. It felt like something he needed to do, and today might be the last peaceful day for a while.

Joe was in his room with Cassandra, and Teddy peeked in before getting into the shower.

"Well, tonight's the night," Teddy said. "You ready?"

"Yes," Joe replied. Looking forward to this fresh start. A year from now, I'll be out of the game. You'll be back in school. Cassandra and I talked about it—she's happy I'm hanging up my guns."

"I'm glad too," Teddy said. "I'll see you tonight. Game room, 6:00 p.m."

He left to take his shower.

The door opened while he was drying off. Cassandra walked in, towels in hand, and froze. Her eyes lingered.

"Oh, baby, I'm sorry... I didn't hear the water," she stammered.

She didn't avert her gaze. Neither did Teddy. What

Betty had said about his "special power" echoed in his head.

Cassandra's eyes dropped lower and didn't rise for several long seconds. Her voice didn't return. She handed him the towel, a slow smile forming before she turned and closed the door behind her.

At breakfast, she was quieter than usual. Her eyes drifted toward Teddy too often. He didn't fully understand what was going on, but he felt the tension like a heat between them.

He hoped she and Joe were okay.

Later, Teddy confronted his drunk stepfather, Harold.

"You gonna let him stay after what he did to Cynthia?" he snapped.

The man swayed but didn't speak.

"I'm gettin' her outta here."

He packed his sister's things and took her to the Trailways bus station. She was headed to Tampa to stay with her father. The siblings hugged. They were the closest out of all five of their mother's children.

Afterward, it was nearly 6:00 p.m. He headed toward the Avenue, the 'Duce humming underneath him. The city felt like it was holding its breath.

As he navigated the alley behind the Wigg Wamm, he spotted a figure in black. The face was covered, but the bandage, the build, Teddy knew. It was the same man from the shootout with Pretty Tony.

And Joe was walking right toward a setup.

"Joe! Nooo! Get back! It's—"

But it was too late.

Pop! Pop! Pop!

The girl fell. Joe grabbed his neck, stumbling. The man turned toward Teddy. Aimed.

Teddy ducked and ran. More shots behind him. He didn't stop.

Joe staggered, tried to run, then fell face-first between two cars. He barely moved.

The man approached, gun raised, and executed Joe with cold finality.

Teddy was frozen. The killer saw him. Came charging. The gun lifted. A shot was fired. Pain exploded in Teddy's leg. But he ran hard. Adrenaline blotted out everything else. He reached Mr. Harry's junkyard and crawled under the fence of tire rims. Mosquitoes swarmed, his leg throbbed, and the shadows grew long.

Then came the monkey.

The surreal image of the monkey grooming the dog, then slapping it into confusion, was absurdly calming. It gave Teddy a strange kind of peace.

Eventually, he climbed over the fence, cut across

Franklin Park Elementary, and returned to the Duce. He sat in the driver's seat, the city humming its oblivious tune. He thought of Cassandra. She would be shattered. So would he.

But tonight, he didn't have time to grieve. Not yet. Not until the war that had just started had its final casualty.

EDWARD WILSON JR

128

Chapter 22

The Beasts We Nurture

"You have to let it go. Try to be more sensible, you're holding on to a dangerous grudge. It could be one that exceeds your abilities and the experience needed to achieve it. Besides, it won't bring Joe back."

Three weeks had passed since Cassandra laid Joe to rest. The earth was still fresh on his grave, just like the wounds she carried inside. She had first met him in high school, he, the electrifying star running back; she, the magnetic cheerleader. Their story had never been simple. On-again, off-again, destined to orbit one another, until about a year and a half ago, when they tried to get serious. But seriousness and Joe's "profession" were oil and water.

She'd known. The night he died, she knew. Not because someone told her, but because some primal pulse in her spirit had throbbed all night and all morning. They'd fought before it happened, over Teddy. Over Joe dragging that kid into danger, into his world.

"That kid," Joe had told her, voice calm but firm, "saved my life in a way no child ever should. I am without power to change the hand fate has dealt me; I can only play it with understanding. If anything happens to me, and you can help him… do it. For me."

That plea lingered, and now here they were.

Teddy's voice was steady, but it simmered with anger. "It might not bring Joe back, but I can't just let it go. And how do you know I won't be able to get them back?"

"Do you even know for sure who's behind it?"

"Joe told me Pretty Tony put a contract on his life. So far as I'm concerned, it's him."

Cassandra sighed. "I still think you should forget the whole thing and go on with your life."

"I can't, Cassandra. And you still didn't answer my question—how do you know I won't be able to get them?"

"I can't answer it, Teddy."

"Why?"

"Because the truth is... I don't know. I kind of like you a lot. I've already lost Joe..." Her voice trailed off into silence.

Cassandra was 27. A woman still cloaked in the glow of youthful beauty. Her eyes were sultry and inviting, her lips full and expressive, her body a statuesque marvel. But behind the allure was a mind in constant motion, analytical, reflective, and deeply feeling.

"How old are you?" she asked softly.

"I'll be 18 next birthday."

"And how long have you been out there, running the streets?"

"Since I was about eight and a half."

"Eight years old…" she whispered. The horror of it pulled her under. "What about your family?"

"Never knew my father. He was killed by the police when I was eleven. My mom lives down in The Bottom, on Lime Street. Mostly drunk."

Cassandra's mind drifted. At eight, she was still learning to fold sheets right, trying to figure out multiplication, worried about bedtime stories, and scraped knees. No child should be living the life Teddy had lived. But this was his reality. The world had failed him. The adults who were supposed to love him, gone. The community that should've supported him, absent.

Who do you blame? She asked herself. The mother? The absent father? The system? Or everyone?

But not the child.

Teddy was still standing. That alone meant something. Maybe it even meant everything.

She glanced at him, and somewhere in her core, an unfamiliar pull stirred. It wasn't maternal. It wasn't sisterly. It was deeper, far more dangerous.

"Teddy… God has given you a very special gift," she said, her voice taking on an almost reverent tone. "If you learn to control it, women will give you their hearts, their bodies, everything. But that gift, when mixed with sex and romance… it can become something dark. A beast. A demon."

She spoke of love as a force that could both heal and destroy. The line between the two is fragile. Once crossed, impossible to uncross.

"I feel it, Teddy. I feel it in the way you look at me. The way I feel when I look at you. You have that thing… that fire. That drug. You don't know what it is yet, but one day, you will. And when you do… just remember what I told you."

Teddy didn't reply right away. He simply smiled. There was understanding behind that smile. And restraint. But Cassandra saw it. The same fire in him that Joe once had. The same danger… and the same promise.

"Thank you for saying it the way you did. I understand better now," he said.

"You're welcome. May I have another hug?"

"You can have as many as you want."

"Be careful with offers like that," she teased, giving a wink. "You might not be able to handle what comes with them."

The next morning, she left a note with breakfast in the oven. She wouldn't be home until after five.

Teddy showered, ate, took out the trash, and then drove the Duce toward Lime Street. Thanksgiving was two days away. As he backed out of the driveway, a cat darted past the tires. Joe's metaphor about danger and Sylvester the cat flickered in his mind. Nine lives. Premonitions.

His mother's house looked the same. On the porch, his sister was washing collard greens, something he hadn't seen in what felt like forever.

"I thought you left."

"Momma called and begged me to come back."

"Is she sober?"

Right then, Inez stepped outside. Her face lit up when she saw him.

"Hey, Ma. What's cooking?"

"Wild coon in candied yams, smothered rabbit, brown rice, black beans. If your sister hurries with them greens, we'll have those too."

He grinned. He had missed this. This version of his mother. When the alcohol didn't win.

"Where's Mr. Harold?"

He is out somewhere. Still drunk, probably. But he's around."

Teddy stayed for half an hour, then left, headed toward Buck's Place. Instead of parking behind it, he walked, hoping to find Frank. He needed someone to buy liquor, but more than that, he needed his friend.

"Mr. Rolland!" he called out.

The old man turned, smiled, and walked over.

"If it ain't Lil' Teddy the sugar cub," he said. Teddy handed him money and a list. "Meet me at the tree."

But when he got around back, Frank wasn't there. Not on the crate. Not near the barrel.

Rolland returned with the drinks.

"Where's Alley Queen?" he asked, referring to Inez.

"She's sober. Liver's going out. The doctor gave her a scare."

Rolland nodded slowly. Then: "You waiting on Frank?"

"Yeah, the old guy with the faded city-worker cap."

"You didn't hear?"

"Hear what?"

"Frank's dead. A cop car hit him while chasing a brown Ford. Knocked him into a Mack truck. Broke every bone. They say it was brutal."

The words hit Teddy like a freight train.

Frank. Gone. Just like that.

Rolland looked at him, hesitated. Then added softly, "Today's the last day to view the body. Boyd's Funeral Home. They did a good job with him."

He turned and walked off, his own eyes glistening with tears.

Teddy stood there, still, the cold weight of loss pressing

in. First Joe. Now Frank.

The world had taken another piece of him, and the fire inside him burned hotter.

Chapter 23

The Burden of Farewell

"The data housed in the complex's archive weren't too extensive on the subject, but enough was obtainable to suggest, to a measurable degree, that the concerns your question raises must have been considered," Stephanie said, leaning back slightly in her chair, her fingers tapping lightly on the edge of the desk.

Although the compilation occurred in the late '60s and early '70s, it appears to obligate the state and local government to create a psychologically healthy, safe, and educational alternative to what you've described in this Teddy kid's quandary. However," she hesitated, looking directly at Cassandra, "I'm reluctant to acquiesce to a position that the government's failure to implement prophylactic measures, or to foresee the potential destruction of the black child's predicament, where such an alternative does not exist, was somehow intended, or racially motivated."

"I don't think I follow you," Cassandra commented, frowning slightly as she leaned forward, intrigued but clearly confused.

"Well," Stephanie resumed, her voice taking on a more deliberate tone, "Let me give you a little history on this black-and-white picture here in our country." She paused, eyeing Cassandra to gauge her attentiveness.

"On May 17, 1954, the United States Supreme Court was confronted with a question addressing two major racially charged social issues. One, which had been the law of the land for over 58 years, was the separate but equal rule, requiring public facilities to provide separate but equal accommodations for black and white passengers, Plessy v. Ferguson, 1896."

Cassandra nodded slowly, her mind processing the words as Stephanie continued. "The second issue, the more recent one, ruled in a unanimous decision that racial segregation in public schools was unconstitutional, and thus, overruled the 1896 decision, Brown vs. Board of Education, 1954, abolishing the old mantras."

Stephanie paused, her eyes scanning the space in front of her. She seemed to weigh her next words carefully. "Despite the fact that the recent rule came in 1954, it took nearly 15 years for the states, especially the southern states, to create and implement the new rule."

She looked up, making sure Cassandra was following, then continued. "Now, as a result of the new desegregation rule, states had to integrate all schools in the public arena. Black and white kids alike were no longer permitted to attend neighborhood schools but were now required to help make up a certain percentage quota in all schools. This resulted in kids, black kids in particular, being bused many miles away from their homes."

Stephanie sighed, her eyes narrowing slightly as she made eye contact with Cassandra, ensuring that she grasped the gravity of what she was about to say. "If you're wondering what this has to do with your concerns and questions about Teddy, please bear with me. All the integration requirements had indirect collateral consequences, which directly address your concerns about whether the state is required to provide a safe environment for black kids to participate in after-school activities. Those indirect collateral consequences are that the only programs or places offering healthy and safe alternatives were the established institutions, such as the YMCA, Christian Youth Outreach, or related programs."

Cassandra's eyes widened as she began to see the connection, but Stephanie wasn't finished.

"However," Stephanie continued, "most of the at-risk kids, black, if you will, live so far away from these offerings that they never get the chance to relish the enormous benefits or positive influences prevalent in such settings. This fact is what really brought the 'at-risk' and the disadvantaged kids to the discussion table, subsequently resulting in additional funds being allocated to address the needs of all kids. I do, however, agree that our city is seemingly dragging its feet in some areas."

Cassandra nodded slowly, her brow furrowed in thought. "I see. That makes sense, I guess," she said softly, processing the information.

Stephanie's face softened as she offered a small smile. "I hope this makes sense to you, Cassandra."

"It does," Cassandra responded, then hesitated before

asking, "But my other concern is, what were you able to find on the requirements for kids staying in school until reaching the age of 16?"

Stephanie's expression darkened, and she leaned forward, her voice lowering in tone. "Now, that's something I am very troubled by. Up until recently, most schools maintained an in-house counselor or truancy officer whose primary responsibilities were to monitor school attendance logs and reports. They were also supposed to investigate any child who violated the minimum attendance standards. But under a recent state budget crunch, the counselor's position in the schools was eliminated, and the truancy task is now assumed by the city's police department." Stephanie shook her head, a touch of frustration in her voice. "Hell, they're already understaffed and overburdened to be concerned with school attendance."

"That explains a lot," Cassandra murmured, her face filled with a mix of anger and resignation. "Thank you for looking into this for me, Stephanie."

Stephanie stood, a wry smile playing on her lips. "Think nothing of it, Cassandra. My lunch break is over. I'll see you later, girl." She gave a playful salute before heading out of the snack room, which served as the complex's dining area.

*   *   *

Later That Evening...

"Young man, please! Do not touch the body." Mr.

Boyd's voice was firm, his words filled with an unexpected urgency. His eyes were narrow with judgment as he stepped forward, his feet making soft, deliberate steps against the polished wooden floors of the funeral home. "Contrary to people's belief, dressing a dead person is not as easy as putting clothes on a live one."

Teddy stood frozen at the edge of the open casket, his hands still trembling from the intensity of the moment. He was only half-aware of Mr. Boyd's presence as he looked down at Frank's lifeless form, his mind clouded by grief. He hadn't expected to feel this heavy, this lost. But there it was, weighing down on him like a thick blanket.

Mr. Boyd stood behind the desk, observing Teddy through the two-way mirror in his office before walking over to retrieve the brown paper bag Teddy had placed beside Frank's body. The bag crinkled under his hand, the unmistakable sound of glass bottles shifting inside.

"This is also not allowed," Mr. Boyd said, his voice dropping as he opened the bag and peered inside. He looked up at Teddy, his eyes filled with both surprise and disappointment when he saw the two-fifths of white port wine. "Besides, what kind of sense does this make? Mr. White is no longer able to consume spirits, son. He's deceased."

Teddy's face flushed with embarrassment, but he didn't move. His gaze remained fixed on Frank, an ache deep in his chest. He didn't care about the wine. He just wanted to do something, anything, for the man who had been his only friend. He reached into his pocket and pulled out a wad of money, peeling off a hundred-dollar bill.

"Sir," Teddy said, his voice tight with emotion, "it might not make any sense to you or my dead friend, but it makes a whole lotta sense to me. He was the only friend I had in this world. To everybody else, he was just a wine head, but to me, he was my friend. I just want to give him a going-away gift. Please."

Mr. Boyd's expression softened just for a moment. He looked at the money but didn't reach for it. Instead, he simply stood still, staring back at Teddy, the weight of the young man's words hanging in the air. Finally, Mr. Boyd sighed and shook his head, his shoulders heavy with a quiet sorrow.

"I can't take it, son." He handed the money back to Teddy. "Hurry and finish your visit. He'll be buried today."

Teddy's throat tightened, and all he could manage was a faint, "Thank you." The tears he had been holding back for so long finally broke free. He turned away, his chest heaving with quiet sobs as he said his final goodbye to Frank, his only true friend in this cruel world.

By the time Teddy left the funeral home, the sky had darkened, and the street outside, The Avenue, was buzzing with the lives of people who seemed to be heading nowhere and everywhere all at once. He blended into the crowd, his face streaked with tears, but he didn't care anymore. Frank would surely be missed, but in that moment, Teddy's heart felt a little lighter, a little freer.

The city was alive. His people, his world, would continue to turn, but the night was still. For Frank, for all the ones lost too soon.

Chapter 24

Echoes on The Avenue

"It was definitely a struggle of some degree," Detective Lewis muttered, crouching near the body, his gloved hands hovering just above the blood-smeared floor. His tone was grim, laced with quiet frustration. "Whoever fired the fatal shot beat our corps on the draw. This guy was trying to position himself to fire his own weapon."

His partner, standing just over his shoulder, observed the scene in silence for a moment before speaking. "What do you make of it?"

Lewis exhaled, rising slowly and brushing dust from his slacks. "I can't imagine anyone wanting to rob the place. That is, unless it was a stash house and drugs were here. But even that notion is diminished by the known fact that this guy here is a user." He nodded toward the corpse, his face expressionless, but his eyes sharp.

Without wasting time, Detective Lewis pulled out his company-issued phone, the screen faintly cracked from years of fieldwork. He dialed headquarters, his voice steady and professional as he requested the Medical Examiner to be dispatched to the scene. Across the room, his assistant had already gotten to work, documenting the scene with his old but reliable Nokia camera phone, snapping photos and tagging evidence with numbered markers.

Call complete, Lewis returned the phone to his jacket and began his own methodical sweep. Each of the three residents living closest to the deceased had already been questioned. They'd provided their names and contact details, but none had witnessed anything useful or relevant. Not even a shadow out of place. Just fear and vague speculation.

*   *   *

"Hi sweetie," the woman purred, her smile sly and suggestive as she leaned into the passenger side window. "What blew you back to me? Have you decided to try this sweet thang of mine?"

The man behind the wheel, cool and deliberate, responded without missing a beat. "Get in. We'll talk about it."

Once she climbed into the seat, crossing her legs slowly and turning to face him, he continued, his voice smooth but direct. "You might find what I have to say very beneficial." He handed her a crisp C-note, folding it neatly and placing it in her palm. "Here's a hundred for the first thirty minutes of your time. I need to rap with you. Let's take a ride."

As the truck eased onto the road, he glanced her way. "The last time we spoke, you told me about someone named Sire who was at the pool room the night of the robbery?"

"Yes, I did," Sweet Touch replied, brushing a braid from her shoulder. "He was."

"Have you seen him since then?"

"As a matter of fact, I saw him a few days ago coming out of the Wagon Wheel."

The name drop caused such a jolt of excitement in Sammy that he nearly missed the on-ramp leading to I-75. He corrected quickly, jaw tight. "Sweet Touch, listen," he said, glancing over, "I'm gonna drive to Punta Gorda and turn around. Are you cool with that?"

"Handsome, I am on your time, bought and paid for," she cooed, her voice like silk dipped in heat. At that moment, she uncrossed her legs, giving him an open and intentional view. She wasn't wearing any underwear.

But none of that mattered to Sammy. Not now. Pussy was the last thing on his mind. His thoughts churned with purpose, with names, with motives. Sire. He had to learn more. He had to know who the hell this guy was.

"Do you often go to Wagon Wheel?"

"Yes," she said casually, running her fingers along her bare thigh. "And so do most of the people who earn their living on the streets of Fort Myers."

"Will he be there when you go?"

"No," she replied. "That was the first time I saw him there."

"Was he alone or with someone?"

"He was with a chick that carried on like she was his woman. And before you ask me, no—I didn't know her."

Sammy pulled a second bill from his wallet, holding it between two fingers. "Okay, here's my offer: I'll give you my number and another hundred bucks. If you see him anywhere or anytime, call me. I'll give you another three hundred then. I need you to be my eyes. If you find him sooner for me, it'll be a nice bonus on top of the three."

Her eyes gleamed, pupils dilating slightly. Greed was like perfume to Sweet Touch—strong, addictive, and motivating. She shifted again, resting her back against the door, legs wide open. Her smooth, hairless skin reflected the faint glow of the dashboard lights.

Sammy tried to resist, but his body betrayed him. His pants tightened uncomfortably, pressure building. It had been years—three long years—since he'd been with a woman. Not since his own passed away from cervical cancer.

A rest stop appeared up ahead. He pulled in, needing a break, needing a moment to cool down. Inside, he bought sodas and returned to find Sweet Touch still poised, legs parted, waiting.

"Woman," he said, shaking his head, "I've got to hand it to you, that pussy do look good."

She smirked. "As hard as you were a moment ago, I was sure you'd want to push that big dick in this hot pussy. Are you sure you don't want to give it a try?"

"Touch, you can kiss it again if you'd like," he said, rubbing himself through his pants. Still, his mind remained focused. Temptation whispered to him, but purpose shouted louder.

Rumor had it that Sweet Touch lived up to her name. One taste and a man was never the same. He couldn't afford that now.

Exit 23 loomed ahead, the turnoff toward Highway 82 and back into Fort Myers. He pulled off and slowed the truck.

"I'm letting you out here," he said.

As she stepped down, something struck her memory. "Oh," she called, hurrying back to his window. "Sire was speaking with Pimpwell as he was leaving the restaurant."

Sammy's expression shifted. He looked at her long and hard. "That's what I call aiming high for your bonus," he said quietly. "Keep our business under wraps, understand?"

The shift in his tone chilled her. It wasn't a request. It was a warning.

"If I couldn't handle the job, you wouldn't have given it to me," she said confidently.

Sammy reached out, gripping her hand in an iron hold. "You didn't answer me. Do you understand to keep yo' mouth shut?"

"Yeah, man, I understand." But fear flickered in her eyes. She was starting to second-guess her decision. Still, money ruled all, and Ho' Bender, her man, would want her to follow through.

Sammy hadn't walked The Avenue in over twenty years. Last time he did, he was tying up loose ends on a contract before disappearing to Pensacola. There, he built something new. A lawn service. It prospered. Eventually, he started one in Fort Myers, too. That one thrived as well. He'd stepped out of the killing game. But for family, for his brothers, Sammy would do it all again without hesitation.

No one recognized him as he walked. He kept his posture low, deliberate. Bought a pack of Kools at Galmer's before heading across the street to the poolroom.

"Well, I'll be damned. Sammy, that you?" East Coast hollered, a grin spreading across his face as Sammy pulled a cue stick from the rack.

"Maybe," Sammy replied, voice dry.

"Lighten up, Sam," said Set-Back, stepping closer. "We ain't see yo' ass since Rodney King got beat down."

"Since when did people on The Avenue become so sensitive?" Sammy responded, more amused than annoyed. He gave Set-Back a look that was sharp and unreadable.

"Look," he said, "I didn't come in here to do nothing but kick some ass on the table, so ya'll ease up."

He played a few games, kept his ears open, and eyes sharp. Then left. He needed Sweet Touch to deliver. Because he had to know: Was Sire the one who cased Rock's crib?

* * * *

"Hello," the voice came through the receiver, calm but urgent. "This is me, baby. Go to the palace. I am on my way. I have Vee's ride. She wasn't there."

A pause.

"Looks like we need not worry about the dude because he's resting in that gangsta lean. Vee couldn't have killed him. Makes no sense for her to leave without taking her car. No. Someone else did our nemesis in, and I'm afraid that someone else now has Vee. I'll see you shortly."

Driving back, Sire's mind replayed the scene at Seville's shack like a film loop.

Who would want to kill Seville, and why?

Why take Vee? Why not kill her, too?

As he pulled into his driveway, Shauka barked from his pen. He paused, then approached to check his food. Tish had already tended to the dog.

"Your bath is ready," Tish called out, stepping into the doorway. "I've had my shower. I also fried some shrimp and made potato logs."

"Okay. I'll be right in."

He soaked in the tub briefly, cleansing the dirt and doubt from his skin. He joined her in bed, sat beside her, and recounted what he'd seen at Gorilla Seville's shack.

149

"We know she was there," he said slowly. "And it's safe to say she's alive, for now. Her panties are still damp."

Tish turned to him, eyes searching. "What are you going to do?"

"Exactly what I'll do, I'm not sure," Sire admitted. "But I'm sure that I'll do something. She did vow to give her life for you or me if it became necessary. I must give her no less. We must give her no less."

He looked out the window, the city lights flickering in the distance. "So I'll hit the streets. There aren't too many people in this town who know the streets of Fort Myers better than I do."

Chapter 25

Velvet Nights and Vengeance

A mechanical whir filled the alley as a thick steel cable lowered an enormous custom cake, white frosting trimmed with gold, onto a pushcart, steam still whispering from its sides. It had just been offloaded from a refrigerated truck backed up to the service entrance of The Palisade Club. The cake was nearly the size of a refrigerator, tiered high with dazzling sugar roses and shimmering edible pearls, but its grandeur was more than ornamental. Hidden inside was the night's most provocative surprise.

The club was already alive with motion. A place of opulence, it stretched two stories high, its bottom floor left in its usual polished form, chandeliers humming above leather booths, soft jazz filtering through. But it was the upper floor, accessible only to the elite with gold-foiled invitations, that had been transformed into a haven of indulgence. The scent of truffle oil, fresh seafood, and aged whiskey perfumed the air. Crates of Dom Pérignon lined the bar. No expense had been spared.

This wasn't just any celebration, it was the birthday of Pretty Tony, the right hand of Chuck Williams, boss of the city's most powerful illicit syndicate, The Outfit. And it wasn't just a party. It was a display of power, wealth, and control. The event had been orchestrated down to the last decadent detail. The Outfit, since Tony's rise, had grown into a multimillion-dollar operation. Tony had brought finesse to the underground walkie-talkies for the crew, new eyes on the street, and a velvet rope approach to security.

But tonight, with Joe Kearse dead, there was a sense of relaxation in the air. An illusion.

Tony Solomon, the man of the hour, did everything big, flashing Tom Ford suits, glinting jewelry, and designer rides he rotated daily. Women followed him like perfume in the wind, drawn by the magnetism of money and the chance to step into the glow of someone who seemingly had it all.

The catering crew, hand-picked from a local agency, wore sharp uniforms: velvet-textured money green. The women's tight pants and cropped tops barely contained their curves, while the men donned slacks and vests, each sporting a gaudy globe pendant in faux gold Tony's signature. Everything was theatrical. Intentional. Just how he liked it.

At exactly 10:00 p.m., a spotlight hit the front gates as a 1989 custom Bentley, painted in velvet green and chrome trim, rolled in with a purr. Tony stepped out, ringed fingers gleaming under the floodlights. Chuck Williams, owner of The Palisade and real boss behind the curtains, waited at the side entrance.

"Happy Birthday, PT," Chuck said, extending a firm hand. His voice carried the weight of age and respect. Five years ago, Tony was a nobody. Now, he was Chuck's most trusted enforcer.

Tony opened the box Chuck handed him. Nestled in crushed velvet was a 22-inch diamond-and-platinum necklace, the size and gleam of it rivaling anything in the club.

"Beautiful, Boss. I'll cherish it for life. Thank you, Mr. Williams."

Chuck gave a nod and a fatherly smile. You enjoy tonight. I've gotta handle a situation in Fort Lauderdale— our sister-truck operation. But I had to be here for this. You earned it, son."

As Chuck departed, Tony settled behind the polished mahogany desk in the VIP lounge, admiring the glimmering globe now around his neck. His thoughts were indulgent, cocky. He should've given me ten of these, he thought with a smirk.

Meanwhile…

Across the street, atop Utopia's Beauty Parlor, Teddy crouched like a predator at dusk. His eyes never left the club. The sentries at the front were sharp but predictable, checking invites, sipping whiskey from flasks. The back, however, was wide open. A filthy, moccasin-infested ditch separated the property from Ford Street. It looked impenetrable. It wasn't.

Teddy slid down the back of the salon and approached the ditch. He cradled Joe's Mac-10 and a .357 Magnum above his head to keep them dry as he waded waist-deep through the reeking water. Suddenly, one of the sentries appeared. Teddy froze.

"Hurry the hell up, Jerry," barked the other sentry. "I ain't missin' that cake!"

"This $150 whiskey's got me pissin' like a faucet," Jerry replied, fumbling with his fly.

Teddy slipped out undetected and found a small utility room unlocked near the back. Inside, the hum of massive air conditioners buzzed. One large duct ran directly into the building, a sliver of light leaking through a gash in its lining.

Peering in, Teddy's jaw tightened. A naked woman was stepping under the giant cake as a cable lifted it. A man in green velvet unhooked the mechanism and began rolling it out.

Teddy moved quickly. He ripped the duct open and followed the man down the hall, stalking silently. When he got close enough, he tapped him on the shoulder. The man turned and froze at the sight of the Mac-10's barrel.

"Strip. Everything but your underwear. Now."

The man obeyed without hesitation.

"Go back to the kitchen. The air duct is next to the freezer. You talk, I kill you. Dip, motherfucker."

Teddy pulled the green uniform over his wet clothes, stashed the guns in a bundled towel, and pushed the cake down the corridor. When he turned the corner, a man in green velvet leaned on a barstool, a shotgun glinting by his side. He merely nodded toward an elevator platform—the dumbwaiter.

Teddy pushed the "up" button. The platform jerked to life. As it rose, light poured in from the glass double doors above.

Inside the lounge, laughter and low jazz filtered through the air. Tony's guests were already buzzing from the booze and the night's anticipation. A glamorous woman with a clipboard and a haircut like Anita Baker approached.

"Come on, baby. How long has she been in the cake?"

"Ten minutes."

"Perfect. She's almost up. Tony's in the VIP. Just follow me."

Stage lights dimmed as the band took a break. The hush gave way to whispers of excitement as the cake was rolled in.

The crowd began singing.

"Happy Birthday to you…"

Tony approached with swagger, a smirk on his lips, soaking up the attention like champagne. When the cake exploded with frosting and sparkles, Mona Louise emerged half-dressed and all goddess. Long, wavy black hair. Skin like caramel and honey. Eyes like sea-glass.

She moved like silk dipped in sex.

The music shifted, the crowd whooped, and Mona's body began to tell its story, sensual, slow, hypnotic. Tony was hooked.

When she beckoned him, he didn't hesitate. She whispered in his ear: "Let's go somewhere private, birthday boy, so I can fuck your brains out."

They disappeared behind the door marked PRIVATE.

Teddy, now back in his own clothes and armed, watched from the shadows. He slipped through the same door, the Mac-10 gripped tight.

Inside, the room was dim, bathed in an amber glow. On the table, Mona's legs stretched wide. Tony was buried in her like a starving man. The sight, raw and primal, sent a strange sensation through Teddy's core.

"Control, Teddy. Control."

He remembered Joe's words: Be sure of what you came to do.

Teddy's eyes narrowed. His mind was clear.

Outside the door, Skinner Jones and Albert Lee had spotted Teddy earlier, changing clothes too openly, too fast. Now they were approaching, guns ready.

But inside that room, the noise of the club faded. The only sounds were heavy breathing, soft moans, and the tension of something about to snap.

Teddy raised the Mac-10.

This night of velvet, gold, and sin was about to turn red.

Chapter 26

The Avenue Burns at Midnight

It's close to midnight, and the sticky summer air clings to the sidewalks like sweat on a boxer's brow. A shabbily dressed bum shuffles along Anderson Avenue, weaving his way through the scattered clusters of nightcrawlers. He clutches a brown paper bag to his chest like it holds the secrets of the world. The green tip of a cheap white port wine bottle peeks out of the torn top. The stench that wafts from his stained coveralls is so vile it creates an invisible force field, people instinctively cross the street or step aside without even realizing they're doing it.

On his face are a pair of battered, knockoff Blues Brothers sunglasses, with one lens cracked and the other missing entirely. Through the exposed socket of the frames, his eye flickers with alertness, calculating, scanning. No one sees past the performance. They see only the stink and the shuffle and the pathetic mumble of a lost man.

But this is no ordinary bum.

As he lingers around George Agent's pool hall, catching stray snippets of conversation and absorbing the tension in the air, the rumor becomes clear, Billy Blanks and one of his brothers are behind Gorilla Seville's murder.

That name Gorilla Seville carries weight on these streets, like thunder echoing down alleyways. Club 82, a fortress of vice and velvet, looms ahead. It's where the powerbrokers and hustlers of Anderson Avenue gather like wolves circling prey.

Inside, the Bassie Court boys dominate the back section, their swagger unmistakable, their arrogance louder than the DJ's bass. They are the only gang close enough to rival Chuck Williams' Fort Myers empire.

And if the whispers are true that they took down Seville, then pride, that ancient enemy, will loosen their lips. Sire knows this. He also knows that in the game of shadows, titles mean nothing. "Aim for the power, not the title," Pimpwell once said. Titles are tombstones waiting for a name.

He leans into the wall of the club, acting every bit the wino. His ruse is nearly flawless.

"What kind of sense that makes?" mutters a man loudly, unzipping his pants beside a dumpster. "All these damn people and the joint got one fuckin' bathroom?"

The man glances sideways and spots Sire, half-fallen against the club wall, swaying in fake inebriation.

"You shouldn't spend all your money on wine, buddy," he says, laughing. Use some soap and water. You funkier than two mothafuckas in a wet room."

Sire doesn't flinch. He keeps playing his part, unmoved, unreadable. Another man comes around the corner, unzipping.

"Man, the Bassie Court crew got the whole damn back of the club blocked off. Sayin' it's some celebration for

Billy. He ain't letting nobody back there even though it's the only bathroom!"

"Yeah," the first one says while zipping back up, "he knocked off Gorilla Seville for 'em."

That's all Sire needs. Tonight, answers will bleed.

Two hours pass.

Billy and three sharply dressed men stroll out of Club 82, laughter trailing behind them like exhaust. A gold Jaguar glimmers in the lot, reflecting the buzzing streetlights. Billy walks past it and heads to his Harley, the chrome growling under the sodium lamps.

Sire waits.

The Jag drives off. Billy reaches for his helmet. That's when the "bum" stumbles forward, suddenly collapsing.

The full weight of Sire's body slams into the motorcycle.

CRASH.

Billy screams as the machine pins him to the asphalt. The kickstand punctures the flesh just above his knee like a meat hook. His voice trembles with real pain now.

"My leg! My leg! Help! Get this 'cycle off me!"

Two men run from the club. Together, they hoist the bike off Billy, revealing the blood, the torn jeans, the twisted limb.

"Call the fuckin' ambulance!" Billy shouts, gritting his teeth.

"No time," Sire interjects. "He needs to be on the way now!"

"I'll use my car!" one of them offers, already rushing to the vehicle.

They load Billy into the back seat. Sire climbs in after him.

But after a few blocks, the driver wrinkles his nose in disgust.

"Yo, man, you smell like hell. You gotta get out."

Sire grins. The mix he brewed, shaving powder, garlic, and onions, had worked perfectly.

"Alright," he says, calm as ever. "Just turn down one of these side streets."

The car turns onto Canal. As soon as it slows down, Sire draws his Beretta. A single shot rings out, missing the driver by inches.

"No sucker. You get out, or you die."

"Man… man, you can stay, it's cool—"

Sire cracks him across the temple with the pistol. The man whimpers, wetting himself. He scrambles out.

Billy fades in and out of consciousness.

When he next comes to, the car is deep in the woods.

Sire stands before him like death incarnate.

"Who the hell are you?" Billy croaks. "You don't know who the fuck I am?"

Sire answers with his boot, right into the injury. Billy screams like a child.

"I know exactly who you are," Sire says coldly. "I know what you and Rock did to Seville. I don't care about that. Where's the girl?"

Billy lies. Sire sees it in the twitch of his eye.

"I don't know what—"

Another kick.

"Okay! Okay! I'll take you. Just get me help!"

Billy calculates. He won't betray Rock. But maybe… Sammy can fix this.

***

"Gentlemen. Ms. Parker, Sgt. Parker."

Chief Daniels' voice slices through the conference room like a blade.

"In thirty days, we've had two homicides in Dunbar, more dope than ever on the streets, and robberies every half hour. The mayor's up my ass. Business leaders are livid. And the people of Fort Myers are scared. We have to fix this."

"Lewis?" he prompts.

"Yes, Chief. Just before this meeting, my top informant reached out. Promised info that could lead to an arrest."

"Good. Welks, kids as young as twelve are slinging crack. I don't want excuses."

Welks answers with steel in his voice. "No excuses. A raid's scheduled. Midnight. Operation Detox."

"Go on," Daniels barks.

"Three outfits: Basie Court, Chuck Williams, and Byron Blanks. Longstanding players. Tonight, we move."

"If you don't show results in a week, you're gone," Daniels growls. "Clean this city up."

*   *   *

"Please... please don't rape me again," Vee sobs. Her voice is raw, eyes wide with horror. "I've only been in Fort Myers for three months. I've been robbed, raped, and kidnapped twice. Just let me go."

Rock stands naked, aroused and drooling, hands on her breast. A sick grin splits his face.

"I ain't gonna rape you, baby," he says. "But I am hoping to get a lil' piece. That fat pussy looks like it needs company."

"You wanna know what I lost when I got robbed?" she says, sensing his weakness.

"My man lost fifteen grand. His best friend lost a diamond."

At the mention of the money, Rock's arousal dies instantly. His face clouds.

"What's your man's name?" he growls.

"Sssss..." she almost says it, Sire, then stops.

"Bitch!" Rock slaps her, knocking her and the chair over.

"Say it! What's his name?"

"I'll tell you!" she screams. "Sire. S-I-R-E. And you better pray he don't catch up to your weak ass."

Fury overcomes him. The belt lands again and again across her skin, bruising the beauty in brutal strokes.

"Rock! The fuck are you doing?" Sammy storms in.

"She's Sire's woman," Rock pants. "She saw too much."

"Does she know you?" Sammy asks coldly.

"No. No, she don't."

Sammy eyes him hard. Then his phone rings.

He listens to the message: Need to see you ASAP. Up on The Avenue 'til 12:00am.

He has to leave

*   *   *

"Girl's safe at my brother Rock's crib," Billy tells Sire, pointing to the cell phone.

"Call him. Now."

Billy dials. It's 11:35 PM. Speaker on.

"Hello?" Rock's voice is calm.

"Rock, it's Billy. I'm comin' for the girl. Have her ready. Ten minutes."

Pause.

"She'll be ready."

Click.

Vee whispers silent prayers, clinging to her faith. Her bloodied mouth tastes of iron and defiance. My man is coming for me, she tells herself. I just need to survive long enough.

When Rock returns, she smiles through the pain.

"What the fuck you smilin' at?"

She quotes Aunt Helen in her mind.

"I came so hard when you whipped me," she lies. "If I'm gonna die, at least fuck me first."

Rock can't help but laugh. She's twisted. He loves it.

He starts untying the shoestring around her wrist.

*　　　*　　　*

Fifteen black SUVs exit an old warehouse. Each carries ten agents, guns ready, eyes sharp.

"Synchronize," Welks says into his mic. "It's 11:50. Confirm position at 11:55. We strike all three outfits at 12:00 sharp."

Every officer responds. The clock ticks down.

Fort Myers is about to explode.

Chapter 27

A King and His Queen

The weight of the night hangs thick in the air as Pretty Tony remains unaware of the presence creeping up behind him. The girl's breath quickens, her body writhing in ecstasy, the noises between them filling the room. The air is charged with heat, the desperation of fleeting moments echoing in the silence of the office. Tony's body is barely contained in his slacks, his lust-driven focus consumed by the girl beneath him, oblivious to anything else.

Then, without warning, the sharp crack of a kick breaks the spell, the force of it ripping through Tony's body. His skin flushes with pain as he yelps in response, a sound that fills the room and spills into the night. His words falter and choke in his throat when he turns to face his assailant, the anger in his eyes freezing when he meets the gaze of Sugar Bear, Teddy.

The cake girl, eyes wide with fear, pushes herself away from Tony, trying to retreat from the danger in the air. Teddy's eyes, cold and unrelenting, scan the room, and then they fall upon the staggering sight of cash. The bills, neatly stacked across the oak desk, are a testament to greed, to power, to lives lost in pursuit of something that can never be taken with you.

Tony's voice trembles as he pulls his pants up, begging

for mercy, explaining in a shaky voice that he had no choice, that the contract was out of his hands. His words are nothing but lies, and Teddy knows it. His anger boils over as he kicks Tony in the chin, breaking his jaw with a sickening crack.

"That's for Joe Kearse," Teddy spits, his voice filled with venom. "You didn't have to kill him, you coward. You didn't have to do that."

The room grows still, the tension as thick as the night air. Tony, in his fear and desperation, offers money and drugs in exchange for his life. But Teddy isn't swayed. His words come slowly, like the sharp sting of a blade.

"You had Joe killed," Teddy says softly, the pain in his chest undeniable. "Now it's your time to pay."

Mona Louise, caught in the middle of the storm, inches her way toward the door, trying to escape the chaos. But Teddy's voice stops her cold. "Do you want to die with him?" he asks, his words cutting through her hesitation. She knows there's no way out now.

With a quiver, she runs, half-clothed, toward the door. But just as she makes her escape, the sound of rushing footsteps and the loud crash of the door opening shatters the moment. Gunshots fill the air. The sentries have arrived.

The noise is deafening as Teddy dives behind the desk, the air thick with the stench of gunpowder and blood. The blasts of the shotgun and the heavy thud of the Desert Eagle reverberate in his chest. But Teddy isn't afraid. He has been here before. His body moves on instinct as he pulls the trigger of the Mac. .10, its bursts sending the two guards scrambling, backing out of the room under the hail of fire.

The room is in chaos, the clamor of violence spilling into the hallways. The guests, the ones who had once been part of the world Teddy had known, spilled from the VIP section like rats fleeing a sinking ship. When the gunfire ceases, Teddy emerges from behind the desk, his heart racing.

With determination, he locks the door and surveys the scene. The money. It's all there, waiting to be claimed. But there's no easy way out. His mind races, and his gaze settles on the air vent above. It's his only way.

He climbs onto the desk, the cool metal of the vent a silent promise of escape. The cramped space feels like a coffin, but Teddy doesn't hesitate. He stuffs his pockets with as much cash as he can carry and climbs into the duct. The passage is narrow, winding through the building like the dark veins of a beast. Every inch of movement feels like a decision between life and death.

Finally, he emerges in the foyer, the night air cool on his skin. He takes a deep breath, his body aching with the weight of the chaos he's left behind. The path to freedom is lined with shadows, but Teddy doesn't look back. He slips out the way he came, his heart heavy with the knowledge that he's left more than just a building of blood behind.

*　　　*　　　*

Hours later, after the madness of the night fades into the

quiet hum of his home, Teddy finds himself standing alone in the dimly lit kitchen. The clock on the wall tells him it's past 3 am, but the world outside feels distant, almost unreal. The shower's too loud, so he opts for a quiet bath, letting the warm water soothe his battered body.

The food Cassandra left for him sits in the fridge, a quiet reminder of the life he's building, a life where someone cares, where someone sees beyond the chaos. He eats hungrily, the flavors rich and comforting. When he finishes, the house is still. The silence is broken only when Cassandra's bedroom door opens, and her voice rings through the air.

"Teddy," she calls softly, concern lacing her words. "You really had me worried about you. I know what you've been through. But I see something in you. I know you're capable of so much more than this life."

Her words sink deep into his chest, unraveling something he's spent years burying. She sees him, truly sees him, and that is something no one else has ever done. As she speaks, her voice carries a tenderness that he can't quite place, a warmth that cuts through the cold walls he's built around himself.

Her gaze lingers on him, and he knows she's not just speaking to him; she's offering him a chance to escape the life that has held him captive for so long. For the first time in his life, Teddy feels the weight of love not as a chain but as a promise.

Their conversation stretches into the night, and though

the words are heavy with meaning, Teddy doesn't shy away. He feels the truth of her affection, the way she sees him, not just as a product of the streets, but as someone worthy of more. For the first time, he feels like something more than the sum of his scars.

Later, as they make love, the world outside falls away. He learns, in those tender moments, what it means to truly connect, to share not just a body but a soul. Cassandra is patient and loving, guiding him through each touch, each kiss, as if teaching him how to live, how to love. And Teddy, in turn, offers her a devotion that he never thought he was capable of.

The next morning, when he wakes to find her gone, a new understanding fills him. His heart is lighter, and as the phone rings and Cassandra's voice fills the air, he knows something has shifted. He calls her "Queen," not just because it feels right, but because he now knows the meaning behind the word.

In that moment, Teddy realizes that his life, his destiny, is no longer a series of disconnected actions driven by fear and survival. It is a journey, a path that he will walk not alone, but with someone who sees the king within him, someone who calls him "Sire."

And as the day unfolds, as he prepares to visit his mother, Teddy understands that the road ahead, though uncertain, is no longer one of isolation. He has found a purpose, a reason to become more than what the world expected of him.

He is, at last, a king. And she is his queen.

Chapter 28

Unforgiven

The night air hangs heavy with tension as the truck rumbles down the deserted road, the steady hum of the engine the only sound in the oppressive stillness. The headlights of Sammy Blanks' F-150 carve through the darkness, illuminating the lonely stretch of highway before him. His knuckles grip the steering wheel tightly, his gaze focused on the road ahead.

Behind the wheel, Sammy's patience is wearing thin, the clock ticking past the time he had set to meet. He doesn't like to be kept waiting, and tonight, he's running on a thin thread of restraint. The moment the passenger door opens and Sweet Touch slides into the seat, Sammy barely acknowledges her presence as he shoots her a sharp, irritated look.

"Get in, girl. You're eleven minutes late. If I weren't anxious to learn what it is you have for me, I'd have left ten minutes ago."

Her breath catches in her throat at the coldness in his tone. She knows better than to protest. "Sweetie, I'm so sorry. Soon after I left you the message, my man showed up and made me take a break. Anyway, I do have something that you can appreciate."

She pauses, searching for the right words, but her voice trembles as she continues. "The reason you don't know who

Sire is is because before he went to prison in 1990, he was known as Sugar Bear."

The words hit Sammy like a punch to the gut, the name Sugar Bear rattling him more than he lets on. His whole body tenses, a jolt of recognition sparking a deep, searing anger that rises in his chest. His grip on the wheel tightens as he feels the familiar rage flood his veins. His heart rate spikes, his blood running hot and furious.

At the mention of the name, his mind flashes back to the scar across his face—a jagged reminder of a promise made long ago. A promise to rid the world of Sugar Bear. The man who had taken everything from him. Sammy barely keeps the truck on the road, swerving slightly as his hands shake with the sudden surge of emotion.

"Hey! Hey, Honey, calm down. You're gonna kill us both if you don't get a hold of yourself," Sweet Touch says quickly, her voice full of concern as she reaches out, trying to steady him.

The words don't seem to reach him, and for a moment, Sammy's eyes harden. He touches the scar on his face without thinking, the roughened skin under his fingertips like a raw, open wound. His mind races as he recalls the days of torture, the terror that had shaped him.

Sugar Bear had left him with a mark that would never fade. And now, hearing that the man—no, the monster—was back under the name Sire, a chill of dread and fury fills him. The world had changed, but the need for vengeance, for justice in his eyes, hadn't.

But for now, there's business to attend to, loose ends that need cutting. He can't afford to let emotions cloud his judgment—not yet. His voice is cold when he finally speaks again.

"I'm okay, Honey. Here's three hundred dollars. Thank you for the tip. Do you want me to take you anywhere special? It's only a quarter after midnight."

Sweet Touch, trying to regain her composure, smiles nervously. "No, sweetie, I think it's best that I head in and call it a night. My man tells me that the streets are too hot tonight. The cops just raided Basie Court and Chuck Williams' place."

Sammy grunts, acknowledging the news with a noncommittal grunt. The streets are always too hot for someone like him, but that's just the price of living in this dangerous world. His focus sharpens again, and he turns to her with a twisted grin.

"Oh. I didn't know that. Sweet Touch, listen, you feel up to making another C-note? Because I think I'm ready to see if that pussy is as good as rumor has it."

The tension between them shifts. Sweet Touch has had a thing for Sammy for a long time, and the moment he makes the offer, she knows there's no going back. This is her chance, the one she's been waiting for.

"I thought you'd never ask," she replies, her voice sultry but tinged with a nervous excitement.

Sammy doesn't waste any time. He drives, his mind still running a mile a minute, but he knows the next steps. He veers off the main road, taking a sharp turn onto State Road 27. As the truck grinds on, they make their way to an old pond—a place Sammy and his brothers used to visit to fish, a place untouched by time. The memories linger, but they don't soften him. Not now.

He drives the truck slowly, carefully, avoiding any marks on the ground that could tie him to this place. When they reach the pond, Sammy pulls over. The moonlight reflects off the water, casting long, eerie shadows. The air smells of damp earth, the night heavy with an almost unnatural quiet.

"Take those hot pants off, Baby, and turn around. Bend over, I want it like that first."

Sweet Touch, feeling the weight of the moment, follows his instructions, her hands trembling slightly as she removes her clothes. But just as she bends over, her eyes closed in anticipation, Sammy's hand, which had been reaching for something else, pulls a gun from his waistband instead. The cold steel of the weapon presses against the base of her skull.

Her body freezes in shock, the world spinning in a split second. But it's too late. Sammy pulls the trigger twice, the sharp sound of gunfire echoing in the stillness of the night. Sweet Touch's body crumples to the ground, lifeless before she even hits the earth.

The darkness around them swallows her, and Sammy stands there for a moment, his breath slow and measured, his eyes scanning the empty pond as if nothing had happened.

The weight of what he's done doesn't hit him, not right away. Instead, he feels a cold satisfaction, like a puzzle piece snapping into place. His hands are steady as he walks around the truck, his heart still racing, but not from fear—rather from the adrenaline that surges through him.

He had done what he needed to do. Another loose string was tied off. Another piece of his past erased.

For now, there is only silence.

Chapter 29

Echoes Before the Fall

The drive from Lehigh Acres is uneventful, the kind of stillness that presses against the windshield like a heavy silence. Teddy glides down the road in the 'Duce, its paint now gleaming with a mirror-like sheen from the latest wipe-down. Every curve of the vehicle seems to glow in the harsh Florida sunlight. It's Thanksgiving Eve, yet the air burns like late July, thick and humid. Teddy's got the AC on full blast, a cold breath against his face as Rick James croons "Hollywood" through the speakers, the beat grooving along with the rhythm of the tires over the pavement.

Teddy drums the steering wheel absently with his fingers. His mind is far from the road.

Cassandra's voice lingers in his thoughts, soft, firm, and always insistent. "You're better than all this. You got a mind that's seen too much not to matter." She tells him that dope money, for all its flash, is just a cheap disguise for a deeper loss. There's something greater he could be. "Take all the things you've seen, all the pain, the struggle, and do something with it. Build, don't destroy."

She'd said it with a look in her eyes that made it hard for him to breathe. Passionate. Sad. Hopeful.

He hadn't understood it all then. Maybe he still doesn't. But some part of her words had made a home in his chest, lying in wait.

A flicker of a memory breaks through Frank. Always Frank around this time of day. He can almost feel the worn canvas of the punching bag in Buck's alley, hear the slap of gloves and the sound of Frank's gravelly voice barking at him to throw "one thousand jabs, hooks, uppercuts." That was Frank training his fists, but sharpening his mind too. Always some lesson hidden inside the sweat.

Teddy exhales deeply and makes a decision. He ain't ready to go home to Cassandra just yet.

He finds himself parking near Buck's Place. The lot is full of folks dancing, smoking, and talking smack. A thick haze of music and weed floats in the air. The basslines from old Al Green records vibrate off parked car hoods, and someone has dragged a speaker out onto the curb.

There, leaning with casual elegance against Mr. Harold's old rust-brown Buick, is Inez, his mother. Her hips sway gently to the music, a cigarette pinched between two fingers, her other hand resting on a near-empty bottle of something strong.

Her eyes catch Teddy, and her face lights up in a way only a mother's could.

"Boy, come here," she slurs with a crooked grin, beckoning with a lazy curl of her fingers.

Teddy walks up and kisses her on the lips, a habit that's as unshakable as it is tender.

"Boy, I done told you 'bout puttin' your lips on me," she says, wiping her mouth with the back of her hand. "I don't know where your lips been."

"I love you too, good lookin'," Teddy replies with a crooked smile.

Their bond is unspoken and untouchable. No amount of drinking could corrode it. She might be lost in the bottle, but she sees him, always has.

He slips her some folded bills, which she accepts without a word, and after some more light teasing with her friends, he heads back to the car.

The Avenue is alive tonight, overflowing with energy and bodies. It's the kind of night that swallows you whole if you're not paying attention. Veterans of the street know to keep one eye open at all times. The uninitiated? Well, they're the ones who end up beaten, robbed, or dead.

Teddy steers the 'Duce toward the Cozy Inn, parking discreetly near Fountain Street. Cassandra's waiting for him, but he can't shake the nagging thought that Pretty Tony's boys might still be out there. It's been two weeks since that thing went down, but paranoia has a long half-life.

He opens the glove box and slides the cold steel of the .357 into the waistband at the small of his back. The weight is familiar, unwelcome.

The temperature has dropped, a chill moving in now that the sun's gone. Still, people roam the sidewalks with drinks in hand, sweat on their necks, and laughter dancing off their lips.

He passes Sam Bo Bo's Greasy Spoon — the line outside stretches down the block. The smell of fried shrimp and chicken punches the air like a second heartbeat. The grease, the spices, the salt, it smells like every memory of late-night hustle.

But Teddy walks past. Cassandra's cooking for him tonight, and that alone makes him grin.

"Hey, Sugar Bear," a gravel-soft voice says behind him.

Teddy turns to see Mr. Hubert stepping out of the shadows, still sporting his wide-brim hat and a smile that doesn't always reach his eyes.

"Everything is everything, Mr. Hubert," Teddy says, reaching to dap the older man.

"You been ghost, boy. Got you an ol' lady, huh?"

"You hit it on the head. She wants me to be more than a hustler, says I got something worth more than that."

Hubert nods slowly. "She sounds like a blessing. You best listen. Streets don't offer pensions or second chances."

He pauses, his expression darkening.

"Folks talking," he says. "Say you might've been the one behind that Otis thing. Chuck's club, too. Folks got long memories and short patience."

Teddy says nothing.

"Keep your eyes open, Sugar Bear," Hubert mutters. "Don't get caught slippin'."

Then he's gone, disappearing into the shadows like smoke.

Club 21 looks abandoned, its front windows dark, a paper sign in the glass: Closed for Repair.

Teddy stares at it for a long moment. He had come to make peace in his own way. A small gesture for Joe. A ghost's gesture.

He moves through a few more clubs, more to be seen than to enjoy. Finally, he heads back to the car, thinking of Cassandra, her warm hands, her sharp mind.

"Yo, Sugar Bear! Man, let me catch a ride to my woman's crib, I'll pay you," comes a voice. It's Mel, grinning and already reaching for a dap.

Teddy laughs. "Keep your money, Mel. Get in."

*   *   *

Larry Starrt had come to Fort Myers with dreams of peace and growth, the clean kind of dreams that get corroded by red tape and racism. A military man, college-educated, and proud, he had believed in the rules of the game. But when those rules failed him, it was affirmative action that cracked the door open.

Now he's Chief. First Black Chief. His office is tight and sharp, just like him.

"Sarah," he says, pressing the intercom. "Get Nygard in here."

181

Nygard walks in with that taut look, always tightly wound, always simmering.

"I'm getting heat from the mayor," Starrt snaps. "Council's screaming about robberies. Businesses are getting hit. It's the same M.O. every time. I want them caught. I want them punished."

Nygard nods, curt and clipped. He doesn't like Start. Starrt doesn't like him. But orders are orders.

Later that day, Nygard issues a command that sends shockwaves across the force: hit the Dunbar community hard.

*   *   *

Teddy's cruising now, sharing a joint with Mel. Jeffrey Osborne's voice croons out of the speakers — "Love Ballad" painting everything soft and slow. Mel exhales smoke and sighs.

"This is some good weed," he says. "You got more?"

"Nah. Fletcher boys had it."

They banter about girls and gas money, and beer. Mel convinces Teddy to stop at the Handy on Fowler.

"I need to call my queen anyway," Teddy says, stepping to the payphone.

When he returns, Mel's carrying a case of Heineken like a prize.

"Let's go," Mel says, eyes darting.

182

"What's up?"

"That bitch wouldn't sell me the beer, said it's after hours. So I slapped her ass and took it."

"Man—" Teddy barely gets the word out before sirens scream to life. Four cop cars swarm like sharks in bloodied water.

Mel bolts from the passenger door, sprinting toward the Edison Bridge, vanishing into the night.

Teddy fumbles for the .357 at the small of his back, desperate to ditch the weapon, but…

"Freeze!" a cop yells, revolver jammed through the open door. "Hands on the wheel!"

Teddy's mind echoes Frank's voice: "Don't ever war with the law. You won't win. You'll die trying."

He's arrested, booked. Armed robbery. Armed burglary. Firearm possession.

Even though the security footage tells a different story, a different man, a different outfit, it doesn't matter.

The gavel comes down. Fifty years.

Cassandra eventually moves on. She marries someone else, and the road back, if there ever was one, fades behind bars and silence.

Chapter 30

The Debt of Blood

On his way back into town, Sammy grips the steering wheel tightly, eyes narrowed, engine growling under him like a caged beast. His thoughts flash to Billy's voice on the phone, urgent and fractured, like something cracked under pressure.

"Listen, Rock... I need some help. I'm on my way to your crib for the girl. Have her ready... give me about 15 minutes…"

The words replay like a strange, discordant melody. Why would Billy call my number but call me Rock? Sammy's jaw tightens, his heartbeat suddenly quicker.

"I need help… I'm on my way… to get the girl…"

He mutters aloud, trying to make sense of it.

"The girl…"

Realization punches him in the gut. Sugar Bear's girl… she's the one Rock's been beating. Billy's trying to warn me... something's gone sideways.

"Shit"

Sammy slams the brakes and whips the wheel into a sharp U-turn, tires shrieking as they rip across the cracked asphalt of Anderson Avenue. The car lurches back toward South Street, urgency pulsing in every muscle.

I've waited over two decades to even this score, he thinks, the bitter taste of vengeance rising in his throat.

*　　*　　*

Billy's pulse thunders as Sire drives, hands locked at ten and two. He tries to stay calm, but there's a twist in his gut when he notices Sire navigating straight to Rock's house. No map. No hesitation.

"How the hell he know where Rock lives?" Billy mutters under his breath.

Still, when Sammy's voice comes through earlier. Cool. Lethal. Steady. It settled something in him. A safety net drawn tight. His three brothers all idolize Sammy. Not just because he's their blood, but because he's a storm cloaked in silence. Sammy taught them to fight, to shoot, to survive. But more than that, Billy respects the way Sammy moves in the shadows. Hunting. Calculating. Killing without blinking.

And that's exactly what Billy needs now. A goddamn shadow with a blade.

The car slows.

Sire's eyes flicker toward the old shell of a house across from Rock's. He smirks slightly.

"Didn't you tell him to have the girl ready when we got here?" he asks Billy.

"Yeah, man, but I didn't say outside. She'll be ready."

Sire lets the car roll past Rock's house, scanning

185

windows, porches, and the stillness of curtains. The street's quiet. Too quiet. He keeps driving, turns into the cul-de-sac, then kills the engine and pulls out his phone.

"Where are you?" he asks, his voice low and sharp.

"I'm at the old recreation center," Tish replies, breathless.

"Okay, drive down the road next to South Street. Park in the woods. There's a pass through the trees that leads to a house a few lots down from Rock's crib."

"The brown one with the bars on the windows?"

"That's it."

Sire ends the call and turns to Billy.

"Call him again. Tell him to bring the girl outside."

Moments later, Sammy pulls up to Rock's house. The air is thick. Charged. Inside, what he sees freezes him mid-step.

Rock is stark naked. The girl, Vee, is still bound, but standing now, twirling her hips in some sick mockery of pleasure. Her eyes are glazed with something between madness and survival. Rock watches her, spellbound, completely unaware.

The gun glints in the open on the dresser, a silent threat. Sammy's stomach turns. *This... this is my brother?*

"Man, your dick is going to be the cause for your death one of these days. Go put some fucking clothes on."

Rock sneers but obeys, sauntering out.   Sammy crosses the room to the girl. Her skin is pale, bruises climbing up her arms like vines. But her eyes. Those are fire. Survival flickers behind the fear.

"Honey, get ready. Gather your stuff. I'm getting you out of here... back to where you came from, or wherever the hell you wanna go."

Vee's lip trembles. Did he just say... getting out?

It's the first sliver of hope she's heard in weeks. Her shoulder throbs. Constant pain. But the words hit her like morphine. She doesn't know if she can trust him, but right now, anything's better than this house of horror.

Sammy's phone buzzes. He steps away to answer it.

"Yes," he says quietly.

"Is the girl ready to go, Rock? I need help," Billy begins, before Sire cuts in, voice hard.

"Just tell him to bring her outside. Fuck all that help shit."

Sammy walks into the hall.

"She's just getting out of the shower, it'll be about 15 minutes longer. Where are you—"

The line cuts. Dead air.

Back in the room, Vee eyes the dresser. The gun. Her breath quickens.

Now.

She dashes across the room and grabs it. Cold steel. Real power. Her hands tremble, but they are steady enough.

Sammy turns back toward the bedroom. Freezes. Vee is holding the gun. Not just holding it. Pointing it straight at Rock's temple. Panic explodes inside him. No, He takes a half-step forward, unsure.

Rock lunges.

Too late.

BLAM

A single shot cracks the air like lightning. Rock stumbles forward, forehead blooming crimson. He collapses mid-step. Dead.

Sammy's brain short-circuits. His brother. Dead.

Vee swings the gun toward him.

BLAM BLAM

Two shots rip through the space he just vacated as he dives out.

Sire hears the gunfire, grabs his weapon, and bolts.

Inside, Vee doesn't look for shoes. Doesn't think. Just runs. Sammy's heart pounds. He needs to go. Police will be coming. But his eyes burn with vengeance.

"I'll make sure they find this bitch... and Sugar Bear too."

Vee searches the house like a trapped animal. Finds a door. A bathroom. Another exit. She opens it. Sees Sammy duck back around the corner, trying to flank her.

She fires.

BLAM

"Fuck" he cries out.

The bullet tears through the wall. His elbow explodes in pain. His gun drops. He grits his teeth and stumbles forward.

He sees a bat. His backup plan.

He grabs it and hides in the shadows.

She'll come to the door. She has to, and she does. Vee dashes into the living room, eyes locked on the front door.

Too late.

Sammy emerges from the closet, swinging. She jerks the bat back, but it catches her shoulder. A scream tears from her throat. Her gun drops. Sammy raises the bat again.

Vee bolts for the door, yanks it open.

BLAM

Miss.

She stumbles down the steps. Another shot.

BLAM

Pain erupts in her backside as the bullet tears into her flesh. She crashes to the ground.

Billy hears everything. He pulls himself from the car, bloodied and aching. Under the driver's seat. A 9mm. Salvation. He grips it with bloody fingers and limps toward the house.

Sire watches from the shadows as Vee falls. He races toward her. Sammy doesn't see him until it's too late.

The Beretta stares him in the face. Sammy raises his own gun, slowly.

Too slow.

POP POP POP

Sire's aim is merciless. Eye. Mouth. Neck. Sammy falls forward, lifeless. Billy sees it. His hero. His brother. Dead. He starts to cry, shaking with grief. Vee is barely conscious. Sire lifts her gently, cradling her weight.

Sirens wail in the distance. A death knell.

Billy watches.

Raises the gun.

One shot. Clean. Right through Sire's head.

"NOOOO"

A woman's voice shreds the night air. Terrified. Final.

BLAM

The bullet leaves Billy's gun. Sire shoves Vee down and dives to the side. He turns. Just in time to see Tish collapse, blood spraying from her shattered head.

Rage becomes him. Sire lifts his Beretta.

POP POP POP POP POP

All five shots punch through Billy's skull. Billy hits the ground, still holding the gun. Sire rushes to Tish.

Too late.

Her body is still warm.

The side of her head. Gone.

She'd once promised she'd die for him.

Now, she had.

Chapter 31

The Debt of Blood

The sky bleeds red as dusk strangles the last light of day. Sammy's knuckles are white on the steering wheel, his veins etched like steel cables beneath his skin. The rumble of the engine growls through the chassis, a beast caged just beneath the hood. Inside the car, a different beast stirs rage, tightly coiled, barely leashed.

Billy's voice echoes in his memory, frantic and cracked, brittle like glass underfoot.

"Listen, Rock… I need some help. I'm on my way to your crib for the girl. Have her ready... give me about 15 minutes…"

The message plays on repeat in his mind, like a warped record skipping over a scratch. But one word sticks out more than the rest.

Rock.

Sammy frowns. His jaw tightens as suspicion prickles his spine.

Why call my phone… and call me Rock?

He repeats the words under his breath, slow, mechanical, like he's trying to force the pieces together with sheer will.

"I need help... I'm on my way… to get the girl…"

His voice trails off. Then—

"The girl…"

A flash. A face.

Vee.

Sugar Bear's girl.

The realization slams into him like a fist to the ribs. His breath catches. His stomach knots.

Rock. That son of a bitch. He's the one who's been hurting her. And Billy, Billy's trying to warn me. But he doesn't know... doesn't know the call went to me. Something's wrong.

"Shit," Sammy growls.

The tires scream in protest as he yanks the wheel into a brutal U-turn. The back end fishtails, rubber streaking across the cracked pavement of Anderson Avenue. His pulse pounds as the car tears back toward South Street, urgency burning in every tendon and muscle fiber.

He's waited twenty-two long years for this. A life spent sharpening blades in the dark. Now, finally, the score gets settled.

Billy sits stiff in the passenger seat, his leg bouncing. Sire drives like he was born behind the wheel, calm, surgical, no GPS, no hesitation. Just eyes on the road and purpose in every turn. Billy doesn't like it.

"How the hell he know where Rock lives?" he mutters.

His fingers twitch toward his own phone, but the earlier call from Sammy replays in his mind. Cool. Steady. No panic.

That voice. That's the Sammy he knows—the one who used to teach them how to hold a knife and disappear. Their older brother, half-shadow, half-wolf.

Sammy was the reason they all made it out of childhood alive.

Billy closes his eyes. Prays this ends right.

The car slows.

Sire leans forward, scanning Rock's street like a hunter sighting prey.

"Didn't you tell him to have the girl ready when we got here?" he asks casually.

Billy nods. "Yeah, man, but I didn't say outside. She'll be ready."

The car rolls past Rock's sagging porch and filthy curtains, every window a dark eye hiding secrets. The whole block feels off. Like something's holding its breath.

Sire doesn't like it. He turns into a cul-de-sac and cuts the engine. The sudden silence presses down like a held scream. He taps his phone.

"Where are you?" His voice is clipped, urgent.

"Old rec center," Tish replies, panting slightly.

"Good. Head down the side road near South Street. Park in the woods. There's a path through the trees. Brown house. Bars on the windows."

"I see it."

Sire hangs up. He turns to Billy.

"Call him again. Tell him to bring the girl outside."

Sammy's car crunches to a stop in front of Rock's house. The air buzzes with static, the kind that comes before lightning strikes. His hand is already on his gun as he pushes open the front door—and freezes.

Rock is naked. Not a stitch of shame. Watching Vee, who sways on unsteady feet, bound and bruised, forced to dance like some broken puppet. Her skin is a canvas of purples and greens, but her eyes—those defy every blow she's taken.

Something cracks in Sammy. A quiet, dangerous kind of fury.

"Man, your dick is going to be the cause for your death one of these days," he says coldly. "Go put some fucking clothes on."

Rock smirks. No shame. No guilt. Just swagger. He saunters off, humming.

Sammy crosses to the girl. Her breathing is shallow. Her arms tremble.

"Honey," he says gently, "get ready. Gather your stuff.

I'm getting you outta here. Back to where you came from…
or wherever the hell you wanna go."

Vee stares. Did he say out? Her mouth parts. The idea is
foreign. Her limbs scream with pain, but hope cuts through
the fog like sunlight through storm clouds.

She nods. Barely. A flicker of life.

Sammy's phone buzzes. He steps into the hall.

"Yes."

"Is the girl ready to go, Rock? I need help—" Billy
starts.

"Just tell him to bring her outside," Sire snaps in the
background.

Sammy frowns. His voice drops.

"She's just getting out of the shower. Fifteen more
minutes. Where are you—"

The line goes dead. Back inside, Vee stares at the
dresser. At the gun. Her heartbeat kicks. She moves.

Cold metal. The weight is real. Familiar. She's never
shot anyone. But she's never been this close to freedom
either. Sammy turns back and stops. Vee is holding the gun.

Pointed at Rock.

Pointed at his brother.

"No," he breathes.

But it's too late.

Rock lunges.

BLAM.

Blood blossoms from his forehead like a grotesque flower. He topples, mid-charge, a puppet with its strings cut.

Sammy blinks. His world lurches.

Rock. His brother.

Dead.

Vee swings the gun toward him now.

BLAM. BLAM.

Two rounds tear through the air. Sammy ducks, heart slamming against his ribs. Outside, Sire hears it all. His weapon is out before the second shot finishes echoing.

Inside, Vee runs. Her feet slap the floor. Sammy's head spins. He needs to move. The cops will come. But so will more trouble.

"I'll make sure they find this bitch... and Sugar Bear too," he growls.

Vee's wild eyes scan every room. Door. Door. Door.

There.

She bolts toward the back.

Sammy peeks around the corner. She sees him.

BLAM.

"FUCK!" he yells.

Pain explodes through his elbow. His gun clatters. Blood spatters the wall like paint. He grits his teeth, stumbles. Spots the bat.

His backup plan. He melts into the shadows, bat gripped tight. Vee bursts into the living room, aiming for the front door.

Too late.

Sammy explodes from a closet. The bat swings, connects with her shoulder. A scream tears from her chest. The gun drops. Sammy lifts the bat again— But Vee is faster. She tears the door open and runs.

BLAM.

Miss.

BLAM.

The bullet tears into her backside. She crashes down the steps, face-first into the dirt. Billy hears it all. Every scream. Every shot. He reaches under the seat. Finds steel.

The 9mm is slick with blood. He gets out. Limping. Determined. Sire races ahead. Sammy sees him—too late.

The Beretta is level.

Sammy raises his own—

POP. POP. POP.

Eye. Mouth. Throat.

Sammy falls. Twitching. Then still.

Billy's scream chokes out of him. The man he worshipped, the shadow-god of their youth, was gone. Vee lies bleeding. Barely breathing. Sire lifts her gently. Her body limp in his arms.

Then—

A scream.

"NOOOO!"

It slices through the night like glass.

Tish.

BLAM.

Billy fires. A perfect shot. Sire jerks—just in time. He shoves Vee down and dives aside. Too late for Tish. She falls, blood spraying like mist. Her eyes were still open. Her mouth was agape. The promise she once whispered into Sire's ear was fulfilled. I'd die for you.

Now, she had. Sire roars. A sound not human.

POP. POP. POP. POP. POP.

Every bullet finds Billy's skull. His body folds, knees first, then face to the dirt. The gun drops from his fingers. Sire crawls to Tish.

Still warm. Too late.

Chapter 32

Echoes and Exits

The early morning sun casts a golden hue over the blinds, filtering slivers of light across the soft carpet of the bedroom. The silence is peaceful, punctuated only by the quiet hum of the air conditioning and the rhythmic beep of medical equipment monitoring Vee's recovery.

In the living room, Sire extends a thick envelope toward the man standing by the doorway.

"Here's five grand for all your troubles, Doc," he says, voice steady with respect. "I really do appreciate you letting us interfere with your vacation like this."

Dr. Salvatore Colon, dressed in a crisp linen shirt and khakis that hint at his intended escape to some oceanside serenity, raises a hand in protest.

"No, no. I cannot accept that," he insists with a gentle shake of the head. "There's no need to thank me. Mr. Pimpwell has already covered all expenses. He asked me to inform you, he'll be on the 10:45 flight tomorrow morning."

He straightens his coat and gathers his small black medical case.

"This is my third and final visit," Sal continues, professional yet kind. "She'll recover just fine in several weeks. Change the bandages twice daily. The medication will last her longer than she'll need. Here's my card. In case of anything."

He places the card delicately on the marble countertop.

Sire walks him to the door, a firm grip offered in a parting handshake.

"Sal, if ever I can be of service… be it as it may, please don't hesitate," Sire says with a sincerity that cuts through the tension of the past week.

The doctor nods, offering a final smile before heading out. The door clicks shut.

Sire lets out a breath, running a hand across his scalp. The weight of what's happened, what's been lost, lingers heavy in the walls. He steps quietly into the bedroom.

Vee is awake.

But she isn't just awake, she's alive.

All her clothes lie strewn across the floor. Pillows nest around her body like clouds cushioning a wounded goddess. Her good leg bent, her back slightly arched, she's massaging herself with a slow, intentional rhythm. Her skin glows with a sheen of sweat and sensual purpose. She's not putting on a show. This is her reclaiming herself.

The sight catches Sire mid-step. A smirk touches his lips. This woman, fresh from hell, still burns. He kneels beside her, says nothing, just offers presence. Then his lips find her wrist, the one she's moving against her own body, and he kisses a path downward, slow and reverent. His tongue brushes her fingertips… then dips between them.

She gasps. Her body jerks with intensity as her climax begins to build. She's so close, on the knife's edge.

Sire's large hand presses down over hers, stilling her fingers inside her. His mouth wraps around her clitoris—suction, rhythm, breath.

Then he exhales against her with a tight-lipped pucker, making a sound like a muted trumpet. Vee lets out a strangled cry as her orgasm consumes her. Her entire body shudders with the force of it.

Tears spill from her eyes. Not just from pleasure, but pain remembered. Survival acknowledged. She'd been brutalized. Dehumanized. Shot. But in this moment, this trembling, electric moment, she felt something close to whole.

And Sire?

He was the only one she'd willingly walk back into hell for. He leans in, careful of her wound. Enters her from the side, slow, loving, present. Her breath hitches again, this time from emotional surrender as much as pleasure. She raises her leg just enough to welcome him deeper. He moves with patience, with reverence.

Each thrust is deliberate. A love letter written in flesh and heat.

Vee clutches him. Anchors herself to the only thing that still feels real.

Sire resists the building tension as long as he can, but after her fourth tremor of release shakes through her, he lets go. A final, powerful release overtakes him.

They collapse into each other, tangled in warmth and quiet redemption. Sleep claims them quickly.

* * *

"I remember when I screamed I hate you…"

Sire stirs, lips curling slightly in his sleep.

The line loops again. Not in his dream, but real. He opens his eyes slowly.

Vee's ringtone.

He groans and reaches for her phone, swiping to answer. "Wake up, Vee," he mutters, still groggy. "Pimpwell's on his way."

She stirs. Together they rise, both sore, both exhausted, but lighter somehow. He helps her to the bathroom, steadying her carefully into the tub. She rests in warm water as he steps into the shower.

Forty-five minutes later, the doorbell rings.

Pimpwell stands on the porch, sharp as ever in a tailored linen suit, signature smirk in place.

"What's happening, my brother?" he greets, locking fists with Sire as he steps into the Palace.

The weight of the week hangs between them. A storm

of grief, blood, and survival.

A full week has passed since Tish fell. Since Vee was torn from captivity and stitched back together by love and luck. The wound still aches, but Vee has been a pillar—not of stone, but of grace. Her strength isn't loud, but it holds Sire together like mortar.

When he grieves, she offers her shoulder. When he breaks, she weeps for him, so he doesn't have to.

"Everything be everything, my brother," Sire says, shaking off the heaviness. "Thanks for sending, Sal. He said it wasn't serious, the bullet passed clean through."

"That's good to learn," Pimpwell replies. "And no need to thank me. You'd have done the same. But... how you holdin' up over Tish?"

Sire's face hardens. Then softens.

"Not meaning to sound cold… but Pimp, we both know how Tish was. She would lose respect for me if I sugarcoated it."

He pauses, a fire rising in his chest.

"It is what it is. She did her part. Now I've gotta do mine. I'll rise. I'll reach the greatness she saw in me. And when I do, I'll sit on my throne. For her."

Pimpwell nods, quiet admiration in his eyes. "Words well spoken, Sire."

Sire's eyes wander across the room to a petite woman

with silky black hair and almond eyes. "Who's this?"

"Oh, that's Kia," Pimpwell says proudly. "Part of the first-place prize. Kia, meet Sire—my brother, my partner."

"Pleased to meet you, Sire," she says with a delicate accent.

"The pleasure's mine, beautiful," he replies. Kia blushes. Pimpwell sees it. So does Sire.

"When do I get to meet Vee?"

"She's in the bathroom. Kia, would you check on her for me?"

"Of course," she says sweetly, already on her way.

The two men step outside onto the patio.

"Sire, cops got the Avenue on fire," Pimpwell warns. "We passed at least three cruisers on South Street alone. They popped the Hall Brothers, hit Chuck Williams, and Byron Blanks. All clean, though. But there's been five, maybe six bodies in three months. You and Vee need to roll. Fast."

Sire nods, jaw clenched.

"Kia and I took care of Tish's remains. Arranged cremation through Boyd's. She'll rest in peace."

Pimpwell hesitates, then continues.

"Kia'll stay at the Palace. Keep things safe. Cadillac, she follow me in? Leased for six months. Don't drive the

Escalade, too hot."

He turns, calling toward the house.

"Kia! Grab the package from the back seat."

"Okay, Daddy," she calls back, like honey on the wind.

Sire chuckles. "She really yours?"

"Her 'manager' thought he'd win Pimp of the Year. Put Kia on the line. I took the bet."

"Fifty stacks?"

"Easy win."

The door opens. Rain begins to drizzle. Kia appears, struggling slightly to support Vee, who limps beside her. Pimpwell rushes to steady them, eyes locking with Vee's. He smiles. "So this is the one who captured my brother's heart. What's your story, Ms. Vee?"

Vee looks him square in the eyes, her voice soft but unwavering.

"I don't know if I hold his attention the way he holds mine. He's got this… raw earthiness. He's wild and gentle. Lethal and kind. I love him. I'm his. Until I catch up with Tish."

Pimpwell leans back, nodding.

"Say no more. A woman who speaks like that? Sire, you only need one Queen. She's all hundred rolled into one."

* * *

Across town, inside a black sedan parked just off the main road, two men sit with eyes locked in a quiet transaction.

"Sorry to keep you waiting," Welks mutters. "Triple raid last week. I was running one. Lucky Byron was clean. Here's three hundred. What do you have?"

Vernon shifts, pulls an envelope from his jacket.

"Billy and Rock Blanks. They killed Seville. He fumbled an ounce of heroin, tried to pull a piece. One of them shot him."

"Which one?"

"Does it matter? Grab them both."

Welks' eyes narrow. "They're dead. All three. Rock. Billy. And Sammy. Byron didn't give us squat. If he had, you wouldn't be getting this money."

Vernon's expression falters.

"Can you give me anything for another hundred?"

No response.

Welks' patience snaps.

"Listen, you little shit. I've covered your ass more than once. Screw me now, and next time you're drowning, I'll throw you bricks, not a rope."

Vernon blinks. Realizes the edge he's dancing on.

"Fine. Someone saw a black guy carrying a bleeding woman. Side or leg wound. That's all I got."

"Who's the witness?"

"Don't know. Don't care." He steps out and walks off, leaving the hundred behind.

* * *

A voice cuts through static on a long-distance call.

"Listen, Ice Man. It's hot out here. Real hot. Fort Myers is cooking. I'm shutting down for now. Getting out of the game."

A long pause.

"Don't try to take over. It ain't safe. Cops are pissed. Doors getting kicked in."

Another breath.

"Black Pearl and Ed the Big Man already paid out. I told them what I'm telling you. I'll be gone. Maybe a month. Maybe six. Stay focused. Stay smart."

And then, silence.

Chapter 33

A King's Offering

"How are you feeling, Baby?" Sire's voice was tender, a gentle rumble beneath the quiet hum of tires on weathered asphalt. The morning sun stretched low across the sky, gilding the horizon in soft gold.

"I'm okay," Vee replied, her voice light but not untruthful. The pain in her leg still pulsed beneath the surface, but it was manageable for now.

"Good," he nodded. "We'll hit the interstate after one last stop."

She turned her head to study him. The lines around his eyes had deepened in recent days, like shadows etched by memory and loss. "How are you, my King?"

Sire's lips curled slightly, though the smile didn't quite reach his eyes. "Is that a loaded question?"

"Maybe… just a little," she admitted. "Ever since Tish has been gone, your spirit seems low. We cannot bring her back, Sire."

He was quiet for a moment, thoughtful. Then, with eyes fixed on the road ahead, he spoke: "Vee, let me explain something to you, my Queen. I was raised by the streets literally. Nothing's ever been permanent in my life except growth. I've long come to understand that change is inevitable."

The timbre of his voice thickened, worn with truth and history. "For over twenty-five years, while incarcerated, I was constantly faced with changing circumstances, some of which broke men completely. But all of it prepared me. Shaped me. I developed the ability to take a loss and still come out being Boss."

He paused. The silence that followed wasn't empty. It was full of Tish's memory.

"So yes, Honey. Your observation is on point. My spirit is heavy. But it ain't just grief. It's the weight of what comes next. We can't let Tish's death be in vain."

The car fell silent after that. The unspoken words hovered between them like a prayer. When they turned onto Lafayette Street, the heaviness lingered, but so did purpose.

"How much is there, Baby?" Sire asked.

Vee pulled a slim envelope from beneath her seat. "Hundred and twenty-five grand."

"Take fifty and put it in the bag with the toys."

They pulled up in front of a modest white and yellow brick house. The paint was tired, peeling like old bark. An aging navy blue hatchback sat in the single-car driveway, its tires soft and weary. Sire got out first, his movement fluid and deliberate, then circled to open the door for Vee. She reached for her crutches without complaint.

The door creaked open as they reached the porch, and a woman stepped outside. Her clothes were plain, their fibers thinned by time and repetition, but she was immaculately clean. A kind of quiet dignity clung to her.

Her face, slender and gentle, tilted slightly, eyes searching, uncertain. Grief had hollowed them, but hope hadn't quite left.

"Mrs. Palmer?" Sire called out.

"Yes… Mary," she answered softly.

"Mrs. Mary, hi. My name is Teddy, and this is Vee. You don't know either of us, but we're here to help you and little Willie Palmer Jr."

Mary's lips trembled. Her hands gripped the edge of the doorframe for support. Tears welled up and overflowed. Her shoulders shook. Her prayers, desperate whispers in the night, had been heard.

Sire stepped forward and gently took her hand. "Everything is going to be alright," he said.

Behind her, a tiny figure emerged, a boy no older than five, his thumb tucked shyly in his mouth. His wide brown eyes flicked from his mother to the strangers. When Mary broke into sobs, the child did too, moved not by understanding, but by the instinct to share her pain.

Vee moved closer to Mary, her crutches clicking on the porch wood. She wrapped one arm around her, steady and warm. Sire bent down, scooping the boy into his arms. "You okay, little man?" he murmured, bouncing him gently.

None of them noticed the dark gray Ford Taurus idling as it passed slowly by. Behind the wheel, Detective Bandy Welks watched with sharp, narrowing eyes.

He'd come to verify the address of the late Willie Palmer Sr., but the faces on the porch demanded closer attention. One in particular

Teddy Hilson.

There was a report from the South Street killings. A man matching Teddy's description had been seen fleeing the area, carrying a bleeding woman.

His gaze shifted to Vee. Her face was unfamiliar. But those crutches? The limp? Fresh injuries.

Suspicion bloomed in the detective's chest like a rising tide.

As the car glided past the house, Sire caught a glimpse of it. His jaw tightened. He had seen Welks.

Inside, Mary finally composed herself, guiding them through the front door. The house was small, humble, but clean and filled with warmth.

"Sweetheart," Sire began, placing the boy back into his mother's arms, "I'd like to ask your permission to adopt your boy as my Godson. We know about your husband's death and his efforts to raise money for the transplant. How close are you?"

Mary clutched Willie Jr. to her chest and lowered her eyes. "We're $36,000 short."

Sire reached into the bag. "Not anymore. In here," he said, placing it gently on the table, "are some PlayStation games, kid notebooks with music, and fifty thousand dollars."

Willie Jr.'s eyes lit up. He toddled over to Sire and leaned an elbow on his knee, grinning bashfully at the mention of PlayStation.

Mary's hand flew to her mouth. She couldn't stop the tears this time. But they were different, born of relief, not despair.

"Teddy... you and your lady are welcome here anytime," she said, stepping forward and throwing her arms around his neck. "You have my permission to adopt Pookie."

Behind her, Willie Jr. echoed the gesture, tears rolling down his cheeks as he mimicked his mother.

Vee quietly moved, wiped away her own tears, her heart swelling with pride and sorrow all at once. Sire was more than a survivor. He was a builder, a provider. A king.

"We gotta leave town for a bit," Sire told Mary gently. "But we'll be back."

Before taking I-75 north, they made one final detour.

The graveyard was quiet. The sky had dimmed to a dusky lavender. Sire laid fresh flowers on plots 50 and 51.

Vee stood beside him, her hand in his

They didn't speak.

They didn't need to. The flowers said enough.

Love.

Loyalty.

And a promise to keep going. For Tish. For Pookie. For everyone who still had a chance.

Chapter 34

Seeds in the Fire

(Four Months Later)

Sanford, Florida, cradled quietly some 25 miles east of Orlando, had for years gone unnoticed, hidden behind the neon shimmer of the larger cities around it. But now, the name was burned into the collective conscience of America and far beyond. The shooting of an unarmed Black teenager, Trayvon Martin, by neighborhood watchman George Liverman, shattered the town's obscurity. Liverman claimed self-defense under the state's controversial "Stand Your Ground" law, but that justification ignited a nationwide cry for justice, outrage blooming like wildfire. Al Sharpton and other prominent voices had taken to the streets and airwaves, urging calm, yet demanding accountability.

Sanford trembled beneath a fragile calm, its streets pulsing with tension, patrolled by an anxious, armored police force. Residents lived in the shadow of unrest, their every breath laden with fear that the town might combust into chaos at any moment.

It was against this backdrop that Sire and Vee arrived, their car rolling eastward along the sunbaked lanes of I-4. As they passed the Seminole County sign, the atmosphere seemed to shift, heavier, electric. A storm, not of weather but of reckoning, hovered just out of sight.

Sire's eyes caught the green-lettered sign of a Holiday

Inn perched beside the highway. Its gleaming glass façade seemed out of place against the emotional grime hanging over the city.

"Are you hungry, Honey?" he asked gently, his voice wrapped in concern.

"A little, but it can wait," Vee replied, brushing invisible dust from her lap, staring out the window.

"I think we should go shop for enough food to last a few days because too much is going on in this city right now. I'd hate to be out excessively when it gets dark."

Vee turned her gaze to him slowly, eyes narrowed in quiet challenge. "Sire, out of all the places in the country we could have gone to, you chose one that is in a complete uproar. Why?"

His voice was calm, resolute. "I have a plan, my dear, one that I spent years researching and putting together while incarcerated. It is totally legitimate, and if it comes together, we'll become very wealthy. This town was chosen particularly because of the chaotic condition and all the attention it's getting. We'll use it to jump-start the biggest movement since Dr. King's March on Washington. A lot of work and dedication will be required. It will be huge, my Queen. We'll also be in a position to make a big difference in the lives of many people."

Vee softened. Her words came slowly, each syllable dipped in devotion. "Baby, that makes a lot of sense. I wasn't questioning you. Anyway, I am down for whatever you want to do. What you choose to do, Sire, I will do it with you. Whatever. In you, I have found the meaning to my purpose. Sire, many women go through life searching for that special something or someone who could capture their full essence. That wonderful meaning that gives shape to all the other meanings in their world. In other words, their purpose. I am in this with you, no matter your call, my King."

Later, a lead from Teddy guided them to a small, freshly painted wooden house in the Georgetown section of Sanford. It stood quiet and proud on a fenced quarter-acre lot off Ninth Street as if waiting for something meaningful to happen within its walls.

As the city braced itself for a march that promised to bring in thousands, Vee shifted gears. The street-hardened edge she once wielded like armor gave way to the sharp elegance of purpose. She moved like a woman born for this moment. The plan was in motion.

Together, they walked into the First National Bank of Sanford and opened a joint business account. Across town, they repeated the process at a smaller bank, setting up the foundations of Eyekon, their vision, their mission, their revolution. At the computer store, Vee's eyes glowed as she ran her fingers over the sleek curves of three laptops and a power-packed desktop. Tools of the future.

Back at the apartment, their days were consumed by internet searches, legal documentation, and business registration. The mundane but necessary bricks of a dream.

"During my long prison stint," Sire shared one night, "in

addition to educating myself, I spent many hours in the prison's library researching the idea for Eyekon, the Union… Everything from what the law requires to how we can change lives. Vee, the potential for such a transformation has been apparent to all for just as long as the prison industry has been in operation."

His voice was low, but electric with intensity. Vee listened with the quiet reverence of a believer.

"You really are special, Teddy," she said, her voice trembling slightly. "You're not simply developing a get-rich-quick scheme. You're sincerely concerned about people. Carlton was a lot like you in many ways."

Vee, with her computer science degree and Black Panther Party experience, developed software to structure Eyekon's internal workings. Every role, every responsibility laid out with methodical precision.

"Baby, who are the people behind the organizing of the march?" Sire asked. She tapped a few keys. "The Reverend O.V. Sapp. Pastor of the Mega Church. The address is 1963 13th Street. No phone listed, but there's a fax and an email."

"Good. Tomorrow we'll make contact. This will be the official launching of Eyekon," Sire said.

The next morning, Vee handled the emails and called the radio station 102 Jams. Soul WBLK also agreed to promote their message at half price.

Later, they found themselves in the cavernous sanctuary of Blessing United Place of Worship. Five thousand worshippers filled the pews, but the Reverend O.V. Sapp commanded them like a symphony. His bass voice seemed born of thunder, and each word wrapped around every listener like a personal message from heaven itself.

Yet something in Sire stirred uneasily. There was power in Sapp, but also something veiled.

After the service, they met Sapp and his poised, graceful wife, Cheryl. Her eyes lingered too long on Sire, her breath subtly catching when their hands touched.

"Tell me more about this union, Mr. Hilson," Sapp asked, eyeing Sire with the gaze of a man accustomed to peeling back layers.

Sire explained everything. The origins, the mission, and the loopholes in the system are designed to fail the formerly incarcerated. He laid out the vision of Eyekon. Reduced recidivism, reentry training, employer incentives, GED programs, and most powerfully, dignity.

The reverend was silent, nodding slowly.

"Young man," he finally said, "I think you have a wonderful idea. I'd also like to come and hear what you have to say."

"That will be an honor, Reverend."

As they left, Sapp watched them disappear into the Sanford dusk. He turned to the glass wall and said quietly, "Get Murdock on the phone. That union has the potential to be the Union of all Unions, and that young man may not know exactly what he is about to create."

Back at Soul WBLK, the station manager agreed to push the message. His own family had been touched by the prison system. He believed in the cause.

At home that night, Sire soaked in a hot bath while Vee cooked. Steak, shrimp, yellow rice, black beans. The kind of meal that says we are home. Things were coming together better than they could have imagined.

"Did you notice Mrs. Cheryl's trance-like gawk whenever she looked at you?" Vee teased.

"Nothing escapes you, does it?"

"She handed you that private number like she was handing over a room key," Vee said, laughing. "Mrs. Holy-than-thou nearly had a religious experience of her own."

"Maybe she did, my love. Maybe she did," Sire replied, pulling her close. "Come on, let's call it a night. I want to see how your breathing will be."

Chapter 35

A Clock Ticking Loud

The television flickered in the dimly lit room, casting bluish shadows against the eggshell-colored walls of the Ninth Street apartment. Sire lounged on the worn leather couch, one arm draped across the armrest, the remote balanced loosely in his other hand. The screen showed a tense press conference filled with reporters, flashing cameras, and one familiar, commanding voice.

"George Liverman has been arrested," the newscaster announced, her tone tight with the gravity of the moment. "He has been given a $150,000 bond."

A sharp cut in the footage switched to Reverend O.V. Sapp, standing at a podium with a banner behind him that read: Justice, Peace, Unity. He spoke calmly but with intensity. His voice filled the room.

"We ask the citizens of Sanford to remain calm," Sapp said, his bass voice steady despite the pressure of the cameras. "This is a step in the right direction. Let the system work. Let us not become what we protest against."

Then came the kicker.

Security officials stood behind him, stern-faced. The anchor cut back in. "This comes amid rising tensions following an alleged ten-thousand-dollar bounty placed on Liverman's head by a group calling itself the New Black Panther Party."

Just as Sire raised the remote to change the channel, Vee burst into the room, eyes wide, breath shallow, her presence charged with sudden urgency.

"What did they just say, Honey?" she asked, her voice clipped and strained.

"You mean about the bounty allegation on Liverman's head?"

"Yes," she said, stepping closer. "But who did they say was behind it?"

"The New Black Panther Party."

Vee blinked. Her expression shifted from shock to deep contemplation, like someone piecing together a puzzle with pieces that no longer fit.

"I thought that's what I heard," she murmured, jaw tightening.

"What is it, sweetheart? Something's troubling you?"

She lowered herself onto the arm of the couch, her fingers absently twisting the ends of her hair. "Sire, I'm aware of the capabilities of NBPP. I spent several years as their secretary-treasurer. At the time Carlton died, I honestly thought that the organization would also die. Then again, I should have known better than to underestimate Ishmael. If the NBPP is really responsible for the bounty on Mr. Liverman, he's as good as dead."

Sire leaned in, the weight of her words hitting hard.

"And the look on my face, love," Vee continued, "is the realization of the urgency that I must locate them before Liverman is found dead. With a dead George Liverman, both the march and our plans for the after-march event will be greatly in jeopardy. I must reach Ishmael and ask him to call off the hit or postpone it until after Eyekon is launched."

"Ishmael?" Sire asked, brows knitting together.

"He is, or was, the second in command to Carlton," she explained. "He was responsible for the safety and security of the organization. Ishmael is a no-nonsense type and is a very focused brother. He also relies on a walking cane, the result of a police man's bullet. The cop had mistaken Ishmael for a robbery suspect, shot him, and shattered his hip. At the time, NFL scouts were trying to persuade Ishmael to forgo his senior year at Virginia Tech and enter the NFL."

Sire shook his head slowly, absorbing the tragic irony.

"The white officer was cleared of any wrongdoing," Vee added, bitterness coloring her voice, "although witnesses testified that Ishmael fully complied with the officer's commands."

"Vee," Sire said, his voice even and urgent, "the march is tomorrow, which doesn't give us much time to work with. The internet should help in finding their home base or at least provide a phone number."

"I was thinking along those same lines," she nodded, already moving toward the laptops set up on the dining table like mission control.

The hours ticked by. Vee sat glued to the screen, fingers dancing across the keyboard, eyes scanning pages of black-and-white text, until finally she leaned back in her chair.

"I found something," she said. "A P.O. Box address. They're based in Tampa, Florida. No physical address listed."

Sire exhaled through his nose. It wasn't much, but it was something.

"When is your college roommate's flight due?" he asked, changing gears.

"Oh, baby," Vee replied with a sigh, "Erika called. She won't be able to be here in time for the initial launch. Something came up that requires her presence. She asked me to give you her apologies."

Sire gave a nod of understanding. "Okay. With the extra help, we should have all bases covered. We also have five thousand Eyekon membership cards, each with a registration number. After registration, it'll take one to three weeks before they receive their card along with a list of employers who will consider them for a job."

He stood and began pacing the room slowly, his mind churning.

"Also, Vee, we must hire an agent. The law requires this. I can run this entire outfit blindfolded, but I can't legally assume any official management titles until January. The law requires a minimum of three years post-felony conviction or release from incarceration. In January, I'll reach that milestone."

Vee smiled, her eyes glowing with quiet pride. "Well, Sire, one thing is for sure. If we follow the plans as you've outlined them, we shouldn't have any problems. I also agree that once this thing takes root and goes forward, quite a few feathers will begin to ruffle."

She chuckled playfully, "The initial fee of $45.00 to join and become a member, together with the $145.00 to $200.00 yearly membership dues, will soon be collected. That, you can take to the bank."

She leaned closer and whispered, "Honey, I've been meaning to ask you. How in the world did you come up with the name Eyekon?"

"That was the easy part, my love," he grinned. "I am an ex-convict. Get it? Eye. Kon. Eyekon."

Vee burst out laughing. "Cute. Really cute. I like that. Thanks."

As the night deepened, Sire stayed at the table under the soft yellow glow of the hanging light. He bent over his notebook, words pouring from his mind as he shaped the speech he would give at the march. Vee had gone to bed, leaving him to wrestle with the weight of the message he would deliver to the world.

Before sunrise, Sire stirred awake to the ringing of his phone.

"It's Cheryl," he said groggily, answering the call.

"She's calling for the reverend. They want us to meet with them before the march starts."

"Meet them where?" Vee asked, rising from bed with sleep still clinging to her voice.

Sire repeated the question into the phone, then grabbed the pen and pad from the nightstand as Cheryl gave him directions.

"They gave me an address to a place located in Midway and told us how to get there. The march begins at noon, so I told them we'll be there by nine."

Vee nodded and stretched. "Do you feel like making breakfast, or do you want to stop by Mickey-Dee's?"

"By the time you finish waking up and dressing," Vee said with a teasing smile, "I'll have something ready."

She leaned down, kissed him softly, and floated toward the kitchen, already moving as the day belonged to them.

Chapter 36

From Chains to Change

"What makes you so sure that this ex-convict's idea is a natural gold mine? I mean, for heaven's sake, the guy's a fucking loser."

The sharpness in Murdock's voice crackled through the phone line like a whip. He was tense, frustrated, and dismissive, his words coated in cynicism. Somewhere in his high-rise office, a half-empty tumbler of scotch sat sweating on the table next to him. The sun outside was beginning its descent into twilight, casting long shadows against the tall glass windows.

"That may or may not be true," came Cheryl's calm reply.

The pause that followed was electric.

"And what the hell's that supposed to mean?" Murdock snapped, annoyance deepening his tone.

Cheryl leaned back in her leather armchair, her tone even and poised, the confidence in her voice like silk pulled taut. "For one, I wouldn't be so quick to classify this one as a loser. Also, I've done the math. If a million people join his union, it will generate nearly fifty million bucks annually."

She let the figure linger in the air, knowing its weight.

"But wait," she continued, her voice laced with a touch of intrigue, "it gets more interesting. Each member will be expected to pay yearly dues, three times the initial forty-five-dollar fee. Twenty million members... that's a billion dollars annually, Murdock."

There was a rustle on the other end. The man was sitting forward now, no longer lounging in arrogance.

"We're approaching 350 million people here in America," she went on, "and according to the government's own data, at least 40 to 60 million are convicted felons. And beyond that, there are millions more with a loved one or close friend in that category. That's a massive demographic."

Her tone turned quiet, serious.

"In other words, Murdock, this 'loser,' as you call him, is sitting on an idea that, if harnessed properly, could put his net worth beyond Warren Buffett and Bill Gates... combined."

There was silence.

Cheryl could hear his breathing now—heavier, shorter. The shift in his mood wasn't just audible, it was visceral.

"Are you still there?" she asked, feigning casualness, though she knew full well she had him.

Murdock didn't answer right away. Finally, he growled, "Orville, in his narrow little vision, only sees the union as a potential problem. Unrestrained. A threat. Which, of course, it could be."

Then his tone twisted, laced with something old and

raw. "But you, my dear... over all these years, you continue to give me reasons to be glad I spared you. If you weren't a colored, I might have married you myself. To hell with that shithead I gave you to."

Cheryl's lips curved faintly in an unreadable smile. "Now, now. You just calm down, O.V., and I have served you well."

She let that hang a moment before continuing, "Listen, Murdock. Visit the Civic Center between 5 and 10. Today is the opening ceremony for Eyekon. This ex-con happens to be quite... charismatic. And by the way, do you want to see me for sex?"

It wasn't a real question. She already knew his answer.

Cheryl had long understood that Murdock didn't like her, not really. But what he did respect, and perhaps even feared, was her mind. Her ability to calculate and foresee. She was once just a pawn to him, a young Black girl out of high school, taken on under affirmative action, working the counter of Sanford's only jewelry store.

She remembered the old store vividly. The ticking of the antique clock on the wall. The smell of freshly polished gold. She'd spend her lunch breaks whispering into the phone, caught up in the sweet nothings of young love.

Then came Murdock's betrayal.

He had recorded her phone calls, playing them back in private. She never knew until it was too late. She had agreed, during one of those hushed calls, to let her boyfriend Toby rob the place. But fate had other plans. A deputy sheriff just so happened to walk out of the next-door store at the exact moment Toby reached for his weapon.

One shot. One life lost. Toby died in front of the store before anything could be taken.

The next day, on Cheryl's day off, she was called in. Murdock played the recording. Cold. Precise. Unforgiving. She stood there, 18 years old and trembling, slowly undressing, tears spilling from her eyes. "Please don't send me to prison," she had begged. "I'll do anything."

She meant it. And he took her at her word.

That was twenty-eight years ago.

"No, no sex," he said now, finally breaking the silence. "Not now. I'll see you around Wednesday. Call me then."

The click on the line was sharp. Final.

Outside the Sapp estate, Sire's car glided through the open wrought-iron gates, crunching gravel beneath the tires as he drove the long, winding driveway. On either side, the lawns spread like emerald carpets—impeccably trimmed, with hedges shaped into regal symmetry.

The peach-colored brick home rose at the end like a well-kept fortress of old Southern elegance.

An older Asian man appeared from the side, his salt-and-pepper beard trimmed neatly. He wore a crisp white shirt, black slacks, and shoes that gleamed like patent mirrors. His demeanor was respectful, alert.

"I'm Lee," he said, bowing slightly. "The Sapps' houseman. Mrs. Sapp has asked me to seat you in the living room. They'll be out shortly. Would either of you care for something to drink?"

"I'll have a glass of water, please," Vee said politely. Sire shook his head.

The living room was tastefully decorated, soft light filtering through gauzy curtains, the scent of vanilla candles faintly in the air.

Cheryl Sapp made her entrance like a vision from another time, wearing a bright blue and yellow sundress, her long hair cascading in soft waves over her shoulders. The white pearls around her neck glowed against her skin like a moonlit halo.

"Hi," she greeted with a warm smile. "Was Lee hospitable?"

"Very much so," Vee replied, returning the smile. "He made us feel truly welcome. Thank you."

Cheryl eased gracefully into a chair, her posture straight, her tone turning businesslike.

"Have you considered my offer?" she asked. "Because of Eyekon's potential financial footprint, the government will be watching. This union isn't a church—there are no tax exemptions. Everything has to be clean. I've already discussed it with my husband. He agrees that if you want this to succeed, you must start on the right foot, legally. I manage his businesses and the church finances. I can help you... If you want my help."

Sire, watching her, thought to himself: Cheryl is fully in control. She knows the weight of what she offers.

When Reverend Sapp entered the room, Cheryl subtly changed her body language. She shifted to the seat across from Sire. Every now and then, when Vee wasn't watching, she opened her legs just enough. Sire noticed. And, he looked.

The Reverend, unaware, addressed them.

"Did you bring your signs, young man?"

"I've lined up fifteen volunteers," Sire responded. "No compensation needed. I covered it."

"And the signs?"

"In the car. I also spoke with the Civic Center manager. They're expecting up to 3,000 people."

"Good," the Reverend nodded. "The local television station called. They'll be covering your speech tonight."

Cheryl leaned forward. "I can't stay more than three months, but that should be enough to get your finances structured. For that time, how does ten thousand dollars sound?"

Sire nodded. "Not bad. I expect five hundred members at least by tonight. Within three months, fifty to a hundred thousand."

They sealed it with a handshake.

The march was powerful, dignified. Trayvon's parents walked between Reverend Sapp and his assistant, grief and pride worn openly on their faces. Cheryl kept to the edge. When they turned onto 13th Street, six men in black berets and leather jackets stood silently in formation. One among them wore a red beret and held flowers.

He stepped forward and presented them to Trayvon's mother, who took them with shaking hands, tears slipping down her cheeks. She mouthed a soft "Thank you."

"That's Ishmael," Vee whispered to Sire. "Red beret."

Sire understands the camaraderie and encourages VEE to go and greet her former comrade.

"Hello Viola, I'm not sure if I should ask you how are you, or what in the hell are you doing here in Sandford?"

Ishmael asks as soon as Vee gets closer.

When Vee approached him, they embraced. She was surprised by the strength in his gait, no cane, barely a limp.

"How 'bout I answer both questions?" she smiled. "I'm doing great. I'm here supporting my new king... his name is Sire. In his effort to launch Eyekon, his union. The large number of people here supporting Trayvon Martin's cause are also fixture of Sire's plans. I tried to locate you, but couldn't."

"You left Fort Lauderdale?" Ishmael asked.

"Yes. After Carlton wounded the cop, before they killed him, the City would not leave us alone. It was either close

233

the NBPP down or relocate. Our founder gave his life for a cause he believed in, and I believed in Carlton. So, closing down the organization was not an option."

"Why were you trying to locate me?"

"To ask a favor. At least, for a few days, anyway. The press has reported that a $10.000 bounty is on George Liverman's head, we need it stopped or put on hold…"

"We?"

"Yes, Sire and I. He is the founder of Eyekon, the union I spoke of earlier. In many ways, Eyekon espouses a strict, uncompromising regimen to mold its members into a unified and cohesive labor bargaining force. These values closely mirror your own, Ishmael: this union also wants freedom for each of its members from the stigmatization that comes with being a convicted felon. The Union's aims are not to be confused with the notion that suggests it is cool to have, or be convicted of, and have a felony record. That would be an inaccurate assumption. However, this Union will be advocating that the mistake of becoming a felon should not be allowed to permanently extinguish the rights to pursue life, liberty, and the pursuit of happiness." Viola continues:

"Eyekon also believes that ex-convicts and felons, who truly demonstrate a desire to reform, will not be free (although their physical sentence has long since expired) until they are able to determine their own destiny. Eyekon wants full employment for our members.

"You're asking me to spare him?" Ishmael frowned.

"No. Just wait. A day or two."

"You sound like you've softened."

"I haven't," she said. "But I've evolved."

Back at the Civic Center, the energy was electric. Hundreds had gathered. Reverend Sapp, at the podium, introduced the evening's speaker.

The lights dimmed.

Sire, Teddy Hilson took the stage.

"Good evening, everyone."

He paused, breath caught in his throat. The weight of the moment pressed down on him like an invisible hand.

"We begin with a moment of silence for Trayvon Martin."

He bowed his head, and the hall followed. Then came the speech. Teddy's words pierced the room, painting a vivid picture of racial disparity, mass incarceration, systemic injustice, and the redemptive power of unity. His voice carried, clear and unwavering, outlining the mission of Eyekon not as a reaction, but as a revolution.

Good evening, everyone. Mothers, fathers, sisters, and brothers, thank you all for attending tonight. Initially, please let us give a moment of silence for Trayvon and his grieving parents." Teddy looks down, closes his eyes, and pauses. He can't help but think of the large crowd in front of him, the culmination of years of planning.

He takes a deep breath before resuming, "Thank you. Now, I am sure that many of you are wondering why I invited you here tonight and if this gathering is a follow-up to the march relating to Trayvon. Well, let me tell you why I asked you here. I asked you here because this union has the potential to change, as well as improve, your life and the lives of your loved ones.

However, before getting into that, I must point out a fact that, sadly, every one of us here who has ever been convicted of a felony has indirectly contributed to what happened to our beloved Trayvon. I know the thought going through your minds right now is how? I will tell you how. It's called hasty generalization, which is a fancy name for a conclusion based on insufficient or unrepresentative evidence.

A stereotype is a hasty generalization, usually derogatory, about a group of people. Stereotyping is a human trait, and because of our tendencies to perceive selectively, we tend to see what we want to see. That is, we subjectively notice evidence confirming our already-formed opinions and fail to notice evidence to the contrary.

For example, if you have concluded that politicians are corrupt, your preconceived notion will be confirmed by the occasional news reports of legislators being indicted or arrested. Even though every day, the newspapers also describe conscientious officials serving the public honestly and well.

Now, more at home with my point: if someone, especially someone who is culturally ignorant to black folks, were to improperly conclude that blacks are corrupt, dishonest, and criminal, their stereotype will be confirmed by the frequent news reports of crime being committed by Blacks. It is immaterial that most of these crimes we commit are against each other.

In fact, Black on Black violence has hit numbers far beyond our imagination and needs to end. From 1988 to 2008, 93% of Black victims were killed by Blacks. The national count of Black males 14 and older murdered in America from 1976 to 2005 was 214,661, according to U.S. Government statistics. That's a mind-blowing number of Black-on-Black killings.

Our being convicted felons – yes, I am one also – has driven up the crime rate, and people like George Liverman will almost always have the edge in the eyes of the law in situations like what happened to Trayvon.

How does this equate to us contributing to Trayvon's death?

We are helping to create the ugly stereotyping. Said a different way, all black folks are criminals.

The laws of this state and most of the states across the country strip the ex-con or felon of his true identity, including the rights of free citizenship. Way back in 1870, the 15th Amendment of the United States Constitution made race no bar to voting rights; the right to participate in any election, including electing a president of his States. But by being a convicted felon, they say you can no longer participate. Additionally, while I'm on this subject, the

Black population is only 12.2 percent of the US, however, the imprisonment rate reflects that between the ages of 1819 only 242 whites, but 1512 Blacks; 20 to 24, 886 whites to 4339 Blacks; 25 to 29, 1001 whites to 6927 Blacks; 30-34, 12004 whites to 7,721 Blacks; 35 to 39, 1,220 to 7,490 Blacks; 40 to 44, 1,121 whites to 6,345 Blacks; 55 to 59, 272 whites to 2,391 Blacks, 60 to 64, 180 whites to 701 Blacks and 65 and older, 69 whites to 287 Blacks.

These statistics are supplied by the Bureau of Justice of the U.S. Department of Justice.

No other race commits more crimes.

Now, I ask you all here tonight to join me. We, as a collective force, can bring change. Change in our community, our city, state, and our nation. Please, do not make the mistake of misunderstanding me or my sometimes pointed presentation. I may be putting extra emphasis on the continuing struggle of the Black race in America, although we have a Black President – neither the purpose of discourse, nor the aims and aspirations of Eyekon, are based on the color of one's skin. We are color-blind.

In fact, our first bylaw is: Each member must learn respect and practice, and total prohibition against discrimination of any kind. The position bestowed upon us by society transcends socioeconomic stratagem, ethnic group, or geographic region.

Today is the official launching of EYEKON, a union and association comprising of two major functions of aims: Firstly, a labor union that aims to improve the access of its members to employment and education through collective bargaining power.' The first step of any union is to get members to join. ' Eyekon' embraces the concerns of other unions: job security, unsafe working conditions, unfair wages, women's rights, equal pay, child labor, and so on. Those of the others.

However, Eyekon's emphasis is to ensure employment of its members without regard to the felony hanging over their heads. In fact, none of the unions today address this issue of ours, and will not. We are considered less than a second-class citizen, and because most places of employment shun people with a felony on their record, the other major unions tend to ignore us as well.

People, the bottom line is that we are a segment of society that is openly discriminated against, and it's time for it to cease.

Eyekon intends to confront this ugly hurdle, which blocks the true highway to reformation to becoming law-abiding and productive citizens. The Florida Constitution states: You have a right to work because to work is to live. I submit to you all that the struggle for equality starts at the first effort to right a wrong.

When Linda Brown and her father went to school in Kansas, it resulted in a challenge led by the legal team headed by Thurgood Marshall, ending legal apartheid in America. When Emmett Till was killed on August 28, 1955, and his mother displayed his waterlogged body in an open casket to show what they had done to her baby, he was

239

speaking from his grave.

In 1957, facing school segregation, the students in Little Rock tested the law. In 1960, students sat in on testing the same law. Each generation must fight every day. In 1965, students led the Selma march after Jimmy Lee Jackson had been killed. John Lewis, now a U.S.

Congressman, the Rev. Martin Luther King Jr., and Hosea Williams were young leaders in that march across Edmund Pettus Bridge in Selma, which brought to a fever pitch the quest for the right to vote. After Emmett Till, we changed our minds about the fight for civil rights and substantially overcame fear.

Secondly, Eyekon will give strong attention to educating its members and requiring those without a high school diploma to obtain a G.E.D. or a trade.

The call for you to partake in igniting the wind beneath the wings of Eyekon is urgent, and the fact that you all are here tonight is a testament that you've paid for breaking the laws of this state. Those of us who did not go to jail or prison but received a felony conviction were somehow able to meet the high standards society demands to merit a break. And you all must remember that after the march on Washington in 1963 for jobs and freedom, a renewed will emerged to fight an unjust system.

So now, what is this day's challenge coming out of the Trayvon Martin crisis? What must happen for it to be a game-changer? Even if they were to successfully prosecute George Liverman, it won't fix the huge debt we all owe

Trayvon and his parents. Everyone here tonight is touched in one way or another by a convicted felon. Right now, all of you have an opportunity to be a part of this groundbreaking history, and you are also in a position to help make Eyekon a reality. Support this Union by joining now! Once again, Thank you very much. GOD BLESS US ALL."

By the end, people were rising to their feet, clapping, weeping, and cheering. Vee stood beside him, pride radiating from her like warmth. Cheryl, too, applauded—but in her heart, something else stirred.

As she watched Sire, something primal and deeply feminine stirred within her soul. What is it about this man... she wondered, that touches me so deeply? And she already knew the answer.

Chapter 37

Fault Lines Beneath the Empire

Murdock Hatchet wore his sour expression like a cursed heirloom, forever etched into the creases of his face like a grim etching on brittle parchment. His hair, as white as freshly fallen snow, was combed back neatly, a ghostly contrast against his weathered, rat-like features—sharp-nosed, twitchy, and dark around the eyes like a rabid predator who'd once known true power but now sniffed at shadows. He was, by all accounts, hard to like. And that suited him just fine.

But last night... last night had unnerved even him.

Sleep had danced around his bed like a taunting lover, always just out of reach. Murdock tossed and turned, tormented not by nightmares, but by something worse—reality. Visions of thousands of faces, lining up at the Civic Center, not in protest or submission... but in unity. Signing their names. Joining. Believing.

Cheryl had been right. That damned woman and her genius brain. She always knew how to sniff out the real deal, and the financial forecast she'd presented him over the phone was no pipe dream—it was manifesting in real time.

But it wasn't the money that had Murdock pacing the marble floors of his estate in the early morning light.

It was the power.

He knew politics. He'd spent sixteen years manipulating the legislative machine as a state senator, and even before that, his family name, Hatchet Jewelry, had ensured wealth beyond need. But control… control was the true currency. And what he saw yesterday was a movement, a union fueled by felons and the forgotten, rising from beneath the system he helped build.

Then the founder, this charismatic ex-con, had done the unthinkable. He'd circled back to the mic after the crowd had begun to thin. He asked for signatures. Signatures to overturn mandatory sentencing laws.

Murdock's blood had run cold.

This was personal.

He wrote the 85 Percent Law. He pushed through the recidivist sentencing clause. His name, his legacy, was stitched into the very fabric of those statutes.

"Over my dead body," he muttered aloud in the quiet of his sunroom, his eyes sharp as broken glass.

"I'll be damned if some street messiah is going to unravel my life's work."

Elsewhere in Sanford, in a high-rise office space nestled within the sleek glass panels of the DuPont Complex, another chapter of the movement was being written.

The atmosphere was festive, glowing with a quiet confidence. The sun cut golden slashes across the polished floors as Sire, Vee, and Erika toasted the second month of

Eyekon's meteoric rise.

Membership had surged past 160,000. The capital was pushing beyond $7 million. Erika's recent addition, an insurance program designed to protect businesses hiring Eyekon members, had gained applause even from corporate circles. The union wasn't just surviving; it was thriving.

But peace is always temporary when change threatens the status quo.

Their celebration was cut short when two sharply dressed men, carrying solemn faces and thick folders, stepped into the reception area. Agents from the Board of Accountability and the Auditor General's Office.

Polite, formal, and chilling.

They requested to speak with Sire privately. Within minutes, the air in the room thickened.

"We'll be reviewing your financial ledgers," one of them said without emotion.

"Asset, liability, capital, and income expense accounts."

The tone wasn't accusatory, but neither was it benign.

Sire leaned back in his leather chair, outwardly calm. "Of course. Our records are open."

But the calm was shattered when the lead auditor delivered the blow:

"Effective immediately, Eyekon's records will be seized. And within ten days, your organization will be temporarily barred from all operations until the investigation concludes."

Sire rose from his chair, anger surging. "On what grounds?"

"A discrepancy," the auditor replied as if discussing the weather. "Between income declared and actual capital on hand. A significant one. That's a violation of both state and federal laws."

Repeated calls to Cheryl's phone met only silence—her voicemail taunting them with its generic tone.

Their accounts? Frozen.

Their future? Jeopardized.

Erika, calm but focused, had already begun tearing into the records. For two straight days, she pored over every transaction, every ledger entry, every deposit slip, and expense log.

When she called Vee and Sire into the conference room, her tone was clinical, but her eyes betrayed worry.

"On day 62, our asset account showed a net income of two hundred thousand. But the earned income for the same period? Seven million. That's not a gap, that's a chasm."

Sire rubbed his temples. "Maybe it was just... an oversight on Cheryl's part."

Vee scoffed. "You don't really believe that, do you?"

Sire gave Erika a look. "Sweetheart. Would you care to

answer that?"

Erika didn't hesitate.

"No. A certified public accountant doesn't accidentally fail to report $7 million. That's not incompetence. It's fraud."

Sire exhaled slowly. "Thank you, baby." He turned to Vee. "Get Pimpwell on the phone. Let him know what's happening. Tell him I need one-fifty for maybe ninety days."

Vee nodded. "Got it."

"And look up a lawyer. Stuart or West Palm. Name's Willie Terry. Retain him. Give him the rundown. I'll be back in a day or so. If I'm not…"

He paused, looking between the two women, the pillars of his mission.

"Eyekon must go on."

He kissed them both gently, then turned to leave. Erika reached instinctively, but Vee held her arm.

"He'll be fine," she said quietly. "He always comes back."

She noticed Erika's eyes, glassy, vulnerable. The emotions blooming behind them were unmistakable. She loved him. And Vee was glad. Together, they would hold the line. For him. For what they were building.

Meanwhile, across the state, the embers of another revolution burned low. In a cramped, dimly lit office in

Tampa, Ishmael Nibblack sat hunched over a sheet of paper, the 30-day eviction notice staring back like a silent countdown to collapse.

Donations had dried up. The organization was underwater. $1,800 was all they needed to breathe again. Yet Ishmael refused to let desperation take the wheel.

He'd already removed Tucker, his sergeant-at-arms. Not because he wasn't loyal, he was. But because he'd violated NBPPs, the sergeant-at-arms violated the NBPP's sacred rule: No crime.

Drugs had paid the bills. But they also paid into the narrative the system expected of them.

Ishmael understood: poverty breeds crime. But so does despair. The system was designed that way. And every time one of them fell into that trap, it proved the system right. He picked up the phone and dialed. The voice that answered was soft, professional.

"Eyekon, how may we help you?"

"I need to speak with Vee Templeton."

A pause. Then her familiar voice. "Vee speaking."

"Ishmael here. I... I'm in a bit of a bind."

He didn't need to explain much. She listened quietly. She didn't tell him about Eyekon's own crisis, or the $110,000 she'd just dropped on lawyers. None of that mattered now.

"How can I help you, my brotha?"

Her voice was warm. Steady. A lifeline in a storm.

"Five grand. That'll stabilize us."

"You still in Tampa?"

"Yes."

"Check Western Union tomorrow. And Ish—thank you. For pulling back on Liverman."

"Give my regards to your king," Ishmael said softly. "He's a winner. Thanks, sis. Take care."

"You too, Ishmael."

Chapter 38

Beneath the Velvet Trap

Candy-apple red and yellow streaked across the quiet morning like a flame against soft gray. Cheryl gripped the steering wheel of the 600 SL Mercedes-Benz, her fingers tight around the cool leather, her knuckles white. She eased through the long driveway, a serpent's path winding away from the Sapp estate, until the tires kissed the road that led into Sanford.

The sky was the color of pale ash, and even the birds seemed to fly in silence. Orville was away on business again, the fourth day in a row, and guilt wrapped around her like a silk scarf pulled just a bit too tight.

Nearly thirty years now.

Murdock Hatchet had scripted every scene of her life since she was a teenager. The director, the villain, the puppeteer. And she, Cheryl Sapp, had been the pliant star of a performance she'd never auditioned for. He had used her, degraded her, and made her body into a vessel of obedience and control. Marriage to O.V. was a façade, a quiet prison cell inside the mansion's pristine walls. She had come to care for him, sure, but love? That wasn't what Murdock had ordered. Love was a luxury she was never meant to afford.

Her eyes flickered to the rearview mirror. Not yet. Not now. But she felt it.

Sire.

He had spent all of yesterday stalking the periphery of her world, the church, the gate, the long road in front of her estate. A panther waits in the brush. He knew she couldn't resist the danger. Cheryl liked to be desired. And when she walked into a room, heads still turned.

Behind her, the low growl of a Cadillac prowled the road. She pulled into the church parking lot, glancing sideways at the stained glass windows like a sinner approaching judgment. She stepped out.

The Cadillac stopped behind her.

Pshhhk. The passenger window slid down.

"Get your stank ass in this car before I change my mind and fuck you up!"

She froze. Air caught in her lungs. Her body screamed to run, but a deeper voice, darker, wetter, hotter whispered go. Always, always those two voices: one warning, one begging. And the second voice always won.

She opened the door.

The barrel of a gun rested in Sire's lap like a sleeping viper. But oddly, it didn't frighten her. No, what disturbed her was the low, thrumming arousal that tickled her ribs. Danger turned her on. Again.

Just like in her office.

Her breath caught in short, wet gasps. Sire smirked. "Freaky bitch," he muttered under his breath. He didn't have to say more. He could feel it.

He took her to the corner room at Motel 6, where he had holed up for three days now. The air inside the room was stale, like a place where secrets had slept too long.

Cheryl undressed in silence, everything except the bra and panties. She sat down, regal yet trembling, in the lone wooden chair facing him. Her eyes shimmered with vulnerability.

"Teddy…" her voice cracked. "I am sorry. Please, let me explain…"

And she did. She spilled it all, every shameful encounter with Murdock Hatchet, the twisted games, the humiliations, the sex. Her words came out as sobs and whispers. Sire listened with his jaw tight. He didn't yell. Didn't move.

He was silent. But behind those eyes, something sharpened.

Betrayal.

Not from enemies. He knew how to handle enemies. No betrayal by someone close was a razor you never saw until it was at your throat. Cheryl had taught him a lesson: never surrender your control center. Ever.

She told him Murdock's truth, his wealth, his reach, and his obsession with destroying Eyekon or owning it entirely. This wasn't a street war anymore. It was chess.

Sire stood. He had heard enough.

An hour later, he was at Radio Shack, buying tools. Then he parked in front of a house for sale, just like Cheryl had instructed. Behind it, a canoe waited. He slipped into the water, paddling silently across the artificial pond.

The Murdock compound loomed.

He entered through the back, no alarm. No resistance.

Inside, the mansion breathed perversion. Sex toys lined the entry table, handcuffs, clamps, things with batteries. And in the master suite, Murdock Hatchet lay sprawled in nothing but a little girl's training bra and silk panties.

Sire's skin crawled.

He didn't speak. He flipped the bed.

Murdock yelped like a hog and scrambled under a chair. Sire kicked him hard.

Beretta is now at Murdock's cheek. "You are being robbed, shithead. If you want to live, take me to the safe behind the Van Gogh picture."

Murdock's face drained. The fact that Sire knew about the safe broke his will. He opened it. Sire emptied the cash, the deeds, and, yes, the black VCR tape. He slipped it into the portable player. His jaw clenched.

There it was.

A black man, hired by Cheryl under Murdock's orders, was doing things to that freak that made Sire want to shoot him twice. But he didn't. He just looked into Murdock's eyes.

"You're done."

Back at the motel, Cheryl hadn't left.

"Get your shit. I'm taking you back to the church," he said coldly.

She didn't speak. Her eyes said everything: You owe me.

In the church parking lot, he handed her the tape.

"You're free," he said. "You can tell them both to kiss your pretty, round ass. I borrowed $150K to hire some lawyers. You've got three days to cover it. Now, get the fuck out of my car."

Tears in her throat. "I'm sorry."

Sire said nothing more.

That night, he packed up the office. Keys slid into the mailbox. Time to move on. Murdock had threatened Cheryl, but now the power balance had shifted. Attorney Willie Terry found a loophole. The fraud case was dismissed. Florida law shielded them for now.

Before leaving Sanford, they all met for dinner. Vee, Erika, Sire. Laughter and promises. Cheryl transferred $500,000 to Eyekon, and Sire was now worth $10 million... and counting. They were heading to Fort Myers, but decided to stop in Tampa first.

In the Cadillac, Erika turned to him. "When will I get to meet Mr. Woody?" she asked playfully.

"That may never happen," Sire said, firm. "Vee told me you're proud to be a virgin. Keep it that way. I'm not the man of your dreams."

"But I'm twenty-four!" she fired back, tears breaking loose. "I'm grown!"

He pulled over at a rest stop. Climbed into the backseat. She collapsed into him, sobbing. He held her gently.

"Erika, baby, don't cry. I know it hurts. But this… sex… It's dangerous. Not physically. Emotionally. If I touch you, if I really touch you… You won't come back the same."

She didn't answer, only cried harder. He whispered in her hair, "Save yourself. For someone who deserves it."

Up front, Vee drove in silence. She understood. Erika wasn't just sweet on Sire, she loved him. Deeply. But Sire was trying to protect her the way he once wished someone had protected his sister.

They reached the NBPP office in Tampa. Ishmael greeted them warmly.

"You're stepping on toes, brother," he told Sire. "But maybe that's what has to happen."

Their dialogue thundered rich with fire, anger, and purpose. Pro-Black but not anti-anything. They all agreed: Eyekon was about justice, not division.

Trey Daniels arrived. An old comrade. Another soldier. When introductions circled around to Erika, Trey asked, "Who's she?"

"She's family," Sire replied simply.

They left Tampa with envelopes exchanged and respect earned. Three weeks left on the Cadillac lease. But Sire wasn't worried. He had control now. Of the money. Of the movement. Of the script. And most importantly, of himself.

Chapter 39

Diamonds in the Rough

Two months passed, and the air around Fort Myers shimmered with change.

The once-modest Eyekon headquarters now buzzed like a hive of focused energy, its sleek glass exterior reflecting the rising sun like a beacon of progress. Inside, 35 full-time employees worked in orchestrated harmony, each commanding a specialized role under the new Board. At the helm sat Teddy "Sire" Hilson, his presence undeniable, regal in his crisp, dark, tailored suit, the weight of his past no longer a shackle but a badge of resilience. His sharp eyes roamed the boardroom with a quiet confidence. The law could no longer bar him from leadership, and the moment had come for him to reclaim what he was born to build.

Three years out of prison and now president and COO, Sire chaired the Board with a firm but visionary hand. Beside him, Attorney Willie Terry, recently rehired, set in motion the long-awaited clemency and pardon process with the State's Parole Commission and the governor's office. The aim was clear: to seal Sire's past once and for all.

The Board's passion ignited real reform. A special finance division was born, its purpose: to craft and secure grants that could breathe life into long-term community projects. The most beloved among them were the "Eyekon 1, 2, and 3" private charter schools, elementary, middle, and high school facilities constructed with ambition and care.

Wide courtyards, sun-drenched classrooms, and murals painted by local artists would one day fill children's eyes with wonder. Parents wept with joy as they enrolled their kids, knowing that only Eyekon members could access these unparalleled opportunities.

Expert educators from across the country were flown in, their resumes glittering with Ivy League and inner-city success alike. They weren't just teachers—they were dream-sowers.

Beyond education, Eyekon expanded into commerce. A brokerage division rapidly acquired local and external businesses, bringing jobs directly to members, replacing despair with dignity.

To ensure holistic development, state-of-the-art recreational centers were constructed, attached to each charter school. After-school hours were no longer a void filled with street corners and silence, they throbbed with basketball games, robotics clubs, dance rehearsals, and laughter.

On holidays, joy spilled into the streets. Thanksgiving turkeys, warm and aromatic, were delivered by smiling volunteers in Eyekon hoodies. At Christmas, thousands of toys found their way into tiny, waiting hands. The sparkle in children's eyes told stories no camera could capture.

Eyekon's value soared $80 million, with major offices in over a dozen cities across the state. The nation began to whisper its name in reverence. Sire, bold as ever, proposed the next leap in national expansion. IPO talks ignited within boardrooms, and projections painted a future where Sire, once a convict, might soon be a billionaire. And still, in the heart of Fort Myers, something even more profound unfolded.

The people no longer looked for a way out of the ghetto. Instead, they saw into it, recognized their grit, their roots, their beauty. They discovered they were, and had always been, diamonds in the rough.

Sire understood. He'd learned that a man didn't have to swim across life's oceans if he had a canoe, and if he didn't, he could build one. Life was about navigating, not just surviving. And that wisdom wasn't his alone; it was earned, taught, passed down.

But then came the storm.

A construction company owned by Vincete Antolini rumored mobster and alleged terror group associate, became the target of a boycott after its refusal to hire any individual with a felony record. Though subtle in public language, the company's policies were seen as racially coded, disproportionately excluding Black men from employment. Word of this spread like wildfire.

The night before the boycott, the atmosphere at Eyekon turned taut. A package arrived, addressed to Mr. Teddy Hilson.

Vee accepted it with a bright smile, her curls bouncing as she walked toward Sire's spacious corner office. She was humming softly until she opened it.

A high-pitched scream shattered the calm.

"Sire!" she gasped, eyes wide, hand trembling.

People burst into the room. Sire's face was steel, unmoving, as he studied the grotesque scene laid out before him. A yellow canary, its tiny chest grotesquely cut open, its head pinned inside the cavity. Blood smeared like a warning across black cardboard shaped like a human form.

BACK OFF was scrawled in crimson. Sire's jaw tightened. He picked up the whole package and dropped it in the trash can beside his desk.

"It'll take much more than an idle threat to stop the boycott tomorrow," he said, his voice low but resonant with thunderous resolve. "Vee, get Pimpwell on the line."

The call connected in seconds.

"Pimpwell speaking."

"What's happening, partner. I've got a situation— Vincete Antolini."

"You mean the Vincete? The mobster?"

"That's what they say. But hell, his asshole points to the ground just like any other man. If it were on his kneecap, then I might worry."

Sire's voice was rough velvet, laced with disdain.

"He sent me a bird. A real one. Head jammed in its chest. Message in blood. Told me to back off."

A long pause.

"That symbol," Pimpwell said quietly. "It's death or life. You do what they want, you live. Ignore it, you've chosen death."

He knew Sire. Knew he wouldn't flinch. But Vincete Antolini wasn't a two-bit hustler, he was cold, calculating, and connected. Men who crossed him vanished like dust in the wind.

"Sire, is this really worth it? This ain't street beef. This is war, stealthy and silent."

Sire's voice came, calm and fire-etched.

"Our seventh bylaw. Eyekon protects its own. If a business refuses to hire one of us over something from their past, we speak up. Even if it costs us everything."

Pimpwell exhaled.

"Let me bring some Darks in from Chi-town. Just in case."

"Appreciate you, but I'm good. I've already hired an ex-Navy SEAL. Serious muscle."

"Alright then," Pimpwell said, voice tinged with respect. "If you need anything, even $150K more, day or night. Oh, and thanks, my lawyer received the million you wired last week."

"Appreciate you, brother."

Later that night, Sire, Erika, and Vee tried to melt the

tension with a movie on their 72" flat screen. Laughter flickered. Popcorn bowls rested on laps.

Erika slipped away to shower. Sire turned toward Vee, hunger simmering in his gaze. The moment they touched, sparks flew. Clothes vanished. Skin glistened. Mouths searched with urgency. Vee's short skirt rose, revealing her naked heat.

"No panties?" Sire murmured, voice thick.

"Didn't need 'em," she whispered back.

But before it could go further, something stirred. A hesitant touch on Sire's hard length. He looked up.

Erika stood naked, eyes wide and haunted, her fingers trembling against his arousal. Her lips parted, unsure but driven. Sire gently pushed Vee aside, rising slowly.

"Why?" Erika's voice cracked, broken. "Why won't you let me love you?"

Tears welled.

"I am not your sister, Sire. I am your woman."

She turned to Vee, pleading.

"Please. Help me. I love this motherfucker. I'm begging you make him understand."

Vee rushed to Erika's side, holding her as sobs wracked her body. Sire stood still. Something in him shifted.

He walked to them, strong arms wrapping around both women. Erika looked up, eyes glistening, heart wide open, and in that gaze, Sire saw everything. He kissed her. Deep. Meaningful. She nearly collapsed. They laid her gently on the sofa. Sire kissed her softly between the thighs and walked out.

The next day, the boycott made headlines.

Channel 2. Channel 11. Local cable.

Reporters jostled for soundbites. Eyekon spokesperson Mary Palmer, regal and composed, faced the flashing lights.

"Is Mr. Hilson concerned for his safety?" one reporter asked.

Mary's voice was clear as church bells.

"Always. But when people are denied honest work because of their past, Eyekon stands beside them. Mr. Hilson faces danger, not to invite conflict, but to inspire peace. Because change begins when someone dares to say: Enough."

And the world listened.

Chapter 40

Ashes of Power, Fires of Loyalty

The G6 jet sliced through the fading blue above the Gulf of Mexico like a silent predator, sleek and commanding. Its engines purred with a confident hum, descending ten miles out from St. Petersburg/Clearwater's private airstrip. The jet, a marvel of executive luxury, seemed almost indifferent to the tension simmering inside its lone passenger.

Trey Daniels sat motionless in his leather seat, the Florida coastline unfurling below like a dreamscape laced with fire. But Trey wasn't admiring the view. His gaze was fixed, his thoughts anything but tranquil.

The weight of Sire's proposal sat on his chest like a stone, heavier than the duffel bag of weapons that waited back home. Accepting it meant power. It meant purpose. But it also meant war. Because Sire wasn't just building a union, he was igniting a movement that threatened the roots of Florida's systemic rot.

No job could offer the kind of money Trey stood to make. But then again, no job came with this kind of danger either. Not unless your name was on a list next to "Public Enemy" and "Dead Man Walking."

Trey had just returned from a weekend locked behind closed doors with Teddy Hilson in Ft Myers. Sire's longtime friend was under fire from lawmakers, from the mob, and from the prison industrial complex itself.

263

Eyekon.

It was more than a union. It was a revolution disguised as structure, offering not just jobs and education, but housing, rehabilitation, and civil rights restoration. Sire's vision was bold. Dangerous. Beautiful.

But it was also in the crosshairs.

Backed into a corner by Florida's political elite who masked their greed with legal procedure, Eyekon was under siege. Their excuse? The state already offered civil rights restoration, just with a mandatory five-year wait after release or conviction. A timeframe so long, most didn't make it to year four without reoffending.

The truth was darker:

Money, Power, and Control.

Four reasons politicians feared Eyekon:

- Profit. With the sheer number of felons in Florida, the union could generate tens of millions annually.

- Scale. If Eyekon went national, and it would, it could eclipse every union in the country.

- Ambition. All of it would fall under Teddy Hilson's command. Billionaire status was a heartbeat away.

- Disruption. Eyekon was tanking recidivism. That meant fewer inmates and less money for the prison industry.

Trey leaned back, exhaling slowly. It all made sense

now. Sire had always seen it coming. They'd spoken of this in hushed tones behind razor wire and concrete walls when they were still inmates. Now, the prophecy had blood in its teeth.

And it was personal.

Months ago, negotiations with a construction giant failed. Then came the boycott. Then came the message.

Sire had been behind the wheel of his prized 2012 Landaulet Maybach 62 S when the call came. The voice on the other end, cool, precise, and disturbingly familiar, had given him one chance.

"Pull the car over. Get out. Walk away. If you want to live another day."

The calmness was what chilled him. Not the words. The voice was smooth, dispassionate. Businesslike. Sire didn't argue. He complied. Fifty feet from the car, his phone rang again.

"Close Eyekon. Or give it to Mr. Antolini."

Sire's answer had been curt, laced with contempt.

"Thanks, but no thanks. I don't need help, especially not from the mafia."

Click.

Boom.

The Maybach ignited in a brilliant, roaring fireball. Chrome, rubber, and glass rained down in twisted pieces.

Sire didn't flinch. He watched the flames, blinked once, and walked away.

The G6 landed softly on the St. Pete tarmac. Trey disembarked swiftly, passing through the single-story terminal with the nonchalance of a man who carried the weight of the world in his chest pocket. Homeland Security gave him a nod. He gave them silence.

Outside, the humid Florida air hit him like a memory. Jaime was waiting. Her smile, warm and teasing, lit up her caramel-toned face. Her eyes, soft brown and full of knowing, watched Trey approach. Her arms opened, and he fell into them, burying his tension in her warmth. His hands tangled in her long, silky hair that cascaded down her back like dark silk over her curves.

Trey had loved her fiercely, even behind bars. She'd waited. She'd believed. Now, they were free together. They walked to the car.

"How's Teddy?" Jaime asked once they were inside.

"He's cool, J. Laying low." Trey's voice dropped. "Still pissed about the Maybach."

"I'm sure he is. But thank God he wasn't in it."

"Yeah," Trey said, jaw tightening. "Thank God."

The silence hung heavy. He could feel her eyes on him.

"They're pushing hard now," he said, "trying to shut Eyekon down or take it. And since Sire won't fold, they're getting violent. But what they don't know is, they're messing with two men who'll bring it right back to them."

"What was the meeting about?" Jaime asked.

Trey glanced at her, pulled back into focus. "Sire wants a security team, something we can roll out across every Eyekon branch. Then he wants me to lead the push to go national."

"Aren't you worried about the bombs?" she asked quietly.

"What do you mean?"

"I mean, is it safe to expand, knowing these people would rather blow you up than negotiate?"

"They'd probably love it if we stopped," he muttered, eyes darkening as they turned onto Westshore Boulevard.

"That's not an answer."

Trey sighed. "Jamie, listen to me. I'm not worried about them. If they come, they get dealt with."

Her voice dropped a note. "So, we're back to your shoot 'em up days?"

He didn't answer.

She didn't press.

She knew. And she pitied anyone who forced his hand.

Their gated community, The Channel, welcomed them in silence. The million-dollar homes stood like monuments to success and secrecy. Their house, at the street's end, greeted them with blooms and trimmed hedges, a picture of peace in an unpeaceful world.

They stepped inside.

The phone rang.

Jaime answered. A moment passed. Then her expression changed. Her mouth fell open. Her eyes went wide. The phone slipped from her fingers.

"Jaime!" Trey caught her as she sagged, limp and trembling.

He cradled her, picked up the phone.

"Hello? Who the hell is this?"

A woman's voice, panicked. Vee.

She'd just left Eyekon HQ late and came home to find devastation. Where Sire's house once stood, ashes. Fire trucks. Police cars. Smoke curling into the sky. Sire's dog, Shauka, was found shot. Beheaded. No sign of Sire. No sign of Erika. Only the charred remains of the Escalade, still parked in the driveway.

Trey lay Jaime down gently. Her chest rose and fell with sobs. He kissed her forehead and whispered something only she could hear. Then he walked outside. Out back, the shed sat quietly. Trey stepped in, brushed dust off the framed photo of Jaime, and flipped a hidden switch. The floor groaned and opened.

Beneath it, cold steel, silent purpose. He grabbed a large duffel, loaded it with precision. Pistols. Rifles. Ammo. Kevlar. All things he swore he'd never need again. He zipped it shut, slung it over his shoulder, and walked back inside. He kissed Jaime goodbye. And drove toward Fort Myers.

(Six Weeks Later)

A billboard stands near the state courthouse, white letters bold and bloodless:

CRIMINALS ARE SCUMBAGS. SOCIETY

HAS NO PLACE FOR THEM. ONCE A

LAW BREAKER, ALWAYS A LAW BREAKER.

THEY SHOULD ALL BE ROUNDED UP

AND PUT TO DAMN WORK. PERIOD.

The world was watching now.

And the fire had only just begun.

Chapter 41

The Cost of Knowing

Hell Week was never designed to kill. It was forged to strip away the illusions of strength, to peel back the skin of bravado until only the core of a man was left, raw, exposed, and vulnerable. It tested more than muscle; it tested the will.

The beach winds tore through the fabric of the fifty-man canvas tents like icy ghosts, carrying the sting of salt and the promise of pain. Sand curled in tiny storms around boots and bedrolls. The air was heavy with anticipation. Fear hovered like a mist.

Few slept.

Most lay in darkness, silently calculating the limits of their endurance. For some, the mental battlefield started before dawn ever cracked. The whisper of waves outside clashed against their racing minds, and the thought of five relentless days ahead was too much to bear.

One by one, cots creaked under shifting weight. A few recruits, their faces cloaked in shadow, quietly stepped out into the wind, heading toward the bell. No instructor stopped them. No one tried to talk them down. If you quit in the tent, you had no business ever stepping on that sand.

Trey Daniels hadn't rung that bell. He had survived it. And the memory of that week, of triumph and pain, clung to his bones like scars. It had been one of the defining chapters of his life. Now, more than ever, those memories revisited him like old ghosts.

"Sir, may I help you?"

The voice was polite but edged with indifference.

Trey had been standing at the reception counter for several long minutes, silent and still, his thoughts drifting between the past and the tense present. He blinked once and returned to the moment. He had a feeling he would need every ounce of that Hell Week strength today.

"Yes, ma'am," Trey said, leveling his tone. "Are you the owner of the construction company?"

Trey Daniels stood just under six feet, his frame lean but muscular, 220 pounds of coiled control. His bald head gleamed under the reception lights like polished obsidian. He had this way of slightly tilting his head when people spoke to him, eyes locking onto theirs like searchlights dissecting lies. It made most people uncomfortable, and that suited him just fine.

"I am not the owner," the woman replied coolly. "I'm his secretary. How may we assist you?"

Trey's voice was calm, his words deliberate.

"My partner and I are in need of a construction company capable of handling a project worth a couple of million dollars."

That got her attention.

Initially, she had assumed the sharply dressed Black

man was another job seeker, overdressed to impress. But now, her expression shifted, greedy curiosity blooming behind her polite facade.

"My name is Irena," she said, smoothing her tone into something more inviting. "Please, have a seat."

"Thank you. I'm Mr. Daniels. Trey Daniels."

He spoke his name like a statement. And it was. Anyone doing a proper background check would find no trace of the New Black Panther Party. That history had been buried. What they would find now was wealth, property, and influence. Enough to warrant interest, if not fear.

"Mr. Antollini will see you shortly. Can I get you water, tea, or soda?" Irena gestured toward the back door of the reception hall, already moving.

"No, thank you," Trey said.

She disappeared behind a heavy oak door, leaving Trey alone in the high-ceilinged reception room. The décor was strictly masculine. Heavy, dark leather chairs, mahogany accents, and dim lighting cast long shadows across the floor. It reeked of quiet intimidation.

Trey glanced up.

A camera. Tucked behind an ornate arrangement of fake flowers. Watching him. Amateurs would have mounted it in plain view for deterrence. But this was covert surveillance, meant not to stop a crime but to observe behavior. To record an advantage. It revealed much more about the one behind the lens than the one in front of it.

Vincente Antollini. A man whose handshake came with a knife. Trey did not trust him. Not today. Not ever.

"Right this way, Mr. Daniels," Irena returned. "Mr. Antollini will see you now."

Trey had just been admiring the Italian scattergun mounted behind the desk. A Lupo. Deep-blue steel. Elegant and deadly. Its polished oak stock glowed under a spotlight like the neck of a violin. It was beautiful, and it had no business being in a business office. He stood and followed Irena into the lion's den.

"Thank you. I wasn't so sure someone would be available on such short notice," Trey said, stepping into the office with smooth confidence.

Antollinni stood behind an oversized walnut desk, dressed in an expensive suit, face creased in equal parts curiosity and calculation.

"How can I assist you, Mr. Daniels?" he asked, voice clipped.

"We're hoping to hire a construction company that could build several structures to serve as classrooms, some to hold fifty students, others up to three hundred, and an auditorium for each."

Antollinni raised an eyebrow.

"That could be quite expensive. You are aware?"

Trey gave a small, humorless smile.

"We are very aware, Mr. Antollini. The question is, can your company handle the job? And if so, how soon can you start?"

Antollinni studied him, lips tightening. He had lived in Fort Myers for over three decades. In all that time, he had never seen a Black man walk in offering millions, unless that man was an athlete or a fool.

"We? What financial institution are you representing?"

"No credit union. Just our bank. We're paying out of pocket. The 'we' is my partner and I."

"And where is your partner, Mr. Daniels?"

Trey did not answer immediately. He met the mobster's stare with a cold, unwavering gaze.

"I was hoping," Trey said slowly, "you would be able to answer that question for me."

Antollinni's face tightened.

"What the hell is that supposed to mean?"

"Teddy Hilson," Trey said. "You son of a bitch."

Antollinni's hand moved. Trey was already moving.

A deafening boom echoed through the office. Trey hit the ground and rolled behind the heavy settee as a shadow standing behind him dropped with a thud. In his hand, a custom P38 whispered its own retort, a sharp, muffled burst.

The bullet slid under the sofa and buried itself in Antollinni's leg.

The gangster howled in pain, collapsing, his weapon skittering across the floor. Now, Trey stood, weapon raised, eyes like black steel.

"You get one question," he said. "And it needs one answer. I won't repeat it. Where in the fuck is Teddy Hilson?"

Blood oozed down Vincente's thigh as he gasped.

"Look, it wasn't my call," he stammered. "I didn't order it. Someone high up, someone federal, doesn't want that union to survive unless it's under their thumb. The Mafia name? That was a mask. A favor in exchange for another favor."

Trey didn't lower the gun.

"A don's son in New York needed a heroin case to vanish. In exchange, we used our name to pressure Hilson. First, they wanted him dead. The Maybach was supposed to be his tomb. I stepped in. I made the call to let him live. Told him to walk away. But someone else, one of them, called instead. Told him to hand the union over."

Antollinni's voice cracked.

"Then they blew up his house. Killed his dog. God knows what they did to him or the girl. And now, now it all looks like my hit, when it wasn't."

Trey didn't blink.

"Do you know where they took him?"

"I swear, I don't know with certainty."

Suddenly, a groan came from the doorway. Irena. Blood soaked her pant leg as she staggered upright, eyes wide with pain.

"Are you alright?" Vincente rasped.

"My thigh's torn to hell. I need a hospital."

Trey did not move.

Antollinni coughed, pointing with trembling fingers.

"There's one camera in this building. Closet to your left. The recording is in there. Take it. And go. I won't stop you."

Then, after a beat—

"Off McGregor Boulevard, quarter mile south of Edison's estate. A compound tied to the Hatchet family. Old Florida senatorial dynasty. My people have reported an unusual level of activity there. It shouldn't be; the Senator is in Washington, D.C.Something's not right."

Trey stared at the bleeding man, then to the shaking secretary, then back to the room heavy with secrets and smoke. He holstered his weapon.

Teddy was still out there. Somewhere in the dark. Somewhere between secrets and silence. And Trey Daniels was going to find him.

Even if he had to burn Fort Myers to the ground.

Chapter 42

The Mind is Everything

With the Biden Administration's blessing and a wave of start-up capital infusing education reform, charter schools across the nation stood like seedlings breaking through the soil after a long drought, ready to blossom. For Teddy Hilson, the timing was prophetic.

As statistics grimly revealed, nearly sixty-eight percent of all males in state and federal prisons lacked a high school diploma. A harrowing truth that screamed for urgent reform. Behind bars, futures wilted. Outside, the cycles turned, generation after generation, locked in a relentless loop.

Elizabeth, Delaware Labrinsky's efficient and soft-spoken assistant, flipped a page in her neatly organized binder, her voice clear with purpose. "There's a troubling, systematic pattern that's been left unaddressed for far too long. It's not just about numbers. It's about lives."

"In 1993," she continued, "the TROY initiative, Teaching and Rehabilitating Our Youth, launched in Miami-Dade County. It was part of the Alternative Outreach School program. That's where teachers first coined the term 'the revolving door' to describe how Black students were repeatedly cycled from school to court.

Teachers, primarily in public schools, would expel Black children for minor infractions, sending them straight into the juvenile system. The same pattern wasn't observed with white students."

Viola Templeton's eyes narrowed, the fire in her gaze unmistakable. She had heard the story before, but each time it stung like a fresh bruise.

"Troubling indeed, Elizabeth," she said, her voice heavy with implication. A pause hung in the air. The clinking of cutlery and murmurs of the upscale luncheon crowd offered a stark contrast to the gravity of their conversation.

Elizabeth, ever respectful, looked toward Viola before continuing.

"Teddy's concern was more than just curriculum. He feared that state-sponsored materials, designed and implemented by those groomed within flawed institutions, would continue to feed children the same hollow narratives. His vision for Eyekon was built on the belief that education, when rooted in truth and quality, could redeem generations."

"That was no accident," Viola said, sitting up straighter, her tone firm. "The design was intentional. After Reconstruction, the so-called 'shot-callers,' those in power, set in motion the educational disparities we're still wrestling with today."

"I wasn't aware of that," Liz said softly. "Where did you learn all this?"

"Teddy Hilson," Viola replied, her voice softening at his name. "He spent more than thirty years in study, research, and planning. What you see today as Eyekon started as a blueprint in his mind. Now it's an umbrella that shelters so much more. Every single part, every department, has a written guide. And yet, it remains open to evolution."

Viola turned toward Mary Palmer, her colleague and longtime ally. "Mary, please, continue with what you've found on the charter school initiatives."

Mary gave a nod, brushing a lock of hair from her cheek. Critics argue that Eyekon's mission focuses too much on race and not enough on academic achievement. They say both should be equal."

"In any event," Viola interjected, "critics will criticize regardless. Teddy's mission is clear. To save the children of the incarcerated. That need is immediate and glaring, like the Miami example you just gave."

She paused, taking a slow sip from her water glass, then set it down.

"And the areas hardest hit? Overcrowded with Black communities. That's the pool we must draw from, not by choice, but by necessity. Blacks have been the primary target of the system, not whites."

Viola's voice lowered, but lost none of its power.

"We recently marked the 61st anniversary of Brown v. Board of Education," she said. "And still, only five percent of U.S. students attend charter schools. These were supposed to be alternatives to failing public schools, but the larger picture shows that equity was never part of the plan. Slavery had barely ended when education for Black children was offered, and even then, begrudgingly."

She folded her arms.

"So frankly," she continued, "I question the notion that diversity should be our chief concern. It's arrogant to throw 'verbal bullshit' at this Union for trying to offer world-class education to the poorest, most overlooked children in America."

Viola, plump, graceful, and commanding, moved like a woman with both urgency and calm. Her yellow-toned complexion often confused others, mistaking her for Latina or even white, but there was no mistaking her conviction. She had once served as Treasurer for the New Black Panther Party alongside her partner until he was gunned down in a shootout with police. Since then, Eyekon had become her mission. And Teddy, her love, though missing, still guided every decision through the manual he'd left behind.

Viola looked at Delaware. "I believe Elizabeth has a strong point about the school-to-prison pipeline," she said. "The real picture? Eyekon is a national powerhouse. Independent. Unshackled. And you, Delaware, are here to lead that."

Delaware Labrinsky, a statuesque man with Lincoln-esque features and a Yale pedigree, met her gaze. "That is exactly what we intend to accomplish, Ms. Templeton-Viola."

"Elizabeth," Viola prompted, "please, continue."

"Yes," Elizabeth said, "As Eyekon's programs grow, what will stand out is obvious. A minority-dominated student body. Some will criticize the perceived lack of diversity.”

“That's because it's true,” Viola responded, without hesitation. “But it's not our doing. White student participation is low because many don't qualify. Black children have been denied quality education since it became legal to teach them. And sixty-five percent of our Union's members are Black, thanks to biased laws from the 'get-tough-on-crime' era of the '80s and '90s.”

Delaware chimed in, his voice calm but resolute. “As a former criminal defense attorney, I've seen more than enough injustice to know that criticism will come cloaked in political pretense and red herrings.”

Delaware had retired from law but never from service. Raised by a lineage, not unlike the Kennedys, he had always admired his father and grandfather, who served the poor faithfully after the Civil War. Delaware, now a mystic at heart, loved teaching. It was his sacred duty. For him, the mind was the final frontier.

“The mind,” he often said, “is everything.

Everything.”

He intended to show the world that brilliance, like beauty, lay in the eyes of those who dared to see.

“That is perfectly fine,” Viola said, her voice nearly melodic. “Red herrings have two heads, and unless you created the lie, you can't guide its path. Also, let me make one thing clear. Eyekon does not depend on the Biden

Administration for funding."

She stood and looked directly at Delaware.

"You, Mr. Labrinsky, are handed a blank check to do whatever is necessary to reach our goals. We want the best for our inner-city students. Make. It. Happen."

Viola snapped her laptop shut. She and Mary Palmer stood, leaving their steak and shrimp virtually untouched, and offered their goodbyes.

Delaware watched them walk across the marble-tiled floor of the high-end restaurant, graceful, composed, and relentless. He admired intelligent women, especially those with class and fire in equal measure.

Elizabeth leaned in, teasing, "A blank check is a sign of confidence, sir."

Delaware chuckled. "I've never accepted anything less than complete control over a mission."

She tilted her head. "You seemed rather pleased with Ms. Templeton. Do you think she's ready to meet God face to face?"

Delaware smiled, then turned contemplative.

"You're right about my admiration," he said. "But as for seeing God... few are ready to handle that truth directly. They must be led to it, circumventingly."

He placed a hand over the leather-bound folder Viola had left. "But that, my dear, is our private agenda. To shepherd the lost sheep. To explore the infinite possibilities of divinity through the universal mind.

He paid the bill, collected the folder, and together they stepped out into the sunlight, leaving behind their untouched plates, but carrying with them the weight and wonder of a revolution in education.

Chapter 43

Through the Green Eyes

She opened the latch affixed to the thick wooden door and peered inside the house-cell. The door led to a small cave-like room, a grotto. A hidden place that does not appear on the registered blueprint of the late 19th-century mansion.

During the Cold War era between America and Russia, the large stately house was primarily used for the safekeeping of Russian nationals, who had been KGB trained, then smuggled into America from Cuba for the sole purpose of embarking upon an espionage escapade.

The property continues to be owned by a Russian oligarch, although the official deed holder reflects an American as the homeowner.

"Are you hungry?" she asked through the opening.

"Certainly. I have been, since last seeing you… especially."

For a good moment, the lissome young woman held the captive's gaze. The attempted intimate advance did not go unnoticed.

"I am not here to be friendly," she said with a barely noticeable accent.

"Nor am I your friend; I will kill you without the slightest hesitation-okay."

Wow! Teddy thought. He actually felt the genuine conviction of this beautiful creature. He had also observed a flicker in her flame. No doubt, this young woman was a killer in the coldest degree. However, it is a given that every human has a weakness, no matter their overall strengths. Teddy had espied a fleeting stirring of emotions... in her eyes. His own confidence began to soar. If memory serves him right, he had been held against his will for nearly a month. One thing was promising: if this humdrum was to come to an end, it must be by, through, or with Ms. Green's eyes!

The look-in latch closed, and shortly thereafter, the huge door opened. Even with the big door ajar, it was impossible to get to her. The specially built enclosure, extending some 10 feet or so from the door, allowed one to enter the secret room-cell without fear of being over taken by a detainee.

"And if I am left with no choice, I will kill your pretty little ass just the same, Ms. Green eyes," Teddy said to her as she entered the opening.

"You ask if I was hungry. That other watchdog only fed me awful-tasting black bread and water."

She placed the picnic basket down and turned to leave, then looked back over her shoulder, saying:

"Now that we understand each other, don't take it personally. Eat and zip it."

When the heavy door thudded closed, a small section along the enclosure parted, allowing access to the food.

Natasha Gruskin was the only child of a man who had wanted a son. Her father loved their country fervently. Feodor had devoted his entire life to the service of Russia. At one point in history, the only thing in the way of Russia's world dominance was America, the United States. Feodor's uncle, Nikita Khrushchev, had gained power after the 1953 death of Joseph Stalin.

Under Khrushchev, the open antagonism of the Poles and Hungarians toward Moscow's domination was suppressed in 1956. He also aided the Cuban revolution, supporting Fidel Castro, but withdrew soviet missiles from Cuba during a confrontation with U.S. President John Fitzgerald Kennedy, September-October 1962. Khrushchev was deposed, October 1964 and replaced by Leonid I. Brezhnev.

However, in 1985, Michael Gorbachev was chosen as the Communist Party General Secretary, and all hell broke loose. By December 1991, after nearly 74 years of communist party domination, on August 29, 1991, the soviet parliament voted to suspend all activities of the communist party. The Soviet Union officially broke up on December 26, 1991.

Three days later, that same year, Natasha was born. Feodor was an exceptional expert in many fields of highly skilled crafts, which led to his being stationed in America. By the time his daughter was 10 years old, the new Russian leader, President Vladimir Putin, eliminated the assignment abroad and ordered Feodor back to Russia. The move by the new leader was not only unexpected, but it was also rumored to be based on suspicious grounds.

Putin did not trust old man Feodor, although in different generations, they both had come up through the ranks of the notorious KGB, that maybe the master spy and recruiter had become a renegade-breached. For a Russian agent, such a designation equated to a forced retirement.

Oftentimes, within five years following this type of dismissal, death was sure to be imminent. Over the ensuing several years, Feodor taught Natasha most of the tricks associated with such dangerous engagements, everything he knew. She had become a very capable and deadly assassin. Feodor won approval to send Natasha back States to serve the Motherland, Russia.

It was only by chance that the skilled killer was called on to serve as an alternative sentry, keeping watch over this black man. She was not told why she wasn't called in to simply kill him; something about needing the captive to agree to a few specifics first.

*   *   *

He saw it! Exactly what he saw is not easily explained in words. But something just happened between those two. Just for the briefest moment, Natasha's guards completely dropped. This equates to an inability to carry out the dire responsibilities of the assignment at hand. Such weakness must not go unreported. Immediately.

Chapter 44

The Blueprint for Justice and Redemption

"Hello. My name is Viola Templeton, and I am trying to reach Detective Bandy Welks."

"Speaking, ma'am."

"Good, thank you. I am calling seeking information, if any, on the status of your investigation concerning Mr. Teddy Hilson and Erika Casselberry. It has been right at a month since their disappearance."

"Ms Templeton, the Union's Attorney, has been receiving weekly updates on what information we can give without jeopardizing the investigation."

"I know, Mr. Welks, attorney Terry advised me that you thought you may have a promising tip. I am simply out of my wits. Teddy was trying to do so many positive things for our city, State, and entire Country. And, I miss them dearly.

"We understand. As a matter of fact, that's true. We are very hopeful that the tip could be a game-changer in our search. I am not at liberty to go into any details; however, we believe that Mr. Hilson and the young lady are both alive. From what we have gathered, a dead Mr. Hilson runs counter to the real goal of his captors. The moment we can give more information will more than likely be when we locate and rescue your loved ones, Ms. Templeton."

"Thank you very much, Detective. Please keep us in

the loop, Mr. Welks."

"We'll do, Ma'am."

Detective Welks concluded before resting the phone in its holder.

Viola, we can't continue sitting and waiting for the cops to find and bring Teddy back to us. Tomorrow will be a full month since Erika and he went missing.

"I know Mary. Has anybody heard from Trey?"

"No, not since last week. He came to Headquarters to review the file on Vincente Antollini."

"Okay. Eyekon's mission must be pursued at all costs; in accordance with Teddy's directions, we, as a collective force, can bring change. Change in our community, our City, State, and our Nation, to echo our Teddy," Viola said.

"Alright," Mary starts with a tone of business:" the million-member milestone had to be drastically reduced. Many of the new associates did not, or could not, measure up to membership rules, which are strictly enforced and must be adhered to. Teddy made it clear that the Union will never be viewed as a supporter of, or safe haven for, criminal conduct. Nor, for those committing them, if Eyekon is to succeed. Our Law 5 prohibits any new member from having been arrested (for criminal conduct) within three years after conviction, probationary sentence, or release from prison/jail following a conviction. The Union is not a supporter of lawlessness. Instead, we are a movement offering guidance, support, and inspiration to those of us who have been tripped up by the system and who sincerely wish to become productive members of society. Some will be allowed to rejoin Viola if they can demonstrate the Union's standards."

"How many have we lost, Mary?"

"At least a quarter of our total."

"Thank you, honey. If you will, Mary, please put all board members on notice that there will be a noon-time conference scheduled for tomorrow, and all are requested to attend."

"Got it," Mary responds as she leaves for her own office.

*   *   *

"A recent article, in Time's magazine, by Reuben Jonathan Miller, titled: 'The Call That I always have to answer,' is a story about one brother trying to be there for the other brother who is locked up in the American prison system. I want to quote a small portion of his article:'… upon release (from prison), people with criminal records are greeted by over 45.000 policies that dictate where they may go, with whom they may live, and how they may spend their time… these collateral consequences prevent these people from fully participating in the labor and housing markets.

There are 19,419 employment restrictions that keep people with criminal records out of the workplace; 1,033 housing restrictions that prevent them from being able to rent an apartment; 3,954 restrictions that limit their civic participation; and 1,612 that constrain their family and domestic rights, which means they may not be able to hold most public offices. They may not be able to sit on juries; there are hundreds of categories of employment for which they need not apply... they may not be able to rent an apartment and will struggle to find a place to stay. In most states, they may not vote.

There are so few places where formally incarcerated people can turn in their time of need...' end quote.

People, we have both our hands filled with tackling the real issues, which expose the elusive evil known as systemic racism and basic human rights. Just because a person commits a crime does not, and should not, mean that person should also lose their basic human rights, as guaranteed by the United States Constitution. This is especially so if the system releases a person back into society after serving their time.

Eyekon is a Union comprising two major functions, the aim of which also has sub-functioning categories: We are a labor union, which is not exclusively limited to, but primarily focuses on, people who have previously been convicted of a felony. Thereby, forming a bargaining power as a recognized group and improving the security of its members through employment, decent housing, education, restoration of voting rights, and other necessary protections. Eyekon differs from your traditional unions, where their concerns focus on limited areas of job security, unsafe working conditions, unfair wages, women's rights, equal pay, child labor, and a few others. Eyekon will also embrace some of those areas on a limited basis, allowing our members to have the option of also joining the established unions of old.

However, most importantly, seek to have our members admitted into a wider spectrum of the workforce without regard to having a felony conviction hanging over their heads.

None of the many unions out there now addresses the issues we have, and they will not. As a felon, we are less than a second-class citizen, which was exactly the intent of President Andrew Johnson's 13th Amendment, helping to rebirth slavery by another name.

More importantly, the elephant standing before the entire Nation, and the clear, but ignored, connection to then and now, is our Nation's original sin. Namely, slavery, and its post-Emancipation manifestations; segregation and oppression of Black Americans, in virtually all aspects of their lives. Said differently, slavery, the so-called Emancipation Proclamation, was withdrawn by John Wilkes Booth, and he died with President Lincoln on April 15, 1865.

The subsequent Black Codes, which predate Jim Crow laws, generally refer to laws enacted immediately after the end of the Civil War and during the period of Presidential Reconstruction by Southern States to 'replace slavery with some kind of caste system, to preserve as much as possible of the prewar way of life. (As Eric Foner observed), The "centerpiece" of the Black Codes was the attempt to stabilize the black workforce and limit its economic options apart from plantation labor. Henceforth, the state would enforce labor agreements and plantation discipline, punish those free blacks who refused to contract (with plantation owners), and prevent whites from competing among themselves for black workers (by, e.g., offering higher wages and better working conditions).

In other words, the Black Codes and subsequent Jim Crow laws (which were first enacted in Tennessee in 1875) have a strong connection and residual influence foreshadowing most of the laws, statutes, codes, ordinances, and rules governing America's society on the books today.

When one hears the words systemic racism, many people have no clue about the true implications of them. The first word, systemic (…being, forming, or formulated as a system; systematized). An action or actions common to a system. The second word, racism (Assumption of inherent superiority…and consequent discrimination, against other races; also, any doctrine or program of racial domination based on such assumption).

Now, when you combine the two, a portrait should enter your mind, allowing a better, more vivid understanding of what is really implied by the term systemic racism.

Alright, before we allow any questions," Viola cautions. "I want to introduce Mr. Delaware Labrinsky, who will serve as the chancellor of our educational arm. He is also an attorney who will now offer more insight on the trove of research material Teddy has left to guide the progress of

Eyekon. Delaware, please,"

"Here, let me connect the dots on the then and now of yesteryears' heavy influence on the state of affairs here in America today. A part of the curriculum that will be mandatory at each of the three levels we will teach, coined as CRT (Critical Race Theory). It is my position that, to understand something, anything, that thing must be broken done to where it first started. Picture this: the strongest part of a mortar, the mixture used for joining bricks or stones, that then becomes huge buildings, is tiny grains of sand. Without that tiny grain of sand, you could not build this building we are all in at the moment.

All things, if they are truly being understood, must be done by finding their origin. Then, and only then, does the chance to change it rear its pretty head.

The Civil War was the deadliest conflict in American History. More than 620.000 persons died in the struggle to restore the Union and eradicate the evil institution of slavery. Sadly, the sacrifices of blood by the hallowed dead produced few beneficial effects in the lives of the emancipated slaves... the 'prize of freedom was effectively denied by the enactment of the Black Codes,' whose intent was the continued subordination of the newly freed slave, of January 1, 1863.

Indeed, the lives of an overwhelming number of Blacks, men, women, and children, for most of the century following the end of the Civil War. Continued to be one of drudgery, illiteracy, and few(or no) educational opportunities. Poor nutrition, bad health, high infant mortality rates, short life expectancies, for those who survived infancy, oppressive discrimination, brutal violence, and lynching (mob murder unsanctioned by state law)

During the nine decades between the 1874 election(between Ulysses Grant and   )cycle(when "conservative Democrats" redeemed controlled of state government from the radical Republicans label of carpet baggers, a Northerner who went to the South after the Civil War to make money by taking advantage of unsettled conditions or by political corruption-scalawags- a white Southerner who, during Reconstruction period (and being a Democrat) acted as a Republican; (to Democrats, the scalawag was even more detestable than the hated carpet baggers), and the Civil Rights Act of 1964 (thus from 1874 to 1964, you have nine election cycles).

It was during this period that Alabama (the leading pro white state in the nation) became a state whose institutions (the systems governing its people) were, frankly, admittedly, unashamedly, and triumphantly dominated by whites.

The theory found daily expressions and constant application. A Caucasian dominance became legally fixed and formalized (as it did), Anglo-Saxon superiority was no less manifest in unstated ways. If a white man and a black man met face to face on a narrow walk, the law said the black had to step aside to let the other pass; a white man's surname was always prefixed with "Mister" or some sort of title. A Negro, never. The Negro did not achieve economic independence.

In a society where the accumulation of money bore an integral relation to the possession of power, the Negro's never. White superiority was no less evident in verbal folklore spawned by, repeated by, and believed by whites: Negro men were naturally lazy.

The emancipation of the African American as property was accomplished at the conclusion of the Civil War with the ratification of the 13th Amendment to the United States Constitution," (…abolishing slavery or involuntary servitude), so it was supposed to be (in December 1865, one month shy of three years following Lincoln's January 1, 1863, emancipation proclamation).

Moving right along. Earlier, I was explaining that at the very beginning of the civil war and the primary basis for it, the South's dispute was that they had the right to keep black folks enslaved, and I said I would tell you the why (why it was so important to the South); here, let us connect some more dots."

In 1903, for a period of nearly 80 years, between the Civil War and World War 2, Black Southerners were no longer slaves, but they were not yet free. In one of the most shameful and little-known chapters in American history, generations of black people were forced to labor against their will.

From almost the first moment, white southerners were responding to try and put blacks back into a position as close to slavery as they possibly could. The old South, which was becoming the new South, could not proceed without the work of African Americans. Their position was, if you had something for free, you damn sure don't want to pay for it now. What happened during that period of time was more terrible than most Americans recognize or understand today. It was a straight exploitation system.

There was only power, force, and brutality. Freedom (for Blacks) had come at a tremendous cost; the war devastated the Southern economy, which, by the way, had supported one of the wealthiest aristocracies (any government in which power is exercised by a small class-the class of people regarded as superior in rank or wealth) in the world-not just America, but the entire worlds (remember this was 1861-ish)

In every southern state, you become a criminal if you cannot prove at any given moment that you were employed. Here is where the dots of then and the dots of now connect with eye-opening awe: Under slavery, most black crime was punished by slave holders, leaving the courts to discipline whites (this is why it appears today that most whites who come before a judge get some kind of leniency, where the key gets thrown away on black defendants).

Consequently, these same states begin to charge fees for prisoners (mostly black prisoners) to companies by the month. NOTE: When you go to the 13th Amendment, one of the troubling things about the text is that it says slavery is abolished except as a punishment for a crime. And within that wiggle room, what you see in it is that slavery is being extended beyond Lincoln's January 1, 1863, Emancipation

Proclamation, freeing the slaves, as it were, by another name."

"Delaware," Viola cut in as the lawyer was taking a sip of water, "I see you have captivated us all with your eloquent delivery of this invaluable information and history, but we must continue next Friday as you've agreed. The day is coming to an end, and we all must get ready to call it a day."

"Sure, Mrs. Templeton, you must have read my mind. Ladies and gentlemen, we will resume where we left off next week. Please save any questions until after next edition," Delaware Labrinsky concluded.

"Thank you so much, Del, for sharing such powerful information on the history; the department confronting black Americans, seemingly at every turn, has begun to have its roots exposed.

Members of the Board, thank you for your attendance and attentiveness. Mary, give us an overview of the status of Eyekon's affairs, starting with our efforts to buy back local neighborhood businesses.

"Statewide, we have been successful on only five occasions over the previous month; one for each of the cities we have branch chapters in."

"Oh-is that so. I didn't know another affiliate had opened. We were in Ft Myers, Sandford, Tampa, Fort Lauderdale, and where?"

"You were away day before yesterday on matters

concerning Teddy," Mary said, "but we're now also being represented in Orlando. We are on track to retake three local gas stations, a cleaners, and a small grocery store, which will provide 10 to 30 jobs," Mary offers proudly.

"Not bad. However, we have got to do better," Viola responds without sounding condescending.

"The more our neighborhoods begin to see us serving them in their neighborhood businesses and stores, Teddy said the easier it becomes to unloosen the psychologically false, misconceived inferior complex syndrome, laid down over five hundred years ago.

He also said that these seemingly unimportant fixtures in society are quite mighty and serve as super glue, keeping blacks mentally accepting and believing that all our needs can only be provided by Master Charlie. This, in turn, makes it almost impossible for these black folks to realize their own unlimited potential.

Systematic racism is simply a by-product of racism (…an assumption of inherent racial superiority or purity of certain races), which ideology drove and continues to drive the core structure of each essential rule of custom, or institution, of the American way of life.

When black kids see ten businesses and owners in their neighborhoods, and they are all white, or a race different than Black, but primarily patronized by blacks, this reality psychologically becomes fertilizer and glue. Which psychologically binds these folks to accept this system, as though it's the only way it's supposed to be.

There is an old saying that they have taken the chains off our wrists and ankles and now put the chains on our minds. It is not enough, Teddy said, that we only free our bodies, we must also free our minds. Much of this programming is readily apparent and right in our faces, getting our attention and pleading for us to address them.

However, much of this programming is not so recognizable. Most are subtle. It is not enough people who confront the system; without also taking on the programmed condition of black people's mental characteristics and attitudes, we're doing nothing. You see, we unknowingly recreate those oppressive systems of society by continuing to look for ways leading to those particular outcomes from which they were programmed.

Just as whites, most white Americans have been reared, bred, and taught to feel and believe that they are superior; the opposite is just as true for blacks, which is a structural component of the system. And this is not a racial dispositional point of view. It is factual.

Yes, Mary, we must do more to take over or build up more black owned businesses in our neighborhoods. Try enlisting community activists, local clergymen, and other effective members of these neighborhoods to join in pooling together resources, financially or otherwise, to make it happen."

"Looks like Teddy really thought this Union through. I see you keep glancing down at the "Blueprint,' Eyekon's Direction Manual," Mary responds.

"That's quite correct. Teddy really wanted to make a difference in not only the lives of Black people but in the lives of all Americans. The man just may be way ahead of his time, that's for sure."

"Is there any real progress on locating him and Erika?" Mary asked Viola.

"We don't know just yet, honey. But his instructions are that, with or without him, Eyekon's mission must go on.

How many inmates were released from the Department of Corrections over the previous 30 days?" Viola inquires, deftly changing the subject from Teddy. God knows she was worried out of my mind, not knowing even if Teddy and Erika are even alive.

"One hundred fifteen statewide; 45 of which cannot qualify to become members," Mary said.

"Of the remaining seventy, only 22 have obtained their GED while incarcerated, and as such, they qualify for temporary housing if they do not have family or friends upon release. The remaining forty-eight will be allowed to sign up for membership on their 180th day of being released, and those who continue to demonstrate an ability to hold down the job we helped to secure.

Also, the insurance arm of Eyekon reimbursed $15,000 dollars damage costs, associated with a business worker, an Eyekon member, over a forklift accident."

"Okay. Fine, Mary, thank you. I apologize for holding those of you up who probably had other engagements, but there are still areas we have not covered, and it is very necessary that you all familiarize yourselves with them so that we all are able to function where and when needed. We will pick up where we left off next week. Mary put someone on finding out more information on those 45,000 policies that dictate where ex-prisoners may go, whom they may live with, and how they must spend their time. We must learn the origin and, more importantly, who were the sponsors of those Bills that became law. I have a feeling we may stumble upon some interesting things."

"I will get right on it," Mary replied.

"Did you want to add something, Mr. Labrinsky?"

"Yes, thank you, Ms. Viola. I want everyone to know that we have purchased several buildings. Well, actually, we bought the land that has a few buildings, and an auditorium intact. The property is now being renovated to occupy our first charter school under Eyekon's umbrella. We hope to open our doors, admitting students, in 4 to 6 weeks."

Everyone chinned in with clapping.

Chapter 45

The Grotto of Betrayals

On the other side of the cave-like recess, Natasha repeated the same thing she did with Teddy, placing a basket of food in the secret room. The two cell-like rooms are essentially one, divided by a four-foot concrete slab. They are identical.

"Excuse me! Hey-you! Hold on," Erika yelled before the thick door closed completely.

"What's going on here, and where is my man?!"

Natasha turned and faced her through the specially built enclosure, coldly staring across the house-cell at Erika. Without answering, Natasha slowly turned to leave…

"Bitch, I am talking to you! Don't you just ignore me? Where the fuck is my man?"

Natasha stopped. A smile was forming on her face. She looked back at Erika and said:

"If I was under a different agenda, I would teach you some manners. I did not bring you or your man here. I would gladly kill you both if it was up to me. Your man is just as safely kept as you are… for now. He is closer to you than you know," she said as she left the grotto.

*   *   *

Natasha was completely unprepared for what

happened next:

"Put your hands on top of your head-NOW! 'Tasha, this is not a game," Peter said sternly.

"I just received orders to place you under detainment for breach of duty abroad."

Natasha knew that this was a very serious accusation, especially having it delivered to her by the relief watchman. The situation usually called for an instant, on-the-spot death. The fact that Peter did not kill her, per the rogue manual, told her that the formal decision, whether or not she should die, was forthcoming, usually, within 24 hours. Ordinarily, once an order has been issued to detain, death was all but certain. Natasha was left with two options: take the cyanide capsule that all abroad are required to keep at the ready,-death before dishonor- or fight, no matter the odds.

"Has my father been harmed?" she asked Peter in a barely audible, but cold tone. Peter took several steps back.

Without answering her, he pointed the weapon at the door to the cell holding Teddy, indicating for Natasha to go in that direction.

"Keep your traitorous hands on your goddamn head. Move them again, and I will put a bullet in it- same as your dead father! Since you seem so fond of Mr. Blacky, you may now join him... for the next 22 hours," Peter said after quickly glancing at his watch.

"Did the same people who killed my father also give the order to detain me?"

Ignoring the question, Peter began to speak in a firmer tone.

"Step on the mat, open the fucking door, and get inside!" When Natasha turned her back to comply, Peter hurried and closed the distance between them, bringing his gun down hard on the back of her head. She hit the floor, nearly unconscious.

Prior to pushing Natasha into the enclosure, Peter removed the Beretta and twin daggers from her listless body.

Inside the grotto, Teddy observed from the far side of the house cell, as his guard from earlier was now being ushered into the confinement with him. Blood was spewing from an ugly gash just above her left temple. Teddy rushed to her as soon as the heavy door thudded closed.

"Easy-easy, Green eyes," Teddy gently spoke. Blood appears to be coming from two different areas.

Natasha pushed away from Teddy, attempting to stand, only to collapse, passing completely out.

Teddy's mind was reeling, attempting to make sense out of the chaos rapidly unfolding before him. Now, how in the hell will he get out of here?

Chapter 46

No Way Back

The M-249 Squad Automatic Weapon (SAW) sat on the passenger seat of the rental car, fully loaded with three 200-round belts, holding 5.56mm bullets. There was also an M-203 grenade launcher. All of which can be fired from a rifle.

The accessories also included a night vision scope and a laser sight. Trey checked and rechecked his mini arsenal before loading them in the carry-on small duffle bag. He pulled in the driveway of a house with a for-sale sign in the yard, several blocks away from the Hatchet's Estate. The walking distance was less than 10 minutes. As the big place came into view, Trey caught sight of a small caravan of heavy sedans pulling off the highway, going in the same direction as the estate. The vehicles were all foreign… possibly Russian.

Dusk was quickly approaching, bringing the ex-Navy S.E.A.L. some added layers of obscurity as he darted through the open gate not far behind the end car. Immediately to the right was a small gatehouse. Upon entering the large electric fence, Trey darted to an area just behind an attendance shed. No one was attending it. He looked on as the cars parked near a garage and four men exited each car. At this point, the odds read 12 totals, and this does not take into account who or what the count may be inside. One thing is for sure, something is going on here.

Before the men could enter the house, someone rushed out from a side entrance, looked the group over until resting his sights on a short, stout man, standing out in front. The two spoke, and the fat guy turned and said something in a foreign language, and three of the group went back to the vehicles while the others followed the house guy back inside the mansion.

Here was a chance to minimize the odds, Trey thought. What if Teddy and Erika are not here? No. He decided to wait to be sure that they were indeed inside the house.

Two of the goons waited at the trunk of the sedan while the other one opened the glove compartment by pressing the trunk release button. One of the men reached in and came out with a twin set of AK-47s, several smaller firearms, and a fold-over pouch.

Upon seeing the hardware, Trey quickly changed his mind and decided to act. He withdrew the steel-plated mini-Billy club and came up behind the man holding the weapons, crashing the baton on top of his head. The guy dropped like gravity had snatched him to the ground. Before the other one could react, Trey aimed the M249 at his face and motioned for the man to stay quiet.

The guy who opened the glove compartment was totally unprepared for what he returned to at the trunk. Instantly, he reached for the weapon dangling from a shoulder holster; that was the last act of his life. Trey squeezed the trigger, and the M249 sent a burst of hot lead, ripping apart his upper torso. During the quick exchange, the other goon holding the AK-47 was attempting to raise one of the weapons in Trey's direction. His efforts came up short: he, too, was cut in half with the SAW gun. However, the man did manage to pull the trigger, bringing a loud, tremendous boom to the quiet evening.

*   *   *

The sound of gunfire seemed to bring Green Eyes fully conscious and alert. She held Teddy's lingering look for a moment before nodding slightly with just a hint of a smile.

"That was a Russian firearm, I heard. How long have I been in here?"

"A little over an hour," Teddy replied.

"What the hell are you doing in here?"

"Keeping you company," she said with a touch of sarcasm.

"Come on, we don't have much time; they're here."

We did not escape Teddy's understanding, nor did the urgency in her tone.

"Listen, she said as she sprung to action, I have been accused of betraying my duty and joining your side. Not to mention that such an accusation also carry the maximum penalty of death. However, I am not an easy kill, and those who made the decision to terminate me are aware."

308

Green Eyes went to the sink, unscrewed the hot water knob, before carrying it to a light switch, or the area with the light switch covered by a plastic ornament resembling a Russian trinket winking an eye.

She inserted the squared bottom end of the knob into the winking eye of the ornament and turned it counterclockwise. Instantly, the special enclosure confining them and the huge door opened simultaneously.

Natasha had studied the Blueprint of the stately house and knew it well. Peter, on the other hand, maybe did not have. Otherwise, he would know what she knew about escaping the grotto, if ever trapped inside. Each sentry was provided with the mansion's prototype. Chances are, if Peter was not aware of how to escape the house cells, he also did not know about the under house tunnel leading to the garage. But first, Green Eyes and Teddy had to make it to the master bedroom's bathroom.

"Okay, listen: as soon as you exit that door, take a right and follow the wall, and it will lead you to the other side of this room. That's where your lady friend is being kept. Step on the left side of the floor mat, and the door will open. Get her and wait at the door for me."

"Where are you going?" Teddy asked,

"To find some weapons; without them, we may not stand a chance. The people they sent are well-trained and very professional killers.

At the sound of gunshots, the men who had entered through the side entrance froze in place. Each reached for their guns. All but the leader and houseman headed back to the parking garage. The first one to exit the door observed his comrades lying on the pavement, dead. He said something to the others, then that one immediately dove to the right side of the doorway as he rushed out; two more repeated the same move on the opposite side of the door. Trey was at the ready. So, he thought. When he fired the SAW at the First guy, the others returned shots in his direction. He felt a searing pain in his left shoulder; the damage was minimal. If he wanted to keep it that way, Trey had better remember his training during hell week, CQB (close quarter battle).

The advantage Trey had been intending on remaining inanimate, not moving at all. Their tactic was to cause indecision on his behalf, where, in most cases, with an untrained person, anyone in the area of the garage would move and expose their location. Trey waited for them to make their next move. From his advantageous point, he had the drop on the first set but hesitated on making the kill shot until he was sure of the exact location of the second pair.

Exactly at the moment he took aim and decided to shoot, a small glimmer of light appeared from an area of the wall, in the area of the garage. A slender female exited the door carrying a twin set of handguns. Moments after she had stepped out and closed the door, gunfire erupted. She hit the ground rolling.

Trey decided that, if they both had the same enemies,

then helping her should come without any shillyshallying. With their bodies fully exposed, the two who were adamant about killing the girl, Trey gave them the business: shooting and killing them both. The girl, who was wedged between a windowsill and a large AC unit, witnessed the two Russians die. Then she saw Trey.

For a moment, neither moved. The second pair of killers rounded the house, and Trey and the female each took one out. Natasha did not know who the bald black man was, but she did know he had saved her life. For Trey, her action of taking out one of the rough necks was convincing enough to say he had found an uncommon ally. The female, who, by the looks of things, was a damn good shooter. She re-entered the door she came out of, her mind was on the safety of the other black man.

Inside, Teddy found Erika, and they were leaving the companion house cell when they met Peter and a short, stout man. Neither knew the layout of the mansion, but that didn't stop Teddy from grabbing Erika's arm and running towards a wide door not far from where they were. The other two men followed suit.

"No! Don't shoot him- our orders are to keep him alive-for now," said the man with Peter.

Teddy heard the exchange. This added momentum to his effort to escape whatever intentions these people had in mind. After entering the wide doors, clearly visible, were several additional doors. This was not the moment for searching or playing musical chairs. The first door opened

311

with ease, and he and Erika entered. It was some kind of break, the restroom-then he saw the monitors. This area is where the watchmen would observe the detainees on the monitor's screen. Teddy could clearly see the house prison cell he and Green Eyes had just broken free from. The monitor screen is split; he also observed the other place where Erika was held.

"Guns!" Erika shouted half. "Guns are over there," she said, pointing behind Teddy. Teddy selected an old-style Uzi machine gun, while Erika opted for a smaller handgun resembling a Beretta. All the weapons were loaded.

Peter was aware that the room had many guns and said as much to the fat man with him. In his haste to meet up with and impress the ranking big man, Peter had neglected to secure the room.

"Houston-we have a problem, as the Americans would say," Peter commented.

"No, you have a problem." The fat man said to Peter.

"You are an idiot!" He shot Peter, leaving a gaping hole in his forehead.

Natasha was about to round the corner when she heard the loud boom. She crouched down and, with extreme caution, inched her way to the edge of the corner. Around the corner, the man who shot Peter was doing the exact same maneuver: it is the standard danger approach move, which is taught in most counter-tactical maneuver classes.

The man knew the layout of the mansion; he had

lived here many times in the early days of his service to Mother Russia. He didn't need to follow them, as their direction of travel would lead to only two possible locations. The garage or the back of the house.

The big man dove in a wide angle around the corner, catching Natasha by surprise, and quickly gained the upper hand on her.

"Drop the fucking gun!" he said menacingly in Russian dialogue. Natasha immediately recognized Viktor. For him to be here meant that this situation with the black man was bigger than previously. It also spelled dire trouble for her. She would rather activate the deadly poison of the cyanide capsule than go through the torture that is sure to come at the hands of Viktor.

Trey did not follow Natasha, instead, he went the way the would-be killers came from. He was still unsure whether Teddy and Erika were present. However, he decided to proceed due to his curiosity.

Upon entering the garage entrance, Trey too heard a loud gunshot. At the ready, Trey moved deeper into the space of the garage. While there were no cars present, the garage easily could house four or five big vehicles. Flowers and other ornaments were spread all over the spacious area. This describes the lifestyle of affluent and influential individuals.

In the far corner was an open door; keeping close to the wall, Trey moved towards it. He was within ten feet of the door when Teddy and Erika burst through in a crouching position with guns at the ready.

"Teddy!" Trey shouted. "What the fuck, man…" with his trademark smile, slightly tilting his head to one side, he answered:

"Well, I'll be a monkey's uncle. Trey," Teddy exclaimed with a mixture of perplexity and appreciation.

We will discuss pleasantries later. At this moment, we need to be prepared, as these competitors are serious.

"Hell, we can get the fuck away from here right now. I came for the two of you. So, let's get somewhere," Trey said.

"Believe me," Teddy started, "there is nothing more that I'd like to do, but I must go back in and get Green Eyes, she is responsible for Erika and my breaking free. If she is left, especially now that I have escaped, she will surely be killed."

"I saw her," Trey offered. "She went back in the house through a side entrance right outside the garage.

"Take Erika and go to safety," Teddy said to his friend as he turned to reenter the mansion.

"No," Erika and Trey said together.

"We-I," Trey began," did not come all the way out here, being shot at, risked my life and to rescue you, just to tuck a tail and run. It isn't happening, partner. Besides, she, Green Eyes, as you call her, has already put me in her debt also: she saved my life," he said, pointing to the dead men sprawling across the manicured lawn."

"And Tish gave her life for you, so will I," said Erika.

Teddy flashed them that smile and bid them to follow as he entered the house.

A metallic sound coming from behind them caused the trio to spin in one fluid motion, firing at the lone goon Trey had hit over the head with the Billy club. The goon had regained consciousness and was attempting to collect and fire his weapon. But somehow, he dropped the gun. The mistake cost him his life.

Teddy and Erika crept down the foyer they had just been in a few moments ago. Trey, who wasn't too happy with this major slip-up moments ago, by leaving one of the henchmen in a position to do damage, wanted to make sure this time that they were safe. If the goon had not dropped his gun, Erika, Teddy, or he would be alive. He waited to ensure no one was behind them.

His instincts were honored, and Trey hit pay dirt: he saw two more men enter the garage door shortly thereafter. Two more were right on their heels. This brought the count to four more killers. Guns were in each of the hands. Trey stepped out from behind a piece of furniture, letting the SAW weapon do its thing. Not one shot was fired among the quadruple.

Inside, one of the adjoining rooms, Viktor had stripped Natasha bare from the waist up. Her hands were bound around a cylinder taken from one of the swirling barstools. A pair of water was sitting next to her feet. An electrical cord with one end peeled to reveal raw wires with a small piece of sponge separating the two ends, the other end was plugged into the wall outlet. Although Viktor trusted that his men had captured or killed the Black union guy, he wasted no time in quickly setting up his torture bench. He needed to know why, and Natasha was compromised.

Viktor was unaware that all eleven of his men had perished, and that he was now on his own.

"Your father died in great strength, he refused to beg for his life. Will you, my little stub?" Viktor said with blandness. He carried on like what he was about to do was as normal as drinking a glass of water. The cyanide capsule was still in her mouth, and she would endure as much of what was coming as she possibly could, then she'd bite the poison and end it all. Even as the reality of her predicament became vividly clean, the words of her dead father echoed down the corridors of her mind: …never give up on believing that, chances will always reveal itself to the one who would believe strongly enough. Doubt was trying to do its thing and crumble her resolve. Viktor was now heading her way.

"Well, Natasha, why did you turn and join that captive?"

"Peter lied", she responded." I was doing my job until learning that my death warrant was signed with that lie. You will be wasting your time torturing me because there is simply nothing else to tell you," she said matter-of-factly.

Viktor was very good at interrogating people; in fact, he was considered the best. He knew she was telling the truth. However, she could not be left to live, and set out on a journey of revenge on him for killing her father.

Natasha was far too dangerous. She is, by far, one of the deadliest assassins created from the elite program in a long time. Viktor chose to personally come stateside because to allow Natasha to live meant he would forever be looking over his shoulder. He went to the table to fetch his gun; he decided against torturing her and instead would simply kill her. Viktor did not make it to his weapon: Teddy rushed through the open door.

"I wouldn't do that if I was you, Fatso," Teddy said. "Leave the gun where it is and live. I do not wish to kill you."

Erika was only a few feet behind Teddy, with her own weapon pointed at Viktor as well.

Viktor had never before found himself defeated on foreign soil, nor had he ever experienced a helpless feeling like the one now. A slow sigh of relief crept into his mind as he thought: any moment now, his men would burst through that door, cutting these black bastards down in any hell of bullets.

"Listen, just give me the girl and I will leave you be. It's as simple as that." Teddy said.

Trey entered the room, looked at Teddy, and said: "I saw three vehicles arrive less than an hour ago. Four people got out of each car; out of the twelve, eleven of them are no

317

longer amongst the living. That one," he said, pointing at Viktor, "is the twelfth one. Plus, when they all first arrived, the man I saw run out to speak with that one, I came across him dead down the hall there."

Hearing this, Viktor knew he was neck high in deep shit

"Take her," Viktor said with a smile. He had a plan forming in his mind. He just needed to buy a little time to execute it.

"Trey," Teddy began," get that gun over behind fat boy, and Erika, keep the sucka covered."

Teddy untied Natasha and tried to hand her the torn blouse. Teddy had set the Uzi down to untie Natasha. Instead of accepting her shirt, Natasha snatched up the machine pistol, walked in Viktor's direction, firing the gun, sending too many bullets to count, into his body until the weapon would fire no more.

Teddy made no effort to contain her. The two had bonded in a way that the word mysterious, fails to describe. Erika and Trey immediately bore their own guns down on Natasha, but Teddy waved them down. He walked over to Natasha and saw the tears forming in the wells of her beautiful green eyes, and all he could do was open his arms, gently wrapping them around Natasha as she cried. Her sobbing was that deep, breath struggling sniveling.

"Teddy," Trey cut in, "brother, we have got to depart from these premises. It's enough death here to put us away for a very long time."

"Green Eyes, baby, you've got to pull yourself together. We are getting the hell away from here. What about you? Is there anywhere we can take you?"

Natasha gently shook her head in negative. Then she said, "I have nowhere to go. My life in Russia died with my father. I was trained to be a killer, nothing else. I no longer have a home or a family."

"Bullshit! I am alive because of you. I will accept you as my family if you want a home where you will be welcomed."

Natasha did not verbally answer. However, both of her arms wound tightly around Teddy's waist.

"Erika, come take Green Eyes' hand. She is now your sister. Lead the way. Trey, let's get the fuck out of here."

"Hold on," Natasha said. She went and opened one of the other two doors. Inside were several reels used to record all that occurs in many areas of the mansion, especially the two house prison cells. She took the entire reel. Then she picked up an iron object and broke the glass monitors and the knobs.

"Now let's go," she said, handing Teddy the reels.

Chapter 47

After the Silence: A Reckoning Begins

"Thank you for coming in to talk with us, Mr. Hilson. We understand how traumatized the past month or so has been for you. We simply want to ask you a few questions, hoping you can provide a lead to maybe catch those persons responsible for what happened to you and your friend. My partner and I have been working around the clock in search of your whereabouts, and when your attorneys called to inform us that your captors had released you, unharmed, we simply had to speak with you," the detective said.

The incident at the Hatchet compound had quietly disappeared. There had been no news reports of any kind. The only proof that anything out of the ordinary ever occurred at the estate was safely tucked away in a four-foot safe in the new house Viola had purchased in his absence. The cops only learned of Erika and Teddy's disappearance when the Union's attorney advised that it was the proper thing to do. While on the surface, the Fort Myers Police Department put on a concerned face, in the area concerning the Union, underneath the cops were furious with Teddy's Union, because of all the attention the Union representatives brought to the department a few weeks before Teddy's abduction. The feud was over an abuse of force incident that was captured on someone's cell phone. The station was refusing to discipline the black and white officers who were involved. Some Union members had picketed the police station, demanding accountability.

"There is only so much I am able to give," Detective Randy Welks, Teddy said.

"I remember hearing my dog Shauka barking. I went outside to investigate, and then a loud boom occurred next to me. I believe it was some kind of stun grenade, because when I regained consciousness, I was in the back seat of a van or SUV. They had bound and blind folded me."

"How did you get loose or released?"

"A hood was put over my head; they untied my hands and told me to get out of the vehicle. We were on I-75, about 10 miles from Fort Myers. I followed their instructions, walked until I found a phone, and then called my people to come get me."

"Did you get a look at the vehicle? Welks pressed.

"I was afraid to disobey their instructions; I didn't want them to change their minds about releasing me."

"Okay, Mr. Hilson. If you can remember anything, anything at all, please contact us. Here is my card."

*   *   *

It's been two weeks now since breaking free from the Hatchet compound, and Teddy was certain that he had not heard the last of those who were responsible for his and Erika's abduction. The new house has been outfitted with state-of-the-art security monitoring apparatus. Even body heat sensory points were sporadically positioned around the property.

321

Usually, when Teddy traveled, either Green Eyes or Trey would accompany him, serving as a personal bodyguard. Natasha was using colored contact lenses to disguise the color of her eyes; her hair had a natural red tint to it, so it too had been camouflaged.

Erika and Natasha had bonded in a special way; Viola was included. However, she had taken the helm of Eyekon and was totally committed to its missions.

Teddy was able to jump right in and immediately began strategizing and prioritizing the Union's agenda.

"Its potential is astronomical. The first thing that we must tackle is: how can Eyekon reduce collateral consequences, and provide tools for success through programs for the convicted felons, who have demonstrated an honest desire for change. Listen, Mary, assign someone to begin searching the Legislative History of a few of the laws that seem to target our community the most. Laws like the three-strike, Prison Prior Releasee, and the 10/20/Life statutes here in Florida".

" While in prison myself, I was a certified law clerk and can tell you, it's a trial. We simply need to know where it begins. Within the Legislative History, we will be able to learn who sponsored the Bill, which subsequently became law, as well as how and why the committee discussing the Bill wanted it passed. The laws we are mostly concerned about are the mandatory minimum laws that can lock a person up for up to life without giving a stand-alone reason. This is too ugly; something has to be wrong in this area, people".

Tomorrow was Friday, and Viola had already put in place a Board meeting. Teddy had waited instead of calling a special gathering to formally introduce himself. The first Friday of his release from the kidnappers, he had foregone attending any of the meetings. But it's time now for everyone to learn who Teddy Hilson is, Eyekon's founder.

"Come here, darling," Viola said softly to her king, "Turn that computer off and let Eyekon rest for a spell. Come hold me, love me. I need some more of what you gave your Queen last night."

Flashing that signature smile of his, Teddy flipped the off switch on the Apple laptop, closed it, and let his house robe fall to the floor as he made his way to his lovely, inviting Queen.

Viola had missed her man in a way that expressed itself in the compassionate way she kissed him. Her soft hand seemed to cause each place on his body she touched to tingle with great anticipation. When their lips locked, nothing else even mattered. Nothing at all. For the next hour or so, they made slow, passionate love until he was absolutely sure that Viola was satisfied. Then he himself exploded in an abyss of pleasure.

Chapter 48

The Cost of Power: A Game Beyond Blood

"What do you mean he did not get it done? The only reason his ass is sitting high as a United States senator is because of me."

"Word is, instead of killing the leader and shutting down the Union, he attempted to take it over".

"That, my friend, is not making any sense at all. Are you suggesting that the Senator tried to take control of the Union? Here it is, a white man from the Deep South, whose family history does not sit too well with black people, and yet, you're telling me this bird-brain wants to control an association built for, designed by, and benefits convicts?"

"Boss, do not overlook the Union's primary breath, which is to resurrect the usefulness of the convicted felon across America. In addition, the leader has found a way to have those losers' voting rights restored. We are talking of millions and millions of potentially eligible voters. If one person can control this kind of political currency, I do not have to tell you that this person would be in a position to have sway over the entire country. An elected official at every level, from a county seat all the way to becoming President, depends on votes. It appears that our man, the Senator, could not resist possessing such power. The entire Russian hit team sent, was wiped out. Additionally, it was rumored that a female hit-woman from the Russians had switched sides and joined the Union leader. My question to you, Mr. Hampton, is, where do we go from here? Do we kill the union guy, or do you want control of this Eyekon? Between lobbyists and campaign financing, you have literally spent tens of millions over the last few years alone. However, if you controlled who would, or who could, get elected, you too could control America. It is time for our boy to be removed."

Chapter 49

Power in the Balance

"One thing is obvious, if they had rather I be dead, I sure as hell wouldn't be standing here with you beautiful people," Teddy was saying to the Board Members. Delaware and his assistant, Elizabeth, are also in attendance.

"From what I have been able to gather and piece together, it seems that someone would rather control our Union than close it down. The question is why, and what's really interesting is that Green Eyes said someone in the U.S. Senate is heavily involved. - They were told to keep me alive until someone came who would force me through torture to hand over the rights of the Union."

Teddy continued.

"The man she killed, she believes, was intending to subject me to some serious convincing maneuvers to compel me to go along with their plans. Senator Hatchet's family and I have bumped heads at the beginning of Eyekon formation. His younger brother, Senator Murdock Hatchet, tried to use Cheryl, the Preacher's wife, out of Sanford, to screw up Eyekon's financial records, and almost successfully forced me to relinquish the helm. He had a hold on her until I paid his kinky-ass a surprise visit, ultimately freeing Cheryl. Last year, Senator J.D. Hatchet was elected to the United States Senate."

"We have a very big election next year between a female

Democrat, who appears to have clinched the Democratic nomination, and a Republican male who is far to the right. The split between both parties cannot be further apart than at any time in the history of politics in America.

Listen, it is against the law to directly influence or otherwise interfere with the free choice of someone else casting a ballot. But here at Eyekon, most of us will follow suit. What this means is that we are on course to becoming a voting behemoth to be reckoned with. And that, my friends, is the prize that could come with the control of Eyekon."

Teddy concluded.

"We must never allow such to occur."

"Okay, let us not turn to Eyekon's business at hand: It is apparent that the system is failing people returning to their communities from prison. More than 600,000 people are released from State and Federal prisons each year, and an estimated 68% are re-arrested within three years."

"Now, how in the hell are they able to accurately estimate that high percentage of people who would be re-arrested within three years?" Mary couldn't resist asking.

"That's a very good question, Mary, and I have put much into uncovering the recipe that helped bake that prediction. Voila, you have a copy of the Union operational manual, don't you?"

"Yes, I do, Teddy."

"Would you please turn to page 31 or 32, the section

on big business. When you locate it, honey, would you mind answering Mary's question for us all?"

"Not at all, Sire."

"Here we are, and you wanted to know how in hell the powers that be know 68% of prison releases will return to prison within three years. Well, it's actually a team effort, spearheaded by big businesses."

"There are 12 major corporations benefiting from the Prison Industrial Complex, although there are hundreds more on a smaller level. McDonald's uses inmates to produce frozen foods, beef patties, processed bread, milk, and Chicken products; Wendy's, Wal-Mart, Starbucks, Sprint, Verizon, Victoria's Secret, Fidelity Investments, JCPenney, and Kmart; American Airlines and Avis Rent-A-Car."

"Actually, it was a consorted effort, Mary, one that required the participation of local, State, and Federal policy makers. Initially, they had to create a situation, an issue, or a problem. Then, they won't fix it right away. Instead, they let it run its course to make sure it causes havoc and that everyone sees it. In turn, this promotes a desired policy or outcome, to be a regulated policy, which involves elected officials, who then campaign on the promise to address and fix the problem. Policy says what a person can do, or cannot do, with regard to the created problem."

"Let us jump the gun here for a bit and say, once one becomes a convicted felon, they are now fair game for the material, or food substance, needed for the voracious appetite of the beast we call Capitalism."

Capitalism, for all of you who do not know, never was, and never will be, a level playing field. Trade and Industry play a big part in this equation. Companies that service the criminal justice system need sufficient quantities of raw materials to guarantee long-term growth. In the criminal justice field, the raw material is prisoners. And, mind you, the Industry will do what is necessary to guarantee a steady supply. For the supply of prisoners to grow, criminal justice policies must ensure a sufficient number of incarcerated Americans, regardless of whether crime is rising or whether incarceration is necessary. {Bibliograph information of where this piece of information came from} [Davis2003, 94][Prison contracts, profiles & parties - Tofts Univ. 2023]"

"That is very interesting," Delaware Labrinsky commented.

Teddy was observing the attendees as Viola shared the astonishing facts of how the System is being exposed.

"This, my friends," Viola continued, "Is why you see so very many hurdles placed in the pathway to re-integrating back into society, by one who is released from prison. If you cannot work or you can't buy food, you starve. Most places, through created policy, cannot rent to convicted felons; you can't do this, you can't do that, you can't go here, you can go there. In other words, you, the convicted felon, are being squeezed in an easily predictable direction or course of action."

"Picture this, if there is no water to your left, a life-sustaining necessity, but looking to your right, you see water; never mind the signs (policy) that say, clean drinking water is not for you, convicted felon. However, you have 10 thirsty souls. Tell me, out of those 10, how many do you think you can accurately predict will walk away, or drink a swallow of this precious water? Exactly my point - not many would be able to walk away – because, for God's sake, we all need the damn water!"

"The system, or the Beast, can accurately predict that nearly 70% (7 out of 10) prisoners released will return to prison within three years. Hell, if you are only provided with a Hobson's choice, it's easy to know what direction someone would go."

"What is a Hobson's choice?" Mary asked.

"Let me, please", Delaware cut in.

The lawyer wanted to be a part of the conversation as well. Delaware was really impressed with the hard work and research Teddy has put in.

"A Hobson's choice is a scenario based on a sixteenth-century liveryman who owned a trading Post Store. And when someone came in to buy a horse, he would say to them: You may buy any horse in the Store, as long as it is the closest one to the door."

Everyone started laughing at the explanation.

Natasha entered the room and made her way over to where Teddy was seated, and said something in his ear. Teddy nodded, and she left. Several moments later, he stood and said loud enough so everyone could hear him.

"The cops are out front asking to speak with me," he said.

Delaware stood and told Teddy that he would accompany him.

Chapter 50

The Fall of the Fourth

The Lincoln Town Car slowed as the lone pedestrian jogged past the driveway opening to the sprawling Estate of the neighborhood's wealthiest resident. The driver, ordinarily, would be sitting in the back seat enjoying his customary Bloody Mary drink while his chauffeur handled the big luxury vehicle. However, Alexandro was sent back to clean up the mess in Florida. In addition to being the car's driver, Alexandro also served as personal bodyguard.

The side road leading from the highway extended for sixty or so yards, permitting a sizable caravan to enter without congestion. The huge, powerful-looking electrical gate, adorned with strange medieval bric-a-bracs, required a ten-digit code to gain entrance to the property.

Senator Joseph David Hatchet often invited members of the U.S. Senate here to iron out partisan differences on the other side of the political spectrum. Oftentimes, his good friend and super-wealthy donor, Macy Hampton, would attend.

J.D. was a staunch Republican, and all things conservative were his primary push.

Both sides, the Democrats and Republicans, had grown increasingly further apart since President Trumden took office. Two years after the Presidential election, Senator J.D.

Hatchet was elected the Majority Leader of the Senate, fourth in the succession line to the Presidency. As the leader of the United States Senate, Joseph knew that people on Capitol Hill feared him. Even as a junior Senator, he was one not to offend in Congress. That was usually the case when wealthy white men became Senators. In Washington, D.C., that was business as usual, so the saying goes.

Today had been especially long, the Senator was thinking, one that started at 3:45 a.m. in the morning. To a greater degree, it was becoming difficult to gain bipartisan support in the House of Representatives and the Senate. The Democrats controlled the House and the Republicans controlled the Senate. This was anything but a productive sign.

However, it was imperative that the Bill the Republicans have been working on become law before election time. So much was at stake. No one had taken the Union's President and CEO seriously at the beginning. As a result, this Eyekon leader is on the brink of establishing, legally, what is perhaps the single most influential voting engine ever witnessed in the history of American politics. He - it, must be stopped!

Senator Hatchet, or J.D. as he prefers, drove the big car through the well-kept buttonwood trees. Directing the vehicle to a place next to his wife's Volvo Station Wagon. He immediately became concerned: He knew his wife would frown on his drinking. On the other hand, what on earth is she doing at home? She should not be here for several more hours, J.D. was thinking as he reached for a mint to cover the Bloody Mary's odor.

Joseph has made too much money to calculate since dealing more directly with Macy. He knew the Billionaire was responsible for much of the drugs that were entering the black communities; a secret governmental undertaking first initiated on a large scale in the late 1960s to counter-balance the growing effectiveness of the Black Panther Party, started by Huey P. Newton and Bobby Seal.

The operation was to serve on two fronts: first, to weaken the growing resolve of Blacks due to the Panthers' heavy influence, and secondly, by creating drug dependents, with the predictable outcome that heavy crime was surely to increase.

Let the crime and drug sale, and drug use run rampant for a good while. Then pass strict laws, on the grounds that law and order must be restored.. This would, of course, allow the police to enter these Black communities and lock up the criminals, or, said differently, people of color.

A sudden movement at the driver's window startled J.D., and standing there were several darkly dressed people who were pointing guns at him.

"What in the world-"

"Shut the fuck up!" The one closest to the window barked menacingly.

"If you want to live, open the car door and get out.

J.D.'s head was spinning. He could not believe this was

happening to him. At any moment now, he would awaken, and this terrible scene unfolding would be gone. The door to the vehicle was yanked open, and a strong pair of hands wrestled the Senator from the Town Car, forcing him onto the pavement. Reality settled in, it was clear - this was not a dream.

J.D. felt the burning pain from his left knee scraping the asphalt.

Thoughts of his own safety quickly vanished as his thoughts turned to his wife, who was all alone in the large house. Was she unharmed or alive and well…

"Take off the watch and ring," one of them said.

"That includes your wallet," the other one added. Daylight was disappearing, and visibility was rapidly diminishing. With the approaching darkness, the shadows from the trees were taking on eerie shapes. J.D. could not put a name on any of the hoodlums, whether they were black, white, or other. Fear began to creep through his body as he tried to acquaint himself with the strange silhouettes on the buildings.

"What's going on?" J.D. managed to say in a voice quivering with anxiety. If you want money, I will give it to you.

Seemingly, not hearing a word J.D. had spoken, the one closest to the Senator pointed the gun at the center of J.D.'s head and pulled the trigger. The powerful weapon was almost jumping out of the shooter's hand.

J.D.'s wife was standing at the window in their second-floor bedroom; she had witnessed it all.

Chapter 51
The Thirteenth Power

The round table was a group of 12 tremendously powerful men; they each wielded much, much raw power. Any one of the dozen could have the President of the United States removed from office, or killed, if that President refuses to play by their rules. It is they who really direct the course of America. Each member has been groomed for the lifetime position since the age of 13.

Although it was only 12 members, their number is actually thirteen, which is also known secretly as the Operation of Wisdom. In other words, 12, and the produced product is thirteen. Esoterically, they are the House of the Rising Sons. The Table's formation was established along the lines of a system deeply shrouded in Secrecy.

Each of the twelve is represented by the Zodiac, from Aries to Pisces; however, when communicating with one another, Aries will be Gad, Taurus will be Asher, and so on until all the names of the Sons of Jacob are expended. The member of the Table, who sits as chair, is Virgo. Or, son of my right hand.

The number 13 is unlucky for ignorance only. All so-called laws of nature may be reduced to 13. The origin of words and their application vary widely. Thus, the origin of twelve is circle or completeness without a break. All operations that produce something may be called twelve, being complete; in order to produce the product, and is therefore, 13. Thus, all machines or factories symbol 12 and the product 13. Attendance at the Last Supper was twelve disciples, and Jesus gave us thirteen.

The Last Supper, represents on one plane of interpretation, the last time of the initiate to be, before his leaving of the body (the cross), the place of Golgotha (the Skull) and is the moment of time when he, the spiritual consciousness takes leave or communes with the twelve attributes of being, in the upper room (head) where a spiritual feast of great beauty had been prepared.

The 13th degree of the Zodiacal sign Cancer was rising on July 4, 1776, when the Declaration of Independence was signed. America commenced her individuality as a Nation with 13 States. The reverse side of the United States Seal shows part of the pyramid of Egypt, the base of which covers 13 acres. There are 13 steps or terraces. The motto over the pyramid, "Annuit Coeptis", contains 13 letters and is Latin for Prosper in our understanding.

Cancer represents the breast and is therefore the Mother sign, or woman. M is from Mem, the thirteenth letter of the Hebrew alphabet, and means woman. The United States plays the part of mother to all people and gathers them under her protective care. This love, however, was strictly forbidden for Blacks. The seventeenth President made sure of this because, in the major cotton States of the deep South, nearly half of all Capital, nearly half of all investments were in human beings. When those human beings were confiscated, when the investments were transferred, in essence, from the Slave holder to the people who were enslaved themselves, that meant a huge loss of Capital to Southern slave holders. A tiny slave holding elite had owned the majority of the region's four million slaves, who vowed never to remove the yoke from around the Black person's neck. Hence, the Thirteenth Amendment was put in place by Johnson.

In 1882, thirteen years after President Andrew Johnson left office, an unknown man appeared in Philadelphia, offering the drawing of a seal, which he suggested be added to the reverse side of the United States Seal. The other side contained thirteen stars, thirteen stripes, and an eagle with aquiver containing thirteen arrowheads in one talon, an Olive branch with thirteen leaves in the other. And the motto E. Pluribus Unum, which contains thirteen letters. The Round Table was established that same year.

This man declared that the Seal would be adopted in the year 1921 (One hundred thirty-nine years later); the digits which all equal thirteen; 1921 and 139 both equal 13.) Secret rumor has it that the man was none other than Andrew Johnson.

Interestingly, not only was 1921 the year of phase two of the Round Table's vow to keep Blacks in bondage, it was also the year that a white mob was instructed to descend on Black Wall Street in Tulsa, Oklahoma, looting, burning down the place, and killing many. This was meant to send a message to Blacks across America, 'Stay in your place.

Macy Johnson was born under the sign of Virgo and, therefore, was the Chair of the Round Table. Or, as the appropriate title ensues: Son of my Right Hand.

"Good evening, Gentlemen. Thank you all for arriving on such short notice. I'd like to have given more time for you to get your affairs in order. However, a week was all I cared to risk. We have a situation," Macy Johnson said.

"It is so dire that I had to expeditiously take corrective measures. Senator Hatchet became a liability and was eliminated. Trouble is, he has been replaced in the Senate."

"That won't be a problem".Gemini-Issachar said.

The ranking Senator stationed under Senator Joseph has long been prepared for the top position should his services ever be needed.

Issachar was in charge of the First Circuit, which covers Washington, D.C. Each of the Round Table's members, in addition to being a body of one, was solely responsible for a particular geographical slice of the United States. How each knew their respective jurisdictional boundary was based on that of the Circuit Court of Appeals for the Federal Courts System. Macy Johnson paralleled the Eleventh Circuit, which covers Florida, Georgia, and Alabama.

"The issue we have and the basis for your presence is not Senator J.D., but instead it is for a newly formed Union for felons and ex-convicts."

"A Union for people with a felony record," Naphtali (Pieces) injected with incredulity. Has AFL-CIO recognized it ?"

"No," Macy responded. "It is an independent affiliation.

"What the Hell-" Taurus - Asher stated, before being cut off by Macy.

"Please, Gentlemen, allow me to lay out the facts before you first, then we can ask questions and find answers. Trust me - We're going to need them."

"Listen, brethren, there is a fine line between being rich and assuring all your children and their children, children will live just as luxurious and opulent as you do - such is the case with us at the Round Table. We are the wealthiest families in the world. In a world where luxury is synonymous with the good life, few families epitomize opulence as you do," Macy said, waving his muscular arms over the attendees. One of his favorite pastime was weight lifting. He was a fairly big man, standing about six feet two, with piercing light blue eyes.

"Our families have built empires through the Thirteenth, which covers diverse industries, from energy to manufactories and prisons. And you, Judah-Capricorn, your family is currently the largest privately owned company in America and one of the biggest oil producers in the world. It's not necessary that I stress how much you and the rest of us want to keep our fortunes. Your family, like mine, and theirs are heavily involved in the politics of America. For example, your two uncles invest heavily in opposing any climate change legislation and are among the biggest Republican Party donors. In just over the Past decade alone, the right has received nearly 3 billion dollars from your family. This new Union threatens the grip that our money has over many of the legislative acts that become law".

"How so?" Gemini -Issachar inquired.

"Votes. The Union leader, Teddy Hilson, a Black man, has convinced a Court that, if there was nothing in the Constitution which prohibits a convicted felon from running for, and if elected, to becoming the President of the United States, then it's a cinch that being convicted of a felony surely do not stand for prohibiting the same from merely casting a ballot."

He pointed out to, and the Federal Judge agreed, that the 13th Amendment only authorizes the free labor of one convicted of a felony.

"Hell, the same judge nearly declared my great, great grandfather's Thirteenth Amendment unconstitutional on the ground of vagueness; he, the attorney for their Union, argued that the 13th Amendment does not say who may work the convicted felons, or who is to be the beneficiary."

"As written, they argued, several excellent points: While the punishment for a crime, line in this amendment, points to the judiciary line, this is the only body legally empowered to convict. However, the "except as punishment for a crime, wherefore the party shall have been duly convicted part is based on race and, as such, is still, nonetheless, unconstitutional because it denies and clearly was intended to deny Black people from participating in the process. Everyone knows, they continue to argue, Blacks were strictly prohibited from serving on a jury in 1865, when the Thirteenth Amendment became law."

The light started to shine in Gemini's head:

"It's anywhere from ten to one-hundred million felons across America; My God, if this Teddy Hilson guy can control this much sway over the engine of our Democracy, our money wouldn't amount to a cup of beans when it comes to who gets elected".

"Indeed, Gemini, my friend, "Macy said solemnly.

"This Union also puts in jeopardy over 50% of the Table's bedrock standings - the central principles on which my great, great, grandfather created the 13th, or Round Table. The people here at the Table and our families are the one percent, whose wealth topples that of the remaining 99%, combined. If we intend to keep it that way, we must make a serious decision concerning this Eyekon. Senator Hatchet was directed to take care of the matter, and he failed.

"However, his intentions may have been well placed: J.D. wanted to take control over the Union rather than shut it down. We put a ton of money into each important election. As a result, it has enabled the Table to control everything from what is, or is not, permitted in the society of America. Including what is to be taught in public education."

"There is more: Taurus, your GEO group PAC spent over five hundred thousand dollars on political contributions in Florida last year, not to mention the $730.000 on lobbying. This Union is attempting to keep before the Public's attention that GEO's Private Prison Group was a part of the American Legislative Exchange Council (ALEC), which participated in creating some of the most aggressive, war-on-drugs policies that increase the Prison population.

"Mass incarceration, thanks to the brilliant plan you put in place, went up on the Federal level, 784% between 1990 and 2010. But my concern for you and Wells Fargo, Fidelity, JP Morgan Chase, Morgan Stanley, and State Street Composition, is that the Stock and Security Exchange (SEC) shows all of you to be heavy financial investors, and who owns two-thirds of CCA (the other major private prison for Profit Company), is on full display."

Since 2000, you all have received nearly forty billion dollars from the taxpayers, and we've almost doubled that amount through our other companies doing business with the prisons. Contact our inside Administration at SEC and have the personal names removed from those accounts connected to investing in America's Private Prison Industries and insert substitutes."

"Now," Macy said in a tone that made all present look in his direction. "Do we kill this Teddy Hilson, or do we figure out a way to take over this Eyekon Union?"

Pices-Naphtali had not spoken a single word since their gathering. The look in his cold black eyes bespoke something more sinister than hate. He was a descendant of Lucinda Comer, a widow.

After the Civil War, she and her sons oversaw the family enterprises in cotton, lumber, and corn. They had owned, perhaps, the biggest share of Slaves out of the four million plus, and when the slaves were freed, their high, high standing as one of the wealthiest families in the South immediately crashed. Naphtali was about the same age as Macy, so Lucinda was his great, great -or great, grandmother. His father and grandfather had been the family members to sit at the Table. Now, he sits at the Round Table keeping the family's legacy alive. Of course, with the brilliance of the Johnson family.

"There is nothing like the good old days, when blacks knew their places", Pices began.

"Killing the Union guy would be nice, considering the hazardous opposition he stands for. However, controlling this Union would be ideal. I say we come at him from multiple angles; we offer him two billion to secretly give over the rights, but openly continue playing the part of leaders."

"What! – Levi?" - Sagittarius jumped to his feet with objection.

"Brethren", Pices said in a very controlled and docile tone, "May I please finish my point first?"

Macy did not take the impertinent interruption with as much docility, but remained quiet.

"Yes- Brethren, please finish your point," Levi said, bowing slightly.

"This, my Brethren," Naphtali continued, "This Eyekon is not a toast to our establishment, but more like a THREAT. And, a real one at that! However, to control such a movement would save us tens of billions of dollars on elections alone, not to mention the thwarting of bringing to light many of the things we'd like kept in the dark".

"Where in the hell are they getting the information from?" Gemini asked.

"The information is interwoven in the fabric of the Country's history. All that one needs is to know what they are looking for." Macy answered.

"Okay. Before Mr. Hilson is approached with the financial offer, he needs to be shaken, bombarded with enough things to make him unable to focus. Send the cops to harass him, auditors to purview their records, and trace his movements. Be sure he knows it. It's time we put his black ass on the defense".

"Pieces", Macy started, "Who, or how, is the financial offer to be carried out?"

"Hell, use one of the Union's members," said Taurus.

Virgo's cell phone vibrated; it had to be extremely important because everyone knew he was not to be disturbed over the ensuing two weeks.

He stood and made his way to the back of the large

room. The brief message had a significant impact.

"Gentleman," he said loud enough for all to give him their full attention: Senator Joseph D. Hatchet is alive - in very critical condition- but alive."

Chapter 52

Shadows in the Storage Unit

"Mr. Hilson, we'd like to ask you a few questions about a series of burglaries. We've lifted a fingerprint belonging to you near one of the crime scenes. I'm afraid we'll need you to come with us to Headquarters," Detective Bandy Welks said sternly. His partner started to reach for his handcuffs, but the Black officer waved him off.

"Sure," Teddy replied calmly. "Do we leave now?"

"That would be our intention."

"Mr. Labrinsky, call my attorney, Mr. Terry, and let him know what's happening. Shall we, gentlemen? Do you prefer I ride with you or drive myself?"

"Riding with us will be fine, Mr. Hilson."

Teddy caught Natasha's eyes burning with defiance, ready to lash out at the officers. He gave her a reassuring smile. "Don't worry. Everything's fine."

Just then, Viola stormed out in a fury.

"What do y'all think you're doing? Do you even have a warrant?" she bellowed.

"Mary! Get Willie Terry on the phone!"

Delaware hurried over, handing her the receiver. "He's on the line, Viola."

"Mr. Terry, this is Viola. The police are here, about to take Teddy, hold on." She turned to the detectives. "What's he done?"

"We just want to talk with him, downtown at the station," Welks replied evenly.

At the Fort Myers Police Department, Teddy was read his Miranda Rights. He was told he could have his attorney present or speak without one. Teddy chose to talk.

"When was the last time you were out on College Parkway in South Fort Myers?" Detective Welks asked.

Teddy thought back. He'd been there at least four times before his abduction and twice since escaping. He rented a storage shed behind the Old Brown Derby restaurant.

"I'm not exactly sure, maybe a week ago. Why?"

"We've had a string of burglaries. Your prints were found on an orange juice can near one of the crime scenes."

Teddy's pulse quickened. His mind raced. That detail meant one of two things. Either the detectives had entered his locked storage unit, where he kept a small refrigerator stocked with canned orange juice, or someone had planted the can to frame him. Teddy remembered sipping one on his last visit, tossing the empty into a box inside the shed.

"What do you mean, near one of the places?" Teddy pressed.

"What was your business in that area?" Welks countered, ignoring the question.

"I rent a storage unit at Lee County Storage. I'm sure you already knew that."

His partner jumped in: "I knew it! There's no way to move that kind of stolen property at once."

"Slow it down," Welks cautioned.

"Would you mind showing us your unit, or do we need a warrant?"

"A warrant? I've got nothing to hide. No, I don't mind. You want to see my storage unit? Let's go."

At unit 703B, Teddy unlocked the door and stepped aside. Welks and his partner entered, with a patrol officer waiting nearby.

"Would you like me to unlock anything for you?" Teddy offered.

He was ignored. Welks simply walked around the small room, scanning the neatly stacked boxes and books. His partner stood at the entrance, watchful but silent.

Finally, appearing satisfied, Welks headed toward the door. Then he stopped, peering into the trash bin beside the entrance.

"What's this?" he muttered.

From the garbage, he pulled out a wallet, a gold wedding ring, and a Rolex watch.

Chapter 53

The Framed and the Brotherhood

"Ms. Templeton, get in," Attorney Terry said through the driver's side window of his vehicle. "They have placed Teddy under arrest for some wild accusations. His bond is set at $75,000."

"Seventy-five thousand… that's strange," Viola said with perplexity.

"What makes you say that?"

"Just yesterday, an envelope arrived at Eyekon's Headquarters addressed to Teddy. It had no return address. Inside was $75,000 and a Monopoly Game get-out-of-jail-free card."

"Why wasn't anything said about that?" the attorney asked.

"Mary was going through yesterday's mail this morning and had recently given it to me. Delaware and I were pondering the matter right before you arrived."

"And you said it had no return address. What about the postmark? What city was it mailed from?"

"There was no postmark, no stamps, nor any other indication showing it went through the Post Office. There was, however, the name FRANK stamped where the stamps should have been," Viola said.

"Now that has my attention. That is an old gesture associated with a group of people with a common interest. Sort of a 'Brotherhood.'"

"What do you mean, Mr. Terry?"

"Freemasons, Viola. At one point, especially from the late 50s to the mid-1970s, communication was often conducted without using phones between the Masons across America, and mailing a missive was often the manner of choice. By simply writing the word FRANK in capital letters, it assured the delivery of it."

"Why does this grab your attention?"

"Well, as of now, we don't have all the facts of what Teddy is being accused of. However, what we do know is that whatever they are trying to place on him is not true. Let's wait and see what is going on with Teddy, Viola before I go into the why."

*   *   *

Senator Hatchet was not expected to survive, but he had not only remained among the living, he was expected to make an almost full recovery. And he was furious. Someone wanted him dead. The only things taken from him were a watch, a billfold, and a wedding band. Money was definitely not what the thugs were after. Hell, he had even offered to give them money. One thing was for sure: J.D. knew he had to take measures to avert additional attempts on his life.

That morning, he had a visitor—a cop who flew in from Florida to inform him that his belongings were found in the

352

possession of Teddy Hilson, the Union guy.

Joseph David Hatchet knew better. If the Table was responsible for the attempt on his life, and all fingers pointed in that direction, then he must return to the beginning. Go back to Union.

"Alexandro," Senator Hatchet called to his bodyguard stationed outside his private hospital room door. "Get me my phone." J.D. placed a call to a woman who was once greatly indebted to his late brother, Murdock. She would be able to get a message to Teddy Hilson. Murdock had shared with him how Cheryl, fresh out of high school, was hired to work in the family's jewelry store in Sanford, Florida. She had played the role of inside woman to assist her then-boyfriend in robbing the place. She had been recorded agreeing to the plans.

Things had gone wrong, and a cop was shot and killed. Murdock never turned in the recording or reported Cheryl's involvement. Instead, it was used as a blackmail truncheon to keep her in servitude and also in an almost successful effort to take over the Union at its beginning.

J.D. had long ago been given a copy of the recording as an insurance policy on the Hatchets' business interests with Cheryl Sapp's husband, the mega TV Reverend and businessman O.V. Sapp.

"Hello, Cheryl Sapp?" J.D. said into the phone. "Could you tell me where you were on February 13, 1995, the day before Deputy Gilyard was shot down outside Hatchet's Jewelry Store in Sanford, Florida?"

J.D. heard the sharp intake of breath on the other end of the line. A deafening silence stretched for twenty or so seconds before the Senator continued.

"Here, let me help you: you were working in my family's jewelry store, and you were on the phone with that murdering boyfriend of yours.

Now, you listen to me and hear me good: exactly one week from today, a flight will be booked for you on American Airlines, for a trip to Washington, D.C., by way of Ronald Reagan National Airport. Room 202 at the Darcy Hotel has been reserved for you and your husband, but you are to come alone. It is located at 1515 Rhode Island Ave. N.W.

The following day, at noon, you are to be at Florionz, an Italian restaurant located within a six-minute walk from the hotel. Enter and ask the doorman for your table. I am Senator J.D. Hatchet, Murdock's brother. I need to talk with you, please."

*　　*　　*

"Dealing in stolen property, Count One; possession of stolen property. And they had an accessory to attempted murder, but it was removed at the last minute," Teddy explained to Viola and the attorney.

"And get this, the property was allegedly taken from Senator John D. Hatchet in Washington, D.C., during a robbery. The Senator was shot in the head. The cops didn't say it, but I know they're aware I was here in Florida when

354

the robbery happened. I also believe they know I can afford to buy a much higher grade of jewelry than that old Oyster Bey Rolex."

"I wonder how the stolen items ended up inside your storage unit," Viola asked.

"Let me guess," Attorney Terry interjected. "There was no sign of forced entry, and the lock wasn't broken, was it?"

"You're batting a thousand, Mr. Terry," Teddy replied.

"I am completely satisfied you're being framed here, Mr. Hilson. But what's most alarming is that the police themselves may be co-conspirators in this vile act."

Chapter 54

Shadows Over the Potomac

The lone passenger in seat 2222 could not put her finger on it. Yet something about the call she had received still gnawed at her, like a whisper crawling down her spine. The woman knew one thing with absolute clarity: this was a high-stakes situation. And so she clung to the advice given to her long ago, never again would she go down without putting up a fight.

The plane roared across the runway at Ronald Reagan National Airport, the steel bird trembling as it lifted into the cool air. The District of Columbia stretched below, its monuments gleaming in the golden wash of afternoon light. Washington, D.C., a city of power and secrets, where the Potomac River silently bore witness to conspiracies that could topple nations.

When Cheryl finally stepped outside the crowded terminal, she felt the air, sharp with autumn crispness, wrap around her. At the curb, a restless line of taxis, Uber drivers, and polished limousines awaited their passengers. Among them, one chauffeur stood steady, holding a sign bearing her name in bold letters.

"Hi, my name is Alexandro, Senator Hatchet's assistant," he said warmly. His voice carried a faint accent, deliberate and measured. What he did not say, that he was also a bodyguard, confidant, and errand boy, remained cloaked in silence.

"Thank you," Cheryl replied, her lips curving with a guarded lightness. "You already know my name. I guess that spares me the need for introductions."

They exchanged no further words as the city unfurled before them. Cheryl sat in the back of the limousine, her gaze fixed on the blurred silhouettes of pedestrians, monuments, and stone facades.

Her thoughts, however, raced elsewhere, back to Murdock, the late Senator of a dynasty that held more than political influence. He had passed her name to his brother, and from that moment her past, her very story, seemed to lie naked in their hands.

When she had received the call last week, and the voice spoke of that unspeakable day in 1995, Cheryl's heart had plummeted like a stone into icy waters. The memory was a wound she kept buried, but now it had been ripped open. She clenched her fists in her lap. No, she thought. She would not be used again. Never again would she be a pawn in someone else's game.

The limousine curved onto Rhode Island Avenue, its wheels humming softly against the pavement, and stopped at the elegant façade of the Darcy Hotel.

"The Senator will visit you tomorrow," Alexandro said, his tone laced with courtesy but shadowed with something unspoken. "Here are a few thousand dollars for you to do some sightseeing, if you'd like."

Cheryl accepted the envelope with a polite nod. "I'll do

that. Thank you." She stepped away, her carry-on slung over her shoulder, and made her way toward the front desk.

Room 202 was spacious yet intimate, a corner room with tall windows that framed the bustling street and the hotel's parking lot below. The evening sky deepened into shades of violet and indigo, pressing against the glass. After a quick shower, Cheryl set out into the city.

Six minutes later, she found herself within the warm, aromatic embrace of a small Italian restaurant. The scent of garlic and simmering tomatoes enveloped her as she sank into a booth. She ordered a Cappuccino, its frothy steam curling into the air, and soon after, a plate of spaghetti with garlic bread and meatballs, the kind of meal that carried the comfort of home in every bite.

But comfort was fleeting. As the night crept on, Cheryl's mind replayed the puzzle over and over: why had Senator J.D. Hatchet gone to such lengths to bring her here? The answer brushed at the edge of her thoughts, the tape. She still had her copy of that damning recording, proof of Murdock Hatchet's hidden appetites. They might have had something on her, but she had her weapon too. A grotesque balance of power, dangling by threads.

The next day, just before noon, a knock shattered the stillness of her room. Cheryl inhaled slowly. It was time. Her fingers brushed over the hidden tape recorder tucked securely behind her blouse, its faint mechanical click echoing as she turned it on.

She opened the door.

"Mrs. Sapp, Cheryl?" The man standing before her was wiry, tall, his presence sharpened by his keen chestnut-brown eyes. His graying hair receded slightly, but thick waves framed his temples. His voice was calm, practiced.

"Yes, Cheryl will be fine, Senator Hatchet," she said, steady but wary. "I can see the resemblance to your late brother Murdock."

A faint smile tugged at his lips. "Thank you. Many have echoed the same sentiment, though Murdock was several years my senior. Thank you for coming. I brought you a gift."

He extended a slim envelope. Inside was a single cassette.

"This is the only remaining copy of the taped conversation between you and your friend on the day that the policeman was killed. Consider it a token of good faith. Because I need your help, Cheryl. Teddy is in danger. The men who hold true power in this country, their reach goes beyond senators, beyond government. They are the real architects, and they will kill to protect what they built. They tried to kill me. They took Teddy. They took his woman."

Cheryl's breath caught in her chest. The walls of the hotel room seemed to lean in closer. This was no political intrigue, this was survival.

She thought of Teddy Hilson, the man who had freed her from decades of blackmail and humiliation. For nearly thirty years, she had endured Murdock's hold over her, shackled by fear. But Teddy had cut those chains. And in that moment, Cheryl knew she could not turn away.

"Whatever I can do that would help Teddy Hilson, Senator," she said firmly, her voice steady as iron, "I will do."

"Good," J.D. replied with a slow nod, appreciation flickering in his eyes. He leaned forward, lowering his voice. "Last week, a detective from Fort Myers came to me. He claimed Teddy had been found with property stolen from me, after I had been shot in the head and left for dead in a staged robbery.

Cheryl, Teddy didn't shoot me. He didn't rob me. But the men who did it are powerful beyond imagination. If they know you're aware of them, you and your family will never be safe. Only I know what I'm telling you."

J.D.'s words hung in the air, heavy and unrelenting.

He went on, revealing to her the existence of Operation Wisdom, of the Thirteenth, the shadowed cabal pulling the strings of American politics. He spoke of their hunger to control the EyEkon Union, of their fear of Teddy Hilson's movement dismantling the hidden spirit of the Thirteenth Amendment itself.

Slavery disguised in legality, voting rights stripped from the convicted, the past masquerading as justice.

And now Teddy Hilson was about to turn that tide. If the Supreme Court ruled that a convicted felon could run for President and win, then why should they not vote as well? It was a question that rattled the foundations of power.

As Cheryl sat there, the city of Washington hummed outside her window, its monuments standing tall, its secrets locked away in stone. Yet in that quiet hotel room, the first cracks in an empire had begun to show.

She did not know if she had the strength for what was coming. But she knew one thing, Teddy Hilson's fight was now her fight.

And somewhere, deep in the shadows of the capital, the Thirteenth had already begun to move their pieces.

Cheryl rose from her chair and walked to the window, staring out at the glowing dome of the Capitol in the distance. A storm was coming. She could feel it in the air, thick and electric. For the first time in years, she allowed herself a faint smile.

"They have no idea," she whispered to her reflection in the glass.

But far below, in the maze of streets, a black sedan lingered at the corner, its engine purring like a predator waiting for the night.

A New Horizon

The gates had closed behind me, but for the first time in 34 years, I did not hear the clank of steel echo in my soul. I heard freedom. The world beyond the prison walls was not the same world I had left, and neither was I the same man who entered. My journey was scarred by mistakes, tempered by discipline, and reshaped by knowledge, but above all, it was guided by an unrelenting belief in transformation.

Walking forward into the Florida sunlight, I was no longer defined by numbers on a uniform. I was defined by the work I had done to rebuild, the education I had fought for, and the people I had vowed to serve. My freedom was not an ending, it was the beginning of responsibility.

The decades I lost cannot be returned, but the decades ahead can be built with purpose. I intend to spend them dismantling barriers, empowering the incarcerated and their families, and proving that the measure of a man is not the weight of his past, but the reach of his future.

And so, I begin again. With pen in hand, with vision in heart, and with the quiet determination that what was once broken can not only be mended, but remade into something extraordinary.

From The Upcoming Sequel
"EyEKON, Blood in the Ledgers"

"……Eighteen months after The Palace became a war room and the streets wrote Sire's lessons in blood and steel, EYEKON has leapt from an idea to a movement with chapters in twenty-seven states. Politicians quote it. Warden unions fear it. Private-prison investors hate it. And somewhere in the noise between applause and crosshairs, Sire learns that building a union for the unforgiven means inheriting enemies old and new—some wearing masks, some wearing suits, and one sitting closer than he ever imagined.

Chapter ….. :

Flags and Ledgers

The flags were a lie, but a beautiful one.

They snapped clean in the late-fall air stars, stripes, and the new one with the gold-on-black EYEKON crest stitched in the corner like a dare. It was a pop-up rally on Freedom Plaza, permit, stage, sound system, cameras, everything done right because the stakes demanded it. From the steps of the Wilson Building down to Pennsylvania Avenue, bodies crowded shoulder-to-shoulder: ex-offenders in pressed shirts, mothers in church hats, men with union jackets that used to say things like Local 149 now wearing pins that said

E. Banners read: WORK IS DIGNITY, SECOND CHANCES ARE POLICY, and 1 in 3 ISN'T A MISTAKE—IT'S A MARKET.

Sire took it in from the side of the stage, hands in his coat pockets, eyes steady beneath a simple black cap. He didn't dress like a politician, or a pastor, or a celebrity. He dressed like a man with places to be after this microphone was silent. Gray wool coat, open. Black sweater. Dark slacks. Clean boots. A scar at his hairline that the cameras would never see but that his enemies never forgot.

Tish checked the clock on her phone and stepped closer. She wore winter white and commanded like a second skin. "You've got seven minutes," she said softly. "The chair's office called—staff wants you upstairs for a prep at two. You hit the hearing at three."

Sire nodded. "Where's Vee?"

"Doing what she does. She'll be on your six when you finish." Tish's eyes took one more sweep of the plaza. "You sure about the last line?"

Sire gave her a look that meant yes and don't ask me why.

A young organizer jogged up, cheeks red from the cold. "Mr. Hilson, you're up in sixty."

"Call me Sire," he said.

He climbed the steps. The crowd roared like a freight train trying to outrun its own weight. It was louder than Tee-

Tot's on payday, louder than Club 21 when the right Al Green cut hit the needle, louder than a cellblock riot when a rumor of freedom slid under the doors. He stopped at the podium and let the noise wash over him.

"D.C.," he said, voice low through the mic, "you look like resurrection."

Laughter and cheers. He let them settle, then he slid the blade in, slowly.

"I was supposed to die a few times. On a sidewalk. In a courtroom. In a cell. Sometimes the world puts a price on your head and calls it law. Sometimes your own will sell you cheap and call it loyalty. And sometimes—"

He paused, eyes finding Tish, then the front row where signs bobbed like buoys.

"—sometimes the only thing between you and an early grave is a promise you made to yourself when no one was listening."

Heads nodded. Old men with prison in their shoulders stood straighter.

"I ain't your pastor, your professor, or your politician," Sire went on. "I'm just a man who learned what the streets taught too late: you can win the game and still lose your soul. EYEKON is a promise. Not that the past didn't happen. Not that we didn't cause harm. Not that we didn't get harmed. But that tomorrow will be bargained in public, not in back rooms. On paper, not on your back."

Cheers flared again. He let the wave crest and fall.

"People ask me what EYEKON is. They expect I'll say it's a 're-entry non-profit' or a 'movement.' It's simpler and uglier. It's a union." A murmur ran through the line of cameras. "A union for the paperless. For the folks at every dock and warehouse, and hotel who get paid cash on a Friday and get fired on a Monday. For the ones with pasts who aren't allowed futures. We bargain for wages. We bargain training. We bargain for credit to buy a damn house. We bargain the price of shame down to zero."

He leaned in.

"And we send a message to anyone profiting off cages—public or private."

Silence. Electric.

"We're coming."

A beat. Then the roar rippled through the plaza, into the buildings, up past the flags that pretended to mean the same thing for everyone.

He ended before seven minutes. The best sermons left space for the walk home.

Backstage, Vee appeared the way storms do—felt before they're seen. Braids tucked under a brim. Dark pea coat. The weight of the concealed hip the metal detectors missed because she never let them find it. She gave Tish a small nod: all clear. Then at Sire: "You got a friendly on the northwest corner with a long lens. Press badge checks out.

Two with earpieces near the middle—private security, not ours. And a suit on his phone behind the platform who keeps saying the word 'warrant' like it's a prayer."

Sire smirked. "That's D.C. It thinks paperwork is God."

"God or gun," Vee said. "They both change behavior."

Tish slid a folder into Sire's hand. "Hearing notes. Don't be nice to the ranking member. He's been on cable all week, calling us a front for 'gang labor.' Use page four—our audit."

They moved through the maze of cables toward the SUV. Sire glanced back at the plaza and then upward at a thin sliver of sky between buildings. He had one of those quiet, private moments men like him never confessed to: gratitude heavy enough to hurt.

He didn't say it out loud. He would say it later when he had a room, a light off, and no one watching.

The hearing room smelled like old wood and damp paper. Portraits of men who had never done an hour in a cell stared down with benevolent disinterest. The seal over the dais was large enough to double as a shield in a different century.

The subcommittee chair, Congresswoman Fanon, greeted Sire with a grip that said ally but not naive. "They'll come at you on the money," she murmured, leaning in as staffers shuffled binders. "They have a witness from a private detention firm and another from the corrections officers' union. One will say you're taking jobs, the other that you're laundering drug money. Answer calmly, answer short, and if they interrupt you—smile like a man with receipts."

Sire sat at the table with Tish on his right, Vee two rows back on the aisle, and their counsel on the left, a young Black woman with tortoiseshell frames and the look of someone who slept with case law under her pillow. Nameplate: TEDDY "SIRE" HILSON, National Director, EYEKON.

Cameras hummed. Laptops opened. The chair banged her gavel.

"Mr. Hilson," she began, "thank you for appearing. Do you swear to tell the truth, the whole truth, and nothing but the truth?"

He did.

The first half hour was procedural theater. Fanon lobbed him questions like softballs with barbed wire. He answered clean: numbers of dues-paying members, MOUs with employers, wage lifts in three metros, recidivism rate reductions inside pilot counties. Tish slid charts like a croupier dealing salvation.

Then the ranking member leaned into his mic.

"Mr. Hilson, you call this a union. I call it a racket. Are you now or have you ever associated with any person convicted of a violent felony currently on your payroll?"

Sire blinked slowly. "Senator, EYEKON is designed for people who were convicted of something. If you're asking me to confirm that I don't hire the people we exist to serve, I can't help you."

Snickers in the press row. The Senator flushed.

He tried another lane. "Isn't it true, Mr. Hilson, that in the early phase of your organization, you funneled cash from unlicensed cannabis distribution to seed your so-called chapters?"

Tish's hand touched Sire's wrist under the table. Steady.

Sire let the smallest smile show. "What's true is that we filed disclosures and audits with the IRS and the Department of Labor, which are in the binder at Tab Six. What's also true is that the people who built steel and trains and shipping fortunes in this country didn't all start with choir money. We are compliant now. We are transparent now. And our books are cleaner than the politics paying for this hearing."

A piston hiss of laughter somewhere in the back.

The detention-firm witness, a man whose cufflinks cost more than the monthly rent of the young organizers outside, adjusted his tie. "Mr. Hilson," he said when it was his turn, "you're playing with fire. You destabilize re-entry contracts, and you destabilize communities. Our facilities provide jobs good union jobs."

"Then stop billing per body," Sire said evenly. "Bill per outcome."

The man's lips thinned. "The world doesn't work that way."

"That's why we built another one," Sire replied.

The clip would run that night. He didn't care. The hearing wasn't the fight. It was the commercial.

In the second row, Vee watched the far door. A man in a soft brown suit she clocked earlier had changed his seat twice. He kept his hands in his pockets too long, then too little. He didn't take notes. He didn't care about the hearing. He cared about the man at the table.

She leaned forward, whispered to the intern behind her, "Text Tish's work phone. Send her the word Cedar."

Three minutes later, Tish's work phone buzzed on silent. She slid a pen diagonally across the page in front of Sire: EXIT C – CEDAR. He gave the faintest nod.

When the gavel fell, the room exhaled. Staffers surged like a tide. Microphones crowded. A reporter with hair like a helmet shouted questions that sounded like accusations; another asked if EYEKON was prepping a mayoral run in a Southern city. Sire kept his head level, his answers brief. "We're running contracts, not for office." "We want jobs, not headlines." "We'll meet with any union, any employer, any city that deals straight."

Vee moved first when the aisle cracked open. "Cedar," she said softly. Sire and Tish followed her angle without looking like they were following anything. They slid out a side door into a narrow corridor that smelled like paint and secrets.

The man in the brown suit missed the turn. Or pretended to.

Outside, the sky had softened into that winter gray that made breath look like ghosts. The SUV idled at the curb. The driver, a former Marine named Mando, opened the door and scanned the sidewalk. Vee's shoulders loosened half an inch. Safe enough for now.

Inside the truck, Tish exhaled for the first time in two hours. "We held. You were surgical."

Sire shook his head. "We were lucky. That's not a strategy."

"Then let's get back to one," she said, and opened the leather folio on her lap. "We've got three immediate fires and one slow burn. Fire one: Our New Jersey chapter lead got a notice. A competitor filed to trademark EYEKON for 'consulting services related to re-entry.' It's a shell LLC out of Delaware."

"Who owns it?"

"Unknown yet. My bet? Someone with a grudge and a lawyer."

"Which is half the city," Sire said. "Next."

"Fire two: A supplier in Texas went sideways. They offered kickbacks to one of our field reps to route contracts through their training center. Our rep reported it. We suspended the supplier and self-reported to our auditor. Clean, but it'll splash."

"And the slow burn?" Sire asked.

Tish hesitated. "A banking partner flagged cash deposits under ten thousand coming in from our Tampa operation. Structured. Not our members using our credit union to move money."

"And they're going to blame us for giving them a ladder," he said flatly.

"They will if we don't pull them down ourselves."

Vee watched the lines of traffic flicker past. Her voice stayed soft. "You start policing your own like cops, you lose the room."

"You don't police your own, you lose the world," Sire replied.

No one spoke for a few blocks. The city flicked by: tourists with maps, a man in a suit arguing into a phone, a woman in scrubs asleep upright on a bus stop bench.

The driver's voice cut in. "We've got a tail."

Sire didn't turn. "Same brown suit?"

"Negative. Gray hoodie, black sedan, two back."

"Run a circle," Vee said. "Then a tunnel. If they stick, we say hello."

They looped the block and slid under the artery that carried half of Washington to Virginia every evening. The sedan came, paused, came again.

Vee cracked the window and let her hand ride the air like she was bored. "You know," she murmured, "when Carlton ran Panthers," she said his name rarely, as a liturgy and a warning "we used to plant a fake tail to see what the real one would do. Decoys make amateurs clumsy."

Sire watched her profile the strength in it, the loss, the edge. "And which one is this?"

"Amateur," she said. "He doesn't know if he wants to be seen."

"Then let's do him a favor," Sire said. "Let him."

Mando took the SUV up and out and then cut right into a public garage—the kind that felt like a trap even when it wasn't. On level three, he parked by a pillar and killed the lights. Two beats later, the black sedan nose-inched around the corner and stopped crookedly, like a lie that forgot its ending.

Vee was out first, hands empty, posture loose. Sire stepped to her right, Tish behind them in the V, folder under her arm like it might explode.

The driver of the sedan got out slowly. Thirties, pale, jaw working a wad of gum into paste. He raised his hands before anyone asked him to.

"Don't shoot," he said, which only people who thought guns were for movies said out loud.

"Why are you following us?" Vee asked.

"Because I was told to."

"By who?" Sire said.

The man swallowed. "A friend."

"Bad at picking them," Sire said. "Name."

The man's eyes flicked to Sire, then back to Vee, like he was trying to choose which parent to lie to. "Dunson," he said finally. "They call me Duns."

"What do you call yourself?" Vee asked.

He blinked, confused. "Uh, Dustin."

"Job, Dustin?"

"Runner," he said. "Messenger. Sometimes I drive. Sometimes I… yeah."

"For who?" Sire repeated.

Dustin shifted. "Look, man. They said Just watch. That's it. They said a package would find you regardless, but it'd be better if someone friendly made sure it arrived."

"What package?" Tish asked.

Dustin turned to the sedan, reached through the driver's window, and came back with a flat black envelope. No stamp. No return. The kind whose corners learned secrets.

He held it out like it might bite.

Sire didn't take it. "Put it on the ground."

Dustin obeyed. Vee picked it up, ran a nail along the edge, and let the contents slide into her hand.

Photos. Three. Glossy. Fresh.

The first was an aerial shot of the rally—crowd, banners, flags. The second was the hearing room, mid-gavel. The third was a close-up through glass of Tish at a conference table—late night, empty chairs but one, a man opposite her whose face was drowned in reflection. The timestamp read 01:12.

Tish didn't move. Vee didn't breathe.

There was a note, too, printed in a font meant to look like a typewriter. We were here before the flags. We'll be here after the lights. Welcome to the real union.

"And who gave you this?" Sire asked.

Dustin stared at the floor. "I don't know his name. He's... old-school. The kind who doesn't text. He said you'd understand if I said: 'A debt paid in blood is interest only.'"

Something turned in Sire's chest. A gear, a knife, a memory.

He stepped closer, so close that Dustin forgot to be brave. "If I see you again without an invitation, you'll be visiting your own hands in a bag," Sire said conversationally. "Do you understand me?"

Dustin nodded fast. "Yes, sir. I swear, I'm just—"

"—bad at picking friends," Vee finished. "Go."

He went. The sedan scraped the pillar paint on the exit like a dog that didn't know its body.

They stood in the diesel-tinged quiet for a moment, the three of them and the envelope like a fourth.

Tish spoke first. "That line."

Sire's eyes were on something far past the cement. "Yeah."

"You think it's the Blanks?" Vee asked.

"Could be," Sire said. "Could be someone who knows our dead like we know theirs."

Tish slid the photos back into the envelope. "The man in the reflection—opposition counsel? A buyer? A plant?"

"Or a mirror," Vee said. "They want you looking at who you trust."

Sire nodded once. "Then we don't blink."

They worked the room at headquarters like field surgeons: cut fast, stop the bleeding, sew what could be saved, amputate what would kill the body.

The D.C. office was an old union hall two blocks from a church that fed people without asking them to confess first. The front lobby still had a wood counter with a glass screen that slid open; the main hall had scuffed floors that had seen more organizing than most Ivy League campuses. Maps covered the far wall, pins stuck like colored rain—Atlanta, Houston, Newark, Jacksonville, Detroit, Phoenix, Oakland, Miami, Chicago. A printed quote above the maps reads Pay attention to who isn't supposed to be in the room and why they're always already there.

Tish convened a midnight audit with their controller and the outside CPA on speaker. "Every deposit over five must trigger a call. Everyone under ten triggers a pattern check. We identify structuring. We file." The controller nodded, exhausted but game.

Vee rewrote the building entry protocol on a whiteboard while three security leads took notes. "Anyone who says they're here for Sire is here for the staff. The threat is the quiet thing at the corner of your plan. Run drills. Then run them again."

In his office, Sire closed the door and locked it. Not because he feared anyone on his side of that door. Because sometimes a man needed to speak to the man he was building out of the man he had been.

He pulled the polar bear rug forward, the one he'd had shipped from Fort Myers because a man could change addresses and still want the same battle reminders underfoot. The safe here didn't hide money. It hid paper. Letters he'd written to men inside. Letters he'd kept from men whose faces he still saw when light cut a certain way through a window. One from Willie's son: Thank you for paying for the stone. I don't forgive the world, but I don't hate it every day now.

He put the envelope beside those letters. Closed the safe. Rolled the rug back.

Pick a fight carefully. End it completely. That was how his granddaddy would say it if his granddaddy had said much at all.

His phone buzzed on the desk. A number with no name. He almost let it ring out. Then he answered.

"Yeah."

A breath. Then a voice like gravel dragged across a church floor.

"You built a flag," it said. "Pretty. Looks good in a lens."

"Who is this?" Sire asked.

"You'll get there," the voice said. "Took you long enough to get here."

"Say something that matters," Sire said, keeping his tone bored. Men like this ate fear and threw back the bones.

"Okay," the voice said, amused. "You want the truth? Here it goes: you can have your union, Sire. Have your wages, have your training, have your little apartments with keys that feel like salvation in the palm. That's all fine. The market loves a miracle. But you mess with custody and you mess with logistics, you mess with beds, you'll learn that every system in this country is a cartel. Hospitals. Colleges. Cages. Same math. Different uniforms."

"You finished," Sire said.

"Not quite. You want to know whose reflection was in that glass across from your woman? Look inside your board. Look at who wanted EYEKON incorporated as a 501(c)(6) instead of a 501(c)(4). Look at who pushed for a credit union first. Follow the person who talks outcomes but counts in headcount. You got a man at the table who is not your enemy. He's worse. He's a friend with other friends."

The line went quiet. The hum of the office heater, the siren three streets over, a printer somewhere down the hall— it all rushed in like the ocean after a shell leaves your ear.

"What do I call you?" Sire asked.

The voice chuckled. "Call me a taxpayer. Call me a kingmaker if you like poetry. Or call me what the street did before you learned to pronounce nuance: the man you don't see until you do."

The click was almost polite.

Sire stared at the phone like it might confess something under pressure. He stood, paced once, and then opened the door.

Tish was there like she had been leaning on the wall a long time. "I heard your tone through two inches of oak."

"Time to know our own house," he said.

"We do that," she said, voice even, "and we will break a few hearts."

"We break them or have them broken for us," Sire replied.

Vee walked up with three files under her arm. "Your board list. Everyone with signature authority. Everyone who ever wanted it, and everyone who'll pretend they never did." She set them on the desk. "We start with love. We end with facts."

Sire nodded. "Run the internal in three lanes. Lane one: finances every conflict form, every side gig, every speaking honorarium, every consulting check. Lane two: communications who's been meeting who without calendar entries. Lane three: history every man or woman who ever made a dollar off custody and calls themselves reform now. We aren't punishing the past. We're predicting futures."

Tish's eyes softened for a breath. "If we find something…"

"If we find something," Sire said, "we don't throw it to the wolves. We fix it if we can. If we can't—"

He didn't finish. He didn't have to.

A young staffer knocked, eyes wide with the adrenaline of being near a myth. "Um—sorry, Mr. Hilson? There's a package at reception. No return. It's… heavy."

They looked at one another. No one smiled.

In the lobby, the night clerk slid a crate across the counter. It was the kind of crate that used to carry oranges in another life and now carried whatever men wanted moved quietly. Slats. Rope handles. A smell like oil and rain.

Vee cut it with a box knife and lifted the lid.

Inside, wrapped in butcher paper, was a ledger.

Old, cloth-bound, edges tattooed by a thousand dirty thumbs. On the cover, in stamped gold, a name no one used anymore.

Henderson Street Mutual Aid Society.

Tish's breath hitched. "That's Fort Myers," she said softly, the past snagging on the present like fabric on a nail.

Sire reached out and brushed the cover with his fingers, the way a man touches a headstone with his palm.

He opened it.

Names. Dates. Sums. Not of money, or not only. Of favors, debts, obligations—who paid for whose lawyer, who bought whose mother's headstone, who kept whose lights on when the city cut them twice in winter. An economy of blood translated into pencil marks.

At the back, a page torn from a different notebook had been pasted in. It was newer. The handwriting was precise.

Legacy is not the statue. It's the ledger. Build yours in daylight. —E.H.

Tish looked at him. "E.H.?"

"Ezekiel Henderson," Sire said. "The old man who ran the block like a benevolent cartel before the police and the hustlers made him choose a side. He chose the children. We never paid him back."

Vee closed the crate gently, like putting a body to rest. "Someone wants you to think you're still the kid who owes. Someone wants you to pay in a currency with no bottom."

Sire nodded. "Then we change the currency."

"How?" Tish asked.

"By putting this on the table when we meet with the city in the morning. By telling them that we will run a public ledger for every dollar, every apprenticeship, every bed we fund. You want to fight a cartel? You make the largest gang in America—public opinion—work for you."

Vee tilted her head. "And the man on the phone? The one who talks in riddles and friends?"

Sire's eyes were clear now. "We flush him out with light and we end him in the dark."

He turned, walked back toward his office, and paused at the doorway like a king looking at a battlefield only he could see whole.

"Tomorrow," he said.

"What happens tomorrow?" Tish asked.

He smiled without warmth. "We stop being grateful we survived and start acting like we're meant to win."

The next morning's meeting was at City Hall, ninth floor, windows that pretended to be generous. The Deputy Mayor for Economic Development had a chin built for press photos and a handshake like tepid tea. He wanted to talk ribbon cuttings, not legacies.

Sire, let him. Then he slid the ledger across the table like a man placing an old map in a young general's hands.

"This is how our people kept each other alive when

institutions chose not to," Sire said. "We're bringing it into the light. A public ledger. We'll publish monthly. You want us in your RFPs? You adopt the ledger. Outcomes, not bodies. Apprenticeships, not press releases. We'll bring our flags. You bring your budget. And your courage."

The Deputy Mayor looked at the book like it might stain him. "And if we say no?"

"Then we say it louder somewhere else," Sire said pleasantly.

On the walk back to the SUV, Vee bumped his shoulder. "You enjoying this?"

He didn't answer. Because a black motorcycle was idling at the curb half a block down, the helmeted rider planted like a chess piece waiting to make a stupid move. And because the helmet turned slowly, and because even through glass and distance, Sire recognized the way a man sits when his body remembers another man's fists.

Billy Blanks.

The world narrowed to a seam.

Tish didn't look, didn't flinch, didn't make the mistake of saying a name out loud in a place where names turned into bullets. She said, instead, "We don't run. We route."

"Down G Street," Vee murmured. "Into the crowd."

They moved with a rhythm born a long time ago on a different street with a different name. The bike revved, edged into traffic, checked once, twice. The rider never took the helmet off. He wanted recognition without confirmation. He wanted to say I can reach you. I can touch you. I can ruin your day, your life, your ledger. He wanted to rewrite the terms of the fight back into something smaller, meaner, familiar.

Sire didn't give it to him.

He put a hand on Vee's back, eyes still on the flow, and said something that could have been a prayer or a promise.

"Let him come in the open."

The bike peeled away, swallowed by a city that ate evidence for breakfast.

They kept walking.

Back at the office, a courier waited in the lobby with a flat package and a signature line. The return address said Potomac Strategies, LLC. Inside was a single sheet of paper and a brass key. The paper had a photo printed in the middle: a storage unit door, half-open, shadows like teeth. The caption read: Unit 13. Tonight. Come alone or don't come at all. Either way, the union pays.

Tish looked at Vee. Vee looked at Sire.

He folded the paper once, twice, like a man putting a magic trick back in the deck.

"Call Mando," he said. "We have an appointment with our past."

He started for the door, then stopped and turned back to

the maps—the pins, the strings, the places where men and women were betting a future on his word. He reached up and pressed a finger into the paper over Fort Myers until the pad of his finger hurt.

"Legacy," he said quietly, to the wall, to himself, to the ledger, to the ghosts. "We're going to make it cost them for once."

And then he walked out, toward Unit 13, toward whatever waited in the dark with his name on it—ready to pay in a currency only the living could spend.

EDWARD WILSON JR

www.ingramcontent.com/pod-product-compliance
Lightning Source LLC
Chambersburg PA
CBHW080600300726

48975CB00010B/2741